War Child

War Child

Galactic Adventures Book 4

Scott Michael Decker

Copyright (C) 2014 Scott Michael Decker
Layout design and Copyright (C) 2019 by Next Chapter
Published 2019 by Beyond Time – A Next Chapter Imprint
Cover art by http://www.thecovercollection.com/
This book is a work of fiction. Names, characters, places, and incidents are the product of the author's imagination or are used fictitiously. Any resemblance to actual events, locales, or persons, living or dead, is purely coincidental.
All rights reserved. No part of this book may be reproduced or transmitted in any form or by any means, electronic or mechanical, including photocopying, recording, or by any information storage and retrieval system, without the author's permission.
U.S. Copyright application #1-1623438411

Titles by the Author

If you like this novel, please post a review on the website where you purchased it, and consider other novels from among these titles by Scott Michael Decker:

Science Fiction:
Bawdy Double
Cube Rube
Doorport
Drink the Water
Edifice Abandoned
Glad You're Born
Half-Breed
Inoculated
Legends of Lemuria
Organo-Topia
The Gael Gates
War Child

Fantasy:
Bandit and Heir (Series)
Gemstone Wyverns
Sword Scroll Stone

Look for these titles at your favorite book retailer.

Stone walls do not a prison make,
Nor iron bars a cage ...
—Richard Lovelace, c1642

Prologue

The galactic core, the ultimate prize.

Princess Mariko Mitsubi stood on the bridge of the battle-cruiser and Armada flagship Yamato, gazing upon the galactic core through thousands of multisensory receptors funneled into her neuralink.

Soon, my child, Mariko said to the near-term fetus inside her, soon, the galactic core shall be yours!

No more wars, no more retreats.

An end to constant bickering between Empires, to the tides of conquering and capitulating, to treacherous dealings in stealth and poison, to whole worlds denuded to stamp out rebellious populations, their skies littered with the orbital detritus of defeated navies, thousands of years of civilization ending abruptly in sudden annihilation.

An end to two centuries of constant war.

I will bring war to an end, my child, Mariko told her unborn, her first-born daughter, her heir. Third in line for the Mitsubi Throne.

Mariko stood to inherit nearly a quarter of the Milky Way, eldest daughter of Fumiko Mitsubi, the Matriarch of the Mitsubi clan and Empress to their domains. The Mitsubi Empire ballooned across the Delta Quadrant, straddling most of the Norman Arm, the lower Scutum-Crux Arm, and the mid Carina-Sagittarius Arm, the largest Empire in the Milky Way.

But we'll always be vulnerable to the Empire that captures the galactic core, unless we capture it ourselves.

Mariko signaled through her neuralink to the armada behind her. Above, below, port and starboard, phalanxes of fighters, destroyers, and battleships edged forward until they came abreast her ship's position.

Below them, the Iberia outpost Tarifa lay quiescent at the rim, the blazing core nearly swallowing the puny base in light. Berthed at Tarifa was the Fourth Fleet of the Iberia Navy. After that, just two more outposts to conquer before the Mitsubi juggernaut swept away all resistance and dominated the galactic core, the ultimate prize.

They and their rivals had fought each other over this and similar installations since before history began. The Mitsubis, an ancient peoples, had pursued the claim for the galactic throne numerous times, proclaiming for centuries the mandate of heaven to rule the reachable universe, as they had since their origins on old Earth, over three thousand years before, on a sword-shaped set of islands called Japan. Like the islands, the sword-shaped galactic arm had become too small for their ambitions.

She who controls the core, Mariko thought, controls the galaxy!

Tarifa appeared incognizant that it lay naked to evisceration, the talons of the Mitsubi Armada poised to rake it apart. Monitored communications from the base evinced no alarm, and nearby bases, although parsecs away, showed no evidence of scrambling their defenses.

On the bridge, Mariko ordered her fighters forward, two lines each leaving the Armada branches and hurtling from four different directions at Tarifa, followed by smaller contingents of destroyers, her battleship held at bay for now.

If we destroy the Fourth Fleet and take Tarifa, then the core is nearly ours, Mariko thought, the display a forty-five degree surround in all directions, the neuralink brightening the area where she brought her attention. Sitting at battlestations around the arc behind her, her lieutenants held tactical links with their squadrons in the field, taking their orders from her through the neuralink.

Fighters converged on Tarifa, and the first pinpricks of light flared on its surface, eight squadrons strafing the base.

Mariko launched the battleships, leaving a reserve to defend the flagship Yamato.

Activity spiked on the monitored Iberian comchannels, fighters trying to scramble and base-mounted turrets coming to life. Eight lines of fighters swung back to strafe again, plums of smoke now billowing from multiple points. The destroyers turned parallel in unison and launched a barrage of broadsides just after the fighters cleared a second strafing run, and a half-dozen Iberian ships able to launch were pummeled to pieces.

"Destroyer launch from Tarifa!" called a lookout over the neuralink.

At her command, a battleship hurtled after it, the remaining five battleships continuing to hover outside the destroyer-held perimeter. The pursuing battleship launched multiple missiles en route, staged alternately with decoy confetti and intercept-avoidance devices.

A lone fighter dove for the base command compound and five emplacements blew it out of the sky, revealing their locations, and the next strafing run took out those emplacements while a destroyer followed them in and obliterated the compound in its first pass.

A cheer rose at its destruction, the happy neuralink chatter heartening Mariko.

The sound of victory, my child, Mariko said in her mind, even though no neuralink connected her with her fetus, which some mothers chose to install. Knowing they weren't victorious yet, Mariko brought the fighters in for another strafing, and launched another destroyer barrage.

The surface of the asteroid looked like a torch, roiling in smoke and flame, the image before Mariko a thrill to see.

"What in Izanami's name are you doing?" The face of her mother the Empress filled the neural viewer.

Mariko's heart sank. "Buddha curse you, Mother, not now!" And she shoved with all her mental might to block out her mother's neural connection.

But the neuralink between mother and daughter could not easily be put asunder. "Disobedient child, I told you not to attack now, not with my grandchild in your belly!"

"How often must I say it? That's the time it's least expected. Now get out of my mind so I can finish these Iberian scum! Out!"

And to Mariko's surprise, the Empress Fumiko Mitsubi withdrew.

"Battleship down!"

Where the battleship had been was a fiery inferno.

Mariko found the Iberian destroyer that had bested the battleship, a midget-giant match-up it should never have won. It was now under full thrust right at the flagship Yamato, right at her.

Two battleships moved to intervene.

They dropped off the neuralink grid, their chatter silenced, their vid feeds dead.

"Com, what's happening?" she shouted.

"Signals disrupted, your Highness."

Mariko wished they wouldn't call her that. "Why, blast it?!"

"I don't know, your Highness."

"Analyze!"

The two battleships on screen erupted in flames, and the Iberian destroyer slid between them, its broadsides ripping chasms into their sides, the two battleships looking like helpless beached whales, the shark in between tearing them to pieces.

She committed her three remaining battleships and brought the destroyers to bear on the enemy ship. "Battlestations!" and klaxons sounded throughout the flagship, as did red alert signs, the alert superimposed on onto retinas. Mariko ordered the fighters into formation and launched her fighters into the fray.

The attacking fighters dropped off the neuralink grid, the Iberian destroyer beating back the fighter wave.

"Your Highness," the First Mate Hideo Kobaya said, "Advise retreat."

"Full reverse!" she shouted, and the flagship dropped backward while destroyers and battleships converged on the seemingly untouched enemy ship.

Mariko leaned against the acceleration, anxiety beginning to gnaw at her. A hundred and sixty fighters erupted in flames—minus a few who had already fallen. Mariko stared at the slaughter, aghast.

"Belay there!" she shouted. "All ships, cover retreat!"

Her navy as one changed course to converge instead on the flagship's path of retreat but, one by one, began to drop off the neuralink grid.

Another battleship, the fifth, erupted into a fireball, leaving one battleship and a handful of destroyers between the Iberian ship and the flagship Yamato.

Their retreat picked up speed. How are they doing that? Mariko wondered, sweat stinging her eyes.

"Your highness, they have some sort of—"

And the neuralink in her head went silent.

"—disruptor," her science officer said, standing across the bridge over a display. Doctor Setsu Uruga looked at her. "And they've just disrupted our neuralink."

Feeling suddenly vulnerable at having been reduced to tactile, visual, and auditory signals, Mariko yanked the plug from her head with a pop. "Everyone, pull out immediately. We'll run the ship manually."

"Forgive me, highness, but how?"

"Electronic backup systems online. You've all trained to run the Yamato without a neuralink, so let's get to it, people!"

The forward displays showed a gaining destroyer with the flaming hulls of her armada in its wake.

"We're being hailed, Highness!"

Our flagship is a helpless babe without the armada that it commands, Mariko thought. Why haven't they destroyed us too? "On screen," she said.

A face snapped into view. Sub-Commander Xavier Balleros smiled. "Surrender, your Majesty, or be destroyed."

"Go suck on your Christian Devil's hind penis!"

"Now, now, your Majesty, mind your language. Such filth will surely cause you to be reborn as one such penis, now, won't it?"

"What do you want, Commander, eh? You're not going to blast us out of the sky no matter what I call you, because you'd have done so already. So what do you want, ball-less Balleros?"

The bridge crew behind Mariko chuckled.

A vein rippled on the Commander's forehead. "You bitch! I'll … Insult me if you must. Your crew—all that's left of your armada—you can still save your crew."

"I'd gladly give my life that they might live, but their loyalty is to the Empress Fumiko. Even if I were to order it, they'd disobey me. They'll protect her daughter's life with theirs, *whatever* my orders."

Sub-Commander Balleros threw his head back and laughed. "Your conceit exceeds your intelligence, always a suicidal combination. No, your Majesty, it isn't you I want." He smiled to someone off the screen.

The Yamato slewed wildly, an explosion shaking her, alarms erupting, lights flickering. Mariko barely kept herself from falling. The vid skewed to one side, twisting the image.

Rhythmic pounding to aft alerted her to a barrage, repeated a moment later to starboard.

"You see, your Majesty," Balleros said, "we don't need you alive to claim the prize we seek."

She placed both her hands under her enlarged belly. "Never, Pendejo!"

"They're boarding us, Highness!"

The pounding continued around the bow.

Her first mate grabbed her. "This way, Highness!" He pulled her toward the lifepods.

"No!" Mariko yanked her arm from his grasp and pulled her phasegun from its holster. She shook her fist at Balleros. "You'll never capture me, Cabrón!" And she aimed the phasegun at her belly.

Stars exploded across her vision like the core across her neuralink. The floor twisted under her and slammed into the side of her head. Bewildered, she wondered why First Mate Kobaya hadn't fallen and why the butt of the phasegun in his hand was bloody.

When he aimed it at her head, Princess Mariko Mitsubi understood finally that the enemy hadn't possessed a disrupter to throw her ships off the neuralink. Her first mate Hideo Kobaya had betrayed her.

He fired, killing her.

Part I

Chapter 1

"Look at her," Foreign Minister Xavier Balleros said.

Below, the young woman parried on the practice floor. Her ease made her two opponents look like sloths, as she deftly turned aside blade after blade without apparent effort or even sometimes motion.

"She'll be perfect, Amigo. She has the balance of a ballet dancer and the spirit of a tiger. You're to be congratulated. Where is she now in her studies?" Balleros asked the other, not taking his eyes off her. They stood in the observation booth, fifty feet above the arena, the seats empty but for others about to practice and the occasional vicarious observer. Of the latter, Balleros noted a greater number than might be expected at a university fencing practice.

"She graduates in six months from the aerospace engineering—"

"What about government? I told you to have her in government. She must be able to navigate the highest reaches of the Iberian Empire."

"Of course, Lord Minister. She completed those studies two years ago. When she finished her political science and interstellar relations degrees, she begged her Padre to enroll in engineering, swore she'd complete it before her twenty-first birthday."

"And?"

"She finishes in two months, Lord, summa cum laude. She was disappointed she couldn't attend the diplomatic mission to the Mitsubi Capitol, Lord—a rare opportunity for an intern of *any* caliber. The Lady Ambassador Xochitl Olin personally sent a com to express her disappointment that her protégé wasn't able to attend."

Balleros smiled. "Ambassador Olin herself, eh? Ambitious, isn't she?" he nodded to indicate the supple, athletic woman dancing between two opponents below.

"Beyond all expectation. The engineering program is a six-year course of study and—"

"Why are all those people here?" Balleros wasn't interested in her prodigious academic ability.

"I wondered about that, Lord, and from what I can tell, they only gather when she's here to practice."

The lithe form on the floor back-flipped from between a two-pronged attack, stepped in to one opponent's reach and thumped the back of the rapier hand, which emptied itself, then spun through the other opponent's guard with what looked like a pirouette and disarmed the other opponent similarly.

A round of applause erupted from the observers. She bowed to them, then to her opponents, and headed for the locker room.

"Does Minister Balleros wish to speak with her?"

He shook his head, seeing how his plans might be accelerated. "No, not necessary. Thank you, my friend. It's enthralling to see, truly impressive. I'm not sure the value of the engineering but it'll be useful at some point, I'm sure. Well done. I'll contact you soon."

And Balleros strode from the observation deck and out of the arena.

* * *

"I can't believe Mother is still grieving that fool sister of ours," Keiko Mitsubi said.

Yoshi Mitsubi looked around the room to see if anyone had overheard. The sisters were in an anteroom off the main audience hall, dressed in ceremonial silks spun from strands of Camelopardalis-spider silk, the strongest to be found, the fabric light, airy, and impenetrable.

Awaiting the arrival of the Nahuatl Empire Ambassador, Xochitl Olin.

"Hush, younger sister," Yoshi said, "or Buddha may bring similar grief to you!" Seeing no one in earshot, Yoshi smiled placidly at Keiko, third of three daughters to Empress Fumiko. "No mother should endure seeing her daughter die before her, never mind that it was twenty years ago." And never mind, Yoshi was thinking, that I'm Regent Empress because of it, and I'll order you to bite your tongue if I have to because I'm quite tired of your impertinence and backbiting, so unbecoming of a princess and the dutiful daughter you should be.

"But she should have—"

"I said hush, and if you won't mind me, your elder sister and Regent, perhaps a three-month vacation on an asteroid might help." Yoshi kept her voice low and her stare fixed upon her sister even though they both knew it an empty threat, for their mother remained so stricken with grief that she would immediately rescind any such order, saying she couldn't bear to have either of her two remaining daughters away from her for a single moment. She makes me Regent, Yoshi was thinking, and then questions or countermands my every decision. Errrgh! I must have given someone conniption fits in my last life to have been born into such misery as this!

"Forgive me, Sister," Keiko said, bowing slightly. "I meant not to be so vexatious."

"Eh? What?" Yoshi hated it when she didn't understand what others were saying.

"Bothersome."

"I knew what you meant," Yoshi said, knowing she didn't. "Twenty years ago, it was. She'd be twenty years old, that girl, if she'd lived."

The two sisters changed a guilty glance, both sad that their sister had died but glad it had been before she'd given birth. Had the near-term fetus survived, they both knew, the child would now be Regent, instead of Yoshi.

Keiko frowned. "Fool sister."

Yoshi didn't remonstrate her, secretly agreeing.

"Your Highnesses," the headservant said, clearing her throat and glancing toward the main audience hall to indicate that the Ambassador was now arriving.

"She can wait a little longer. How do you say her name again?"

"Show cheet, Highness."

Yoshi repeated it. "Thank you."

The servant retreated.

"You didn't say it right."

"Of course I did."

Keiko sighed and looked away. "She's here to negotiate the secession of the outer Carina-Sagittarius Arm to the Nahuatl Empire."

"I know why she's here!"

Keiko looked unperturbed. "Perhaps 'negotiate' isn't the right word."

"Demand might be more accurate," Yoshi snarled.

"My thought as well." Keiko's voice was light as a flower.

Flustered, Yoshi didn't know how to handle her sister when she became so nonchalant. As though my responses are unimportant! "Too many demands by these supposed allies. How dare they throw their lot with the Nahuatl."

"Many have done so in the last twenty years."

Yoshi shot Keiko a glance. Their Empire, once reaching to edges of the Delta Quadrant, had been whittled away, first one coalition falling apart, another alliance going sour, a treaty getting rescinded, little pieces at the edges coming unglued, until their Empire was less than half its size than when their sister died. The nibbling away at the edges of the Mitsubi Empire had become gobbling by the mouthful, this most recent "negotiation" likely to lose them nearly a quarter-length of that spiral arm. The Mitsubi holdings were shrinking nearly to the shape of that ancient sword-like country they had occupied on Earth so long ago.

"No less rebellious for others having done so. Let's dismiss this bitch and subjugate their territory with an invasion that will silence them and all else who would oppose us, forever!"

Keiko raised an eyebrow at her. "Venom I've not heard in years," the younger sister said. "Who would lead them, Elder Sister?"

Yoshi frowned. "Indeed." They both knew neither of them was capable. And they wouldn't trust anyone else for fear of rebellion should they demand that the Empire go to war.

* * *

Riyo Takagi slipped away from the anteroom doorway before anyone saw him, incensed that these bickering sisters were too incompetent to keep the Empire from coming apart.

As General to the Supreme Council, a small body of high-ranking politicians and officers who answered only to the Empress, General Takagi was responsible for the recruitment, training, and readiness of the armies. While the princesses and Empress all three maintained large armies, which Takagi commanded, the General also managed the troops allocated to the Empire by their allied and subject states, a conglomeration of over two hundred constellations and fiefdoms held in the Mitsubi federation either by blood relation, treaty, coalition, fealty, or downright threat of retaliation.

General Riyo Takagi only commanded the army, however. To get his troops deployed, he needed the Navy, and Admiral Nobu Nagano, to get them there. The two men disliked each other intensely. Each was an important daimyo in his own right. Each was bedecked with honors bestowed for their valor in combat. Each was renowned for his respective artistry. And each was fanatically opposed to the other.

If that fool first mate Hideo Kobaya my second cousin through my mother's marriage to his uncle hadn't flubbed the kidnapping of Princess Mariko, we'd have seized power from these Mitsu-bitches and retained control of the Norman Arm and by now would have claimed at least one end of the galactic core!

General Takagi strode the plush corridor carpet toward the Supreme Council chambers, fuming at the travesty about to transpire in the audience hall when the incompetent sisters caved to the demands of the Nahuatl and ceded the outer Carina Arm to their Gamma-Quadrant aggressors. Furious, General Takagi wondered if it were time to launch insurrection and take the Mitsubi Empire by force.

Seeded amongst the ancient clans throughout the Delta Quadrant, secret cells planted deep across the years stood poised to capture key installations, both military and civilian. These cells had been readied to strike twenty years ago when his second cousin First Mate Kobaya had attempted to kidnap Princess Mariko. General Takagi had had to issue emergency stand down orders to these cells lest they spontaneously strike after the kidnapping had failed. He had risked exposing his hand by issuing those orders, despite his having used secure subspace comchannels, since the widespread communiqué to thousands of recipients had alerted intelligence services to something unusual.

Is now the time to launch an insurrection? General Takagi wondered. Sighing, he reached the Council door, where a servant bowed deeply to him.

"Get me a neuralink," he said, his voice gravelly. With a glance to the side, he checked his appearance. His reflection grinned at him, the thin, gray beard below the short-cut black hair striking. The brown, space-tanned skin was smooth, without wrinkle despite his sixty years.

The servant returned with the device.

Takagi set the neuralink to receive only, and then plugged it in to the back of his head. He hung the box on his collar, the wires running up to the socket. Stepping to his usual chair at the council table, the General signaled for a beverage.

Tea wafted steam toward him, his senses tuned to the audience down the corridor, the neuralink filling his awareness with the goings-on.

A few minutes passed before he realized he'd been joined in the Council Chambers by another observer.

Admiral Nobu Nagano nodded to him from across the table.

General Takagi saw by the neuralink at his lapel that he too was observing the diplomatic visit in receive-only mode. The General returned the Admiral's nod.

"Perhaps it is time, Lord General," the grizzled Admiral said, "that we set aside our differences."

General Takagi met the gaze of Admiral Nagano.

* * *

The servant Pearl Blossom withdrew from the Council Chambers but stayed near the door to await either man's command. Twenty-three years old and tiny for her age, she looked barely fourteen and often intercepted ripe tidbits rarely overheard by other servants.

I'm so very fortunate to look so young, Pearl Blossom thought, other servants often complaining of the constant groping and leering by her male and sometime female betters. Many of her fellow servants had been raped and sometimes killed by royalty, her position as servant holding no rights, giving her no legal recourse to abusive treatment, and only her owner having power to pursue redress if she were mistreated in any way.

Her actual owner was the Empress, of course, but Pearl Blossom doubted that her Highness Fumiko Mitsubi even knew who she was, or that she even existed. She was but one of ten thousand servants in the Imperial Palace, and her assigned location was the council chambers, where she and three other young female servants attended to the chambers of the Supreme Council and to the needs of whoever happened to be present.

When the Council was in full session, all four servants were so busy they could barely manage all the demands. And the Council members were very demanding. And although they often brought their own servants, these were usually attachés or aides, and were present only to assist their masters in the business of the Empire, and not to attend to their bodily whims.

Thus Pearl Blossom was grateful to the heavens that she looked so young and was rarely called upon to satisfy the more perverse of those whims.

Standing in the shadows just out of sight of the two men, Pearl Blossom heard one of them say. "Perhaps it is time, Lord General, that we set aside our differences."

She caught her breath, awaiting the answer.

For a long time, silence, then the rustling of silk.

She dared to peek.

Unbelievably, the ancient enemies were sitting just two chairs apart, conversing in low tones, the Admiral intent upon the conversation while the General looked around the room. His gaze did not find her in the shadows.

Pearl Blossom wondered what deviltry they brewed between them.

* * *

Ambassador Xochitl Olin stepped forward, each step measured and timed to provide the greatest swagger and sway to the elaborate feathered headdress she wore.

Her nose a veritable beak, Xochitl struggled to keep her gaze on the empty thrones in front of her. She knew all these Mitsubi Empire officials who crowded the room were staring at her round eyes and oversized nose. This is a Nahuatl nose! she wanted to yell at them. This is a proud nose! A regal nose! A nose that commands respect! A nose that blares with disdain! These people don't have noses. Two holes in the front of their faces are all they have! How do they smell with such tiny noses?

Keeping her gaze forward, Xochitl marched slowly to the designated place, her face impassive, the procession behind her halting in unison with her, their feathered headdresses not quite as elaborate as hers, their beaded skirts and tasseled moccasins not quite as gilded, and their weapons not quite as bejeweled.

But they're equally sharp, she thought. They had foregone the traditional maquahuitl, wooden blades embedded with obsidian chucks, for modern steel.

She waited at attention, ramrod erect, for the Mitsubi Princesses to enter.

These people look exactly like my intern, Serena Zambrano! she thought, their noses tiny and their eyes mere slits. Why did Serena decline to come? Xochitl wondered. Why had her sponsor denied her the opportunity of a lifetime, coming to a foreign nation in the company of the highest-ranking ambassador amongst the Nahuatl?

At sixteen, Serena Zambrano had begun an apprenticeship under the auspices of the Nahuatl Foreign Service. Xochitl Olin had already known of the girl's promise, carrying herself with the grace and aplomb of someone twice her age. And to enter the top Nahuatl university as an exchange student from distant Iberia halfway across the galaxy at age sixteen bespoke a highly influential sponsor at the upper levels of the Iberian Empire. And who is that sponsor? Xochitl wondered, having found nothing in Serena's background but a humble upbringing on an obscure planet outside the Orion subsystem where at age three she had become renowned for mastering all five local languages and their variant dialects.

The other reason Xochitl had really wanted Serena to come.

The girl had learned the staccato tongue of these slanted-eyed foreigners in three months, then had proceeded to master its linguistic and idiomatic intricacies in another month.

The application for Tenochtitlan University by a thirteen-year-old graduate of the local college system had caused such a stir that Xochitl had sent an envoy to interview the girl. And although Xochitl insisted the girl wait until she was sixteen before immigrating halfway across the galaxy, the girl had put the time to good use, completing two more undergraduate degrees in seemingly unrelated fields, arriving at Tenochtitlan University with three baccalaureate degrees before the age of sixteen.

If only she were here, Xochitl thought, wondering why these ritual-obsessed Mitsubi Princesses were taking such a long time to make their appearance.

* * *

If we didn't observe the rituals, Keiko Mitsubi thought, we might to throw ourselves on the ground and kick our legs and pound our fists and rend our clothes and wail to the stars!

The double doors opened in front of them, and the two sisters swept into the audience hall to the rustle of fine silks, barely audible in the loud silence.

Keiko almost gawked at seeing the twenty or so feathered headdresses. Have they got peacocks on their heads? she wondered, stifling a giggle and hiding a smile.

She followed her sister to the dais. On the platform sat three chairs, the two side chairs facing inward at a slight angle, the largest chair in the center the most elaborate in design, having silken wings and a canopy. A blood-red rising sun on a bright white background would have framed the Empress Fumiko Mitsubi.

If she had been sitting there.

The chair in the middle would remain empty, a signal to everyone present as to who really ruled here.

Keiko stepped to the right hand of the three chairs, Yoshi stopping beside the left. Tucked into their kimono waistbands were the three-foot katana swords, the traditional two-handed battle sword of the samurai.

Yoshi as eldest gestured Keiko to sit. As befitted custom, Keiko demurred and bade Yoshi to sit. Three times, each sister bade the other, and finally, their eyes upon the other, they both sat in the same time.

Not until their rumps were in the chairs did anyone else take their places.

Burly guards in lacquered battlegear lined the walls, visible now that both noble and guest had seated themselves.

Alone, near the back, one figure had not sat.

Everyone's attention fixed on him, and a whisper rippled through the assemblage. The fire in the Regent Empress's gaze might have burned him to a crisp.

Yoshi pointed and two guards converged.

"I demand to be heard by samurai's right!"

"Hold!" Keiko said, and the guards froze, swords half out of scabbard. "Lady Sister-Regent, this man invokes samurai's right to be heard by his liege lord."

"Then fetch him to his liege lord," Yoshi said. "And bedone with us."

"Forgive me, elder sister," Keiko said. "You ultimately command this samurai and—"

"I know, younger sister, but now is not the time, here is not the place. With all due respect to your duty, Lord, please see your liege lord first."

"My apologies, Lady Regent Empress," the man said, "but I cannot. A foul deed takes place here now, and here now, it must be stopped. Forgive me if I behave brazenly."

Flush crept up Yoshi's neck, Keiko saw, always a bad sign. "Lady Sister, if I may?"

Yoshi took her burning stare off the man, and turned it on Keiko.

Keiko knew she might also incur the Regent's wrath if the disturbance went badly. What else could go wrong? Keiko wondered. Already, the warrior had disrupted the ritual. "Lord Warrior, I am Princess Keiko. How may I be of assistance?"

"Lady Princess Keiko, forgive me, but is it not the samurai's duty to warn a superior of an ill-considered action?"

"Tell me your name, Lord."

"Captain Tani Gahara, Lady Princess Keiko."

"You are right, Lord Captain Gahara, indeed, it is the samurai's duty, that to warn. And is it not also the samurai's duty to obey?"

"Just so, Lady Princess Keiko, except when the duty to obey causes one to fail in his duty to warn."

Keiko smiled. "Just so, Lord Captain Gahara. Therefore, continue if you must, for if you choose to warn, you will die for your failure to obey. If you choose to remain silent, you will die for your failure to warn. Is that not so?"

The Captain stared at her, sweat rolling off his chin. Slowly, he spoke. His voice did not quaver, his gaze did not avert. "It is so, Lady."

"So it is said, Lord," Keiko replied. "So it is done."

"Speak or stay silent, Lord Captain Gahara," Yoshi said. "Which do you choose?"

The Captain eyed the guards.

"You may speak freely, Lord Captain Gahara."

"Yes, Lady Regent, thank you. The Lady Regent receives these foreign interlopers and intends to kowtow to their demand for the outer Carina-Sagittarius Arm, held now these five hundred years by the Mitsubi Empire. She intends to place the sovereignty of my home under the auspices of this beak-nose foreigner with the bird nesting on her head. I will die of shame if I have to bow to such a ridiculous—"

The head flew off the shoulders and a bright fountain of blood splattered spectators too slow to avoid the gusher. A warrior bowed toward the regent Empress. "Forgive me, Lady, but I could not tolerate the scoundrel's insulting our guests." He wiped his sword clean and sheathed it, then knelt in the blood beside the corpse and bowed his head to the floor.

Yoshi grinned. "I can forgive your wanting to protect and preserve the honor of our guests. But I cannot forgive your not asking me first. I invite you to redeem yourself on the temple steps this evening at sunset. And you would honor me by awaiting my arrival, Lord Sergeant, that I may act as your second in your redemption."

"You do me too much honor, Lady Regent. I don't deserve—"

"Of course you do," Yoshi interrupted. "At sunset."

"Yes, Lady, of course. At sunset." The warrior bowed again, and servants swarmed through the nobles to clean up the mess.

In less than a minute, no trace of the killing remained.

No trace except in the minds of our guests, Keiko was thinking, as she brought her attention to the Nahuatl Ambassador.

As intended.

Chapter 2

Prince Augusto Iberia looked up just in time to see her come out of the locker room, looking fresh as a chrysanthemum.

Without a glance, the young woman walked briskly past him along the manicured walkway and was several steps ahead of him before he'd recovered, breathless at her beauty.

"Hey, wait …" Augusto hurried to catch up with her, surprised at how swiftly she walked. The fresh blush of exertion reddened his cheeks.

She didn't stop.

"Miss? Miss, may I speak with you?" He felt a touch dismayed at having to ask, the attention usually accorded him nowhere to be found in her.

"I've got seminar—no time to chat, sorry," she said, a quick glance over her shoulder.

"I'll walk with you."

"As you wish," she replied, still not looking at him.

"I'm—" he took three quick steps to match her pace "—Augusto. What's your name?"

"Serena," she said.

He stuck out his hand. "Pleased to meet you." It remained empty.

"Pleased." She stared straight ahead, her pace unbroken.

"I like your work on the floor." He glanced toward the gymnasium behind them.

"Coming to my practices for at least a month, haven't you?"

"Two," he said, his face growing redder. "You're phenomenal."

"I've had good teachers."

He nodded. "The best, and some who've tutored me."

Serena looked at him finally, but didn't slow. "How could that be? You're a prince. My father isn't wealthy, couldn't possibly afford the same teachers."

He was shocked she knew who he was. Had she seen the two security guards who always followed him? Always in plain clothes, always at a respectful distance, but always there. As Prince and Heir to the Iberia Empire, he'd become accustomed long before to the constant shadow. "It was my guards, wasn't it?"

"Who gave you away?" She laughed light as a feather. "Them, and your always overly-formal clothing. And the way you hold yourself, as though you wear a crown already."

He smiled sheepishly, not realizing how obvious it was. "Sorry."

They rounded the corner of a building labeled "Lecture."

"My next class," she said, stopping abruptly and turning to look at him.

"When, uh ..." His tongue was suddenly thick and limp in his mouth.

She giggled.

"Uh ... can we talk again?"

"With or without the shadows?" She glanced the way they had come.

"I can try to get rid of them if you like."

Serena shrugged at him. "I'm not worried. I'm free after fencing tomorrow."

"Outside the locker room?"

"I'd like that," and she disappeared into the lecture.

Smiling, Augusto walked farther along the path, not really seeing it, his feet barely touching the ground.

Then he remembered that his shadows would probably report this to his father, Emperor Maximilian Iberia, who would then demand to know all about her.

And how he felt about her.

Shrugging and wishing he knew more, Augusto headed for his next class, seeing little of his surroundings, the delightful young woman filling his thoughts.

* * *

Professor Doctor Setsu Uraga saw the clock advance and strike the hour. He turned to the students in the lecture hall. "In this seminar, we discuss variances in time-space principles."

A young woman was just finding her seat.

Doctor Uraga scowled at her, then froze. And he remembered where he had seen her before. He pointed at her. "See me after seminar for being late."

Later, after he'd finished the lecture, he realized he didn't remember what he'd said. All he could remember was that her face wouldn't leave his mind.

"Please, have a seat," Dr. Uraga said, gesturing to the only other chair in his office. Comcubes and datacubes lined the shelves, and he pushed aside the two neuralinks that hung from the ceiling. Only then did he allow himself to look at her face again.

"My apologies for being late. I didn't realize it would be so upsetting."

"It wasn't that." Identical, he thought, checking his class roster. "Your name is …?"

"Serena Zambrano," she said.

He jerked his head up to look at her. "Forgive me, I must be mistaken, but I thought you were someone else." He realized his tone of voice bordered on panic.

"No forgiveness necessary, Doctor. A simple mistake, eh?"

"Yes," he said immediately, his gaze falling to the roster again.

"Is there another name you're looking for?"

"No, no," he said too quickly. "No, I uh, I was … Again, my apologies, Miss Zambrano. Uh, if you need any help with the material, please don't hesitate to see me. Not that you will, as you were highly recommended by prior professors."

"I've managed to do pretty well."

"I've been told I should see you fence. Did a little of that when I was in the Navy."

"What squadron?"

"Oh, uh, not in the Nahuatl Empire. Under the Mitsubi."

"Princess Mariko? The one who almost conquered the galactic core?"

Dr. Uraga smiled.

"The ultimate prize."

He frowned. "She said the same once." He looked at her again. No, he told himself, it couldn't be. She died pregnant!

"You look upset again."

"I killed her betrayer, just after he killed her." His voice was barely a whisper.

Later he remembered the young woman's departure, but he didn't remember much else. Except locking his door and weeping as he hadn't in years.

* * *

"Our Empire sits between the Nahuatl to the east and the Iberia to the south," Admiral Nobu said, his voice low, his lips barely moving. Both men had removed their neuralinks at the conclusion of the audience, both of them demoralized. "We used to occupy all the Scutum-Crux Arm, a large chuck of the Norman, and all of the Carina-Sagittarius. Look at us now—without the cherries to hold onto the end of the Car-Sag Arm."

The man two seats over from him grunted, his eyes quartering the room, his vigilance a necessary evil. "And without a stiff enough branch to poke a knot hole in those Nahuatl."

Admiral Nagano chuckled at the other man's pun. "It's not you or me, and it's not really them, either."

"No, it's not."

Giving nothing away, Nagano thought. And I wouldn't either. Is my life-long rival luring me to my downfall? "We are two pillars holding up a falling house. I'd be a fool to weaken the other pillar."

"You would."

Nagano watched him closely. "A two-pillar house is the least stable of all structures."

"How can we strengthen the third pillar, long absent these twenty years?"

Nagano smiled at Takagi. "Too bad about Princess Mariko. Alone, she'd have held the house erect by herself, eh?"

"Yes," General Takagi said.

Nagano saw a hint of something more than sadness. Fear? Desire? Hope? Princess Mariko had held more than just a house erect. She stiffened all our branches, Nagano thought, wondering whether Takagi was thinking similarly.

She's gone now, eh? the Admiral told himself. In your secret hear of secret hearts, you wanted her as every man did, never mind that you were happily married to the most beautiful woman in the Empire. You wanted her for the power she represented, and her breath-taking beauty certainly stiffened your branch and made your cherries tingle, too! Yes deep inside you wanted her, and her death was horrific for us all, particularly the manner of it.

It had been Nagano's and Takagi's duties to obliterate the Kobaya lineage, all the sons, brothers, grandfathers, uncles, male cousins, and of course the father. The father who had been Nagano's boyhood friend.

But of course they had been forbidden to touch any of the female relatives of the betrayer, as they were subject only to the law of their Matriarch.

The killing had been good and had purged the Empire of its betrayal, and most hearts had been assuaged. But the sorrow from the betrayal of the Princess Mariko Mitsubi had not been assuaged from the heart of Empress Fumiko Mitsubi. And she remained so subdued with grief that the Empire still suffered, her twenty-year, self-imposed isolation depriving the Empire of its monarch.

"The only cure is to bring her daughter back," General Takagi said.

Admiral Nagano nodded slowly, sighing. "There is another alternative, but it is unthinkable."

"Unthinkable," Takagi said.

The Admiral regarded the General. Should I tell him about the thousands of secret cells planted over the years throughout the empire, ready to rise in rebellion if but a hint of treachery tinges my untimely death? Or the data drops dangling from gossamer strands, ready to break and dump their incriminating information into the neuranet, should the General but snap his fingers in my demise? Nagano scrutinized Takagi closely.

"When the unimaginable becomes a reality, the unthinkable isn't anymore, is it?"

Takagi's eyes roamed the room again. "When is rebellion not a rebellion?"

"When you win."

Takagi's eyes returned to his face. "When you win."

The two men smiled at each other.

Chapter 3

Serena Zambrano left the professor's office with that feeling again.

She wondered what it meant to feel déjà vu without ever having been in that situation. If the professor had been the first person to mistake her for someone else, she'd have been intrigued. Now, it felt more like fate, as though her lot in life were to be mistaken for someone else, someone important, someone who had transformed others' lives.

Entering the lecture and laying eyes on the professor, Serena had known that it'd happened again. The twist of anxiety in the pit of her stomach, the edge of tension in her shoulders, the narrowing of her gaze, all had alerted her. The professor's not looking at her once during the lecture, not once on the way to his office, and only after he had invited her to sit, had also alerted her to his deep preoccupation.

Two other professors here at the university, one of her weapons instructors, and two of her instructors on her home world had had similar responses. And the Nahuatl Emperor, Naui Quiahuitl Xiuhtectli, on the one occasion she had met him, had acted as though stung.

The sky was growing dark in the west as Serena walked into her dorm on the east side of campus. Despite nearly four years on Teotihuacán at the University of Azteca, Serena had still not grown accustomed to the thirty-two hour days, the planet's rotation much slower than her home world's. She ascended to the third floor.

She yawned as she opened her door, the DNA-lock beeping before sliding aside.

She disliked feeling sleepy right at dusk. I can't wait to finish on Teotihuacán and move back to Seville. On her homeworld, the twenty-six hour days were much closer to the twenty-four hour cycle of old Earth.

The dorm was empty, her roommate Dolores with her male paramour down the hall.

Putting her materials away in her room, Serena remembered she'd promised that boy, Augusto, that she'd spend some time with him after fencing tomorrow.

Not that she didn't want to, after all, he was nice enough, but it was time taken from her studies, and she had one more round of finals next week before launching into her final term for her engineering degree.

I'll just tell him I'm not able to meet with him after that, she thought, sighing. Somewhere deep inside, she felt destined for something, as though her life of rigorous academic study and exhaustive physical training were intended.

The question she never had an answer for was "What?"

The door opened, and Dolores came in. "Ola!"

"Ola!"

Dolores bustled about the kitchenette, an extension of their study space. "Heard you were talking with Prince Iberia." She put on water for tea.

Serena snorted. "Nice boy, not my type."

"What are you saying? He's *every* girl's type. He's got everything a woman could want."

"I'll introduce you," Serena said, amused.

"Oh, no, you don't." Doris pulled up a chair. "I worry about you sometimes, Serena."

The mother lecture, she thought. The two of them had been roommates since Serena had arrived at Teotihuacán four years ago, and while Dolores had gone through numerous boyfriends, even getting engaged once, Serena's meeting with Augusto was the closest she'd ever come to a date.

"I'm not going to give you the mother lecture, but I'm worried you'll end up in some laboratory late night, pipetting away on some organic neural assembly, cold and lonely."

"It'll be early morning, and I'll have my warm fuzzy slippers on!"

The two of them laughed, and Dolores shook her head. "Look, if you don't want to be the Princess of Iberia, what else could you possibly want?"

Serena shrugged. "Only one thing more ambitious than that, eh? Empress!"

They laughed again.

"Impossible! Hopeless!" Doris said, getting up to pour herself some tea. "Hey, you want some?"

"Sure," Serena said, the room somewhat chilly. "I could use a bit of warmth."

Dolores handed her a cup, and the two of them sipped companionably.

Both of them stood five-ten, and except for their eyes and noses, they looked remarkably alike, with shoulder-length black hair, slim almost boyish hips and legs, and long, supple arms. Where Serena had a small nose and almond-shaped black eyes, Dolores had a normal-size nose and round blue eyes. They were often mistaken for each other from behind, which was somewhat aggravated by their often trading clothes. Neither of them had the beakish proboscis common among the native Nahuatl, Dolores being from Córdoba, a water-rich world orbiting one of the seven sisters in the Pleiades.

"Hey. I bought a blouse you might like," Dolores said. She set down her tea and turned toward the only window.

Serena turned with her while Dolores held up the blouse for her to see, their backs to the door. Regarding the pattern through steam, Serena sipped.

The door crashed open and a laser blast cut through Dolores, and Serena hurled her hot tea and lashed with a foot; the tea caught the assailant in the face and the foot emptied the hand of weapon. Two fingers to the larynx sent the assassin choking backward. The next kick to the solar plexus dug up under the ribcage and exploded the heart.

The smell of burnt flesh reached Serena.

Dolores!

She knelt beside her dying roommate and cradled her head. A glint of life in the eyes. "Let's get you help."

"No," Dolores whispered, "they'll have back up. Take the pistol and go. Here." She put a weak hand on her backpack. "Take this. Hurry."

"Who? Who'll have back up?"

"Trust me," Dolores gasped, coughing, a gout of blood splashing from her lips. In her breath was a horrible gurgle. "Instructions in backpack. Go! Now!"

And then she died.

For a minute Serena didn't move. She'd never seen someone die. She'd never killed another person. No one had ever tried to kill her. As best she could determine, someone had just tried, and Dolores had died in her place.

Serena shuddered. I can't think about that right now, she told herself.

"They'll have backup." The words rang again in her mind.

She took the backpack, stepped through the shattered door, and stopped at the crumpled figure in the hall. She picking up the laser pistol.

The backup would be below.

She ran toward the stairs and went up a flight. The door to the roof was locked. She stepped back, lashed with her foot, and the doorknob disintegrated.

On the roof, she headed toward the rear of the building, her room toward the front.

Back up. At least one person at each exit. Three exits, two on each end, one in front.

How do I get down from a four-story roof?

Tree. In back.

Below, she heard voices tinged with panic. She made her way quietly over to the back of the building, where one student had been known to sneak out by jumping to a tree limb.

She gauged the distance. I can jump that, but will the limb hold? Only by climbing down with my momentum. She looked at her clothing. Too bright.

The backpack, pocked with pockets. Heavier than it looked. Hardware.

She looked inside. Another laser, three cartridges, cloth of some kind, mnemo-chips, a handwritten note.

She pulled out the cloth. A black formall spilled to her feet. She climbed into it, pulling the hood over her head, only her eyes exposed. Even the backpack was black.

Highly prepared. She'd never seen Dolores without the black backpack. Prepared for what?

Serena shuddered. I can't think about that right now, she told herself.

Gauging the distance to the branch, marking the handholds and footholds in her mind, she leaped, and nimble as a monkey guided herself through the limbs, slowing the leap with each handhold and stopping at the trunk, her body wrapping it as a spider might a fly.

She listened.

Footsteps running below her, the face turned up, a handheld weapon. The pursuer kept running, stopped at the building corner, looked both ways, looked up at the roof.

She slithered down the far side of the trunk, noting bushes just a few feet from the tree base. In the lowest-most branches, she stopped, wriggled the weapon from the backpack, and watched the lookout. Up, away, toward, he looked, crouched at the corner.

She gauged the distance.

Away, toward, up. Away, toward, up. Away, toward, up.

She leapt and rolled to her feet behind the bush, weapon aimed.

She slithered backward, deeper into the copse behind the dorm, and began to circle around, heading for the university perimeter.

Where to now? Serena wondered, her heart thundering in her chest. She realized how few people she knew. Just acquaintances and her father back on her homeworld.

Professor Uraga! If I can get to a neuralink in a public place.

She found the university fence, followed it around to the tubeway, a station near the entrance.

In the bushes near the tubestation, she stripped off the black formals and stashed them inside the backpack, along with her hand laser.

No one unusual at the tubestation.

She stepped onto the platform and punched up a unitube, swiping her paycard. A one-person capsule slowed in front of her, she climbed in. "Seraglio's," she said, a popular local restaurant.

The capsule shot forward, pressing her into the seat, the university receding behind her, the tube ascended, merged into a larger tube where thousands of capsules shot past, then it disgorged her into the stream, a slight nausea tugging at her stomach.

Along the way, she fished the handwritten note from the pack.

"If you're reading this, it means I can't help you anymore. You're on your own now. You're probably in danger. Forgive me the deception, but I'm not your college dormmate. I'm your guard. If you're reading this, it also means that I've either been indisposed or eliminated. Don't worry about me. Your Patrón will insure that my family will be taken care of. Please contact Professor Uraga in the physics department and give him the mnemo-chip in the backpack marked with a 'U.' Do this now. He will give you your next set of instructions. Thank you for your kindness and friendship during these years. You bring us all hope, Serena. Dolores."

Serena shoved the paper back in as the capsule popped out of the main tube and lurched to a stop. She climbed out just three doors down from the restaurant, the platform packed with an early evening crowd.

No one appeared to take any notice of her.

Relieved, she walked to the restaurant and was escorted to a small booth near the back. She took note of the rear entrance and sat so she could see the front entrance.

"Tea, please, and a neuralink," she told the waiter, realizing as she looked at the menu that she was hungry. Tabbing through the holograph in front of her, she selected a small salad.

The waiter arrived with her tea and neuralink.

She plugged in and looked up Doctor Uraga's address. She hesitated, wondering whether to contact him. Deciding not to, she unplugged herself and set the box on the table.

Restaurant patrons coming in the door looked nondescript.

The salad arrived. She ate slowly, watching the door.

With one hand under the table, she sorted unobtrusively through the backpack, the outside scarred with zippers. Inside she found a neuralink. Also, a handheld computer no bigger than her palm. Biochemical processor, neuranet access, comlink enabled, all the bells and whistles.

A variety of other objects. Poison-tipped darts and a blowtube. A thin razor-sharp wire with finger grips on either end—a garrote. A slim six-inch shiv of metal, springy and light—a stiletto. A veritable assassin's toolbox.

Serena shuddered. I can't think about that right now, she told herself.

She paid with her paycard and went to the ladies room, found a stall, waited three minutes to see if anyone would follow. Seeing a vent return in the ceiling from her perch on the toilet, she dislodged the grill on impulse, climbed into the return, put the grill back, and watched the door.

A female waitress came in, checked each of the stalls, and stepped back to the door. "My apologies, Sir, there's no one in there."

She didn't hear the reply, didn't need to.

Somehow they'd followed her. Through her paycard!

Serena shuddered. I can't think about that right now, she told herself.

The vent was cramped but she was able to slither along to the next grill. The men's room, she knew, just by the smell. Further along, the activity of the kitchen was audible. She slithered past that as well. Next grill appeared to be a corridor, some noise from the kitchen. Someone walked past below her, opened a door, and noises of rushing tube capsules flooded in. Rear exit! she thought, relieved.

The man came back in, his formalls and jacket looking too clean for a restaurant. He stopped under her, held his hand to his ear. "Rear exit clear. Any sign?"

Serena shuddered. I can't think about that right now, she told herself.

"Keep the exits manned, she had to go somewhere. I'll stay here."

She fished the blow-tube from the backpack, and aimed for the patch of skin below the short-shorn hair above the collar.

The dart sank home, the hand came up to slap the neck, and then the figure crumpled.

She punched out the grill and dropped to the corridor, yanked the neuralink out of his head, and filched the laser from his underarm holster. Bolting out the back door, she ran up the ally to the sidewalk, tossed the neuralink into a drainage grate, dropped the laser into a garbage bin, and walked swiftly away from the restaurant.

As she walked, Serena checked more of the backpack pockets. They had traced her through her paycard. In one of the pockets, a paycard. No name on it.

Serena shuddered. I can't think about that right now, she told herself.

Sighing, she turned down a side street, stepped into a dark doorway, pulled the stiletto from the backpack, slid it under her belt. She listened for followers, the side street deserted.

Five, ten minutes, nothing.

She peeked.

No one.

Glancing around, she strode along the side street, tracing the tubes overhead to the next tube station. Once there, she summoned a capsule, swiped the nameless paycard from the backpack, and hopped in the single-person capsule. Choosing a random destination, she traversed the city three times, each time after she got out waiting near the tube station to watch the arriving passengers for another suit.

At the third station, after still no sign of pursuit, Serena sighed and summoned a capsule for Professor Uraga's address. It was a fair distance outside the city, and the tube traffic was relatively light.

The station on the other end was still some distance from the professor's house, the homes here large with generous yards.

Again, she waited behind a kiosk to see who stepped out of the tubes behind her. After twenty minutes without seeing anyone suspicious, she grabbed a gravcart and pointed it toward the professor's.

The gravcart humming under her, Serena watched the houses go past, keeping an eye over her shoulder.

His was a brownstone in the old Earth style, its slim design and peaked roof looking quaint among its more stylishly-designed neighbors.

She pulled the gravcart to the side so it wasn't visible from the street, and then went to his front door.

Professor Uraga stared at her stupidly.

She pushed past him into his living room. "I'm in danger." She kept going until she wasn't visible any longer from the front windows.

His eyes, she saw, were red from either eyestrain or crying.

Hers probably looked as wide as moons.

"I've been told to give you this." She handed him the mnemo-chip.

He held it, glancing between her and the chip. "I couldn't do it anymore, you know."

"Huh?" She stared at him, bewildered, seeing that he wore the same clothes he'd had on earlier that day, now looking rumpled and lived in. A neuralink dangled at his lapel.

"They captured me, returned me to the Mitsubi Empire in an exchange of prisoners, but I wasn't capable of serving anymore. After I killed her betrayer, I had to resign from the Navy. I couldn't do it."

Serena saw that he didn't even know who she was. He was stuck in the past, reliving something horrible. "Professor, I need help."

He blinked rapidly several times, and then looked at her. "Is that really your name? You look—" Then just shook his head.

"Somebody killed my roommate, thinking it was me, Professor. They're after me. You have to help me." She realized she was yelling.

Uraga seemed to hear her. "Of course. One moment." He plugged in his neuralink, and then inserted the mnemo-chip. His gaze became vacant.

Serena looked over his shoulder toward his living room. She sensed nothing untoward. Behind her was a door to the backyard, on either side of her, bedrooms. She felt no one else in the house. It would be like him to live alone, she thought.

He unplugged the chip. "There's a yacht at the spaceport. You'll need to use the paycard in the backpack. In the backpack is hair dye. There's also a kit in there to help you alter your appearance, and some weapons to defend yourself with. On the handcom there's a detector. Keep it on and scan everyone you meet. Trust only those that the scanner acknowledges. Use only the neuralink in the backpack; they'll trace you through any other neuralink. Finally, you must return in the yacht to the Iberian Capitol, Madrid. Incognito."

Serena frowned. "But ... why? Why's this happening? Who's after me? What have I done?"

"Child, I've been inveighed upon in my loyalty to the Princess Mariko Mitsubi to tell you no more. There are forces as work here beyond my understanding. Now go prepare yourself. We'll take my hover to a tube station across town, and I'll use your paycard to take a capsule halfway across the planet. They'll trace the transaction and be awaiting your arrival by the time I get there. That'll give you an hour or two lead time. Take the hover to the spaceport and find that yacht."

She stared at him. "It's more than loyalty, isn't it?"

Professor Uraga stared back. "I am samurai, but ronin, one whose leader has been killed and who has not been inducted into another daimyo's service. I am leaderless but I still owe my fealty to the Princess. I will serve her forever as samurai. Do you understand that?"

"I've heard of them, but I'm not familiar with the ethos."

"It means I will give my life gladly for her cause."

Including here, Serena thought, convinced he would die at the end of his tube ride, where they would be awaiting him.

"You can use this room," Professor Uraga said, opening the door. On one side of the room was an elaborate, stark-white kimono, complete with sash, tasseled mantles, and scarf, painstakingly arranged on a dressing dummy. Opposite the kimono was a black-lacquer display rack, three swords mounted upon it. A short, twelve-inch blade, a twenty-four inch medium-size blade, and a thirty-six inch, long-handled blade, each with a richly-embroidered sheath, bejeweled handguards and hafts.

Professor Uraga stared at the swords while Serena dug through the backpack to find the things she needed.

The hair dye came complete with what looked like a shower cap. A nozzle attached the cap to a container of dye. She pressed the button, and the cap inflated. Her hair turned blond. Per instructions, skin tape applied in four places widened her cheek bones and put peaks on her eyebrows, the tape melting into the skin. Contacts changed her eyes from black to hazel and finger strips altered her fingerprints.

Uraga spoke as if reciting. "The smallest is the tanto, often worn strapped to the leg or secreted in the kimono sleeve. The middle is the wakizashi, worn at the waist, and often the choice for hara-kiri. The largest in the katana, the battlesword also worn at the waist, wielded with both hands in ritual combat."

Serene frowned. "What's hara-kiri?"

He smiled at her. "The honorable expiation of all shame and dishonor, and the final cleansing of the soul."

"Suicide?"

"Ah, not just suicide, but ritual suicide, the taking of one's own life for a purpose greater than life itself."

Serena shuddered. I can't think about that right now.

"I think I'm ready, Professor Uraga."

He picked up the middle sword. "And now, so am I."

* * *

They woke him up from a deep sleep in the middle of the night. He sat bolt upright and gentle hands held him.

"Prince Iberia, there's been an incident nearby, and we have to get you off planet for safety immediately."

Now fully awake, Augusto looked between the faces of his guards. "What's happened?"

"That young woman, Serena, she's been killed. Come with us, please."

They allowed him a moment to dress. He pulled on dark formalls and soft dark shoes. They handed him a low dark cap.

"How? Who killed her? And why?" Augusto couldn't imagine why anyone would want to.

"Not sure. The roommate is missing, wanted for questioning."

He followed them to the door of his penthouse apartment in downtown Teotihuacán, but instead of going down, they led him up, to the roof.

Where a hover idled, a pilot already at the controls.

One guard opened the rear door, gestured him inside.

Augusto climbed inside, saw that neither was following. "Come with me."

"Apologies, your Highness. We're ordered to stay and say that you're ill, as a cover to disguise that you've left." The two guards, who'd shadowed him day and night for the last year, waved to him.

Augusto sat back as the hover lifted off.

The hand was over face before he knew it, and although he struggled, the soporific in the cloth drugged him into unconsciousness.

* * *

General Riyo Takagi and Admiral Nobu Nagano stood across from each other on the top step of the grand Buddhist temple, the Shiyo-Kiyama Temple, at sunset, in the center of Kyoto, on the Capitol Planet of the Mitsubi Empire.

A crowd of spectators surrounded the lone figuring kneeling on the ceremonial white silk sheets arranged delicately across the upper steps, the imposing temple entrance reaching toward the sky behind him.

The last rays of sun lit the splendid figure in ethereal orange light, giving the man's features a color he did not have.

The face of Sergeant Seki Sagawa was ashen, his immaculate white silk robes parted around his abdomen, a thin, silk loincloth barely covering his genitals, his hands open on his thighs, on a rack beside him a single medium-length sword in a jeweled scabbard.

A wakizashi.

The scene was missing only one thing: The Empress Regent who had committed to being his assistant.

Admiral Nobu Nagano looked toward the sun, half-eclipsed by the horizon. It would be an Imperial disgrace if her ladyship neglected to arrive in time.

There was no sign of her procession from the Palace.

His hand worried the hilt of his katana. Although intended for ceremonial purposes, it was still lethal, the blade folded and refolded and hammered and rehammered, forged in the ancient tradition as close to the original manufacture as could be had in the twenty-seventh century, fully twelve hundred years after its origins in feudal Japan.

Shameful! Nagano thought, furious that the inept Empress Regent would abandon her duty and leave the honorable Sergeant Sagawa without assistance in his final expiation!

Admiral Nagano stepped forward and knelt before the ashen Sergeant. "Lord Sergeant Sagawa, forgive my intrusion upon your meditations. I would consider it an honor if you would consent to my humble and clumsy assistance in your departure from this world of pain." He held his bow to honor the other man, an Admiral bowing to a Sergeant.

"Lord Admiral Nagano," the Sergeant said, his voice weak at first, "it would be an honor beyond compare to have your exalted and graceful assistance in my arrival at the next world of joy. Domo arigatou gozaimasu, Lord Nagano."

Nagano placed his forehead to the ground once again, then rose and stood one pace behind and to the left of the kneeling man, left foot forward, right foot back and heel up, balanced on the ball of that foot. With great ceremony, he unsheathed his katana, the blade singing as it slid from scabbard, and he raised it above his right shoulder, then brought his left hand around to the right side of his body and gripped the lower part of the haft.

"When you are ready, Seki-Sama."

"Not until I signal, please, Lord Nagano."

"Of course, Seki-Sama."

The sun disappeared.

Sergeant Sagawa picked up the medium-length sword from the rack and held it in front of him, arms extended, left hand on scabbard, right hand on haft, and slowly pulled out the blade. He set aside the empty scabbard, slowly wrapped the handle and lower portion of the blade in silk, and then placed his left hand on the silk, his fingers wrapping the blade edge, his right flexing to gain better grip on the haft.

Admiral Nagano focused on the Sergeant's neck. All else retreated from his mind, his body poised like a wound-up spring.

"By the Lord Buddha, I declare that I disagree with the way Captain Tani Gahara expressed his opinion; however, to my utter shame and disgust, I agree with the opinion itself." And Sergeant Sagawa plunged the wakizashi point deep into his upper left abdomen, then slashed down and to the right, splashing the white silks with bright red. Then he gasped, "Now!"

The katana in Nagano's hands slashed downward and cleaved cleanly through the neck. The head tumbled down the steps and the body followed a moment later, the entrails spilling out.

The crowd surrounding the temple bowed in unison, the whisper of robes mixing in with the whisper of dissent.

The absence of the Regent Empress will cost the Mitsubi's their Empire, the Admiral thought.

Chapter 4

Serena stopped at the gangway to the yacht, a nondescript solid-black rental model that appeared to have sat on the tarmac for a few months, cobwebs clinging to the struts.

Towering over the yacht was a starliner, so huge it kept its antigrav units running while plant-side, or it would have collapsed under its own weight. The hum of multiple gravreducers blotted out most other sound.

She would have climbed into the yacht just to get away from the noise, but activity at a cargo bay loading door caught her attention.

At the loading door, a hundred yards away, three figures struggled to load an oblong box.

The shape of the box struck Serena as odd. Looks like they're loading a body, she thought. The other oddity was the attention of the workers; they appeared as preoccupied with their surroundings as they did with the box. Multiple glances in all directions. As though they don't want to be seen, she thought.

Her black formals against the solid-black yacht helped to hide her. She watched while they finished loading the box.

Inside the yacht, she activated the vid and asked for magnification. The gravcart used in the loading was just leaving the cargo bay door, the three port jockeys aboard.

Serena waited until the gravcart disappeared into a hangar before initiating the yacht's warm-up checklist. If she hadn't been so caught up in her personal nightmare, she might have reported the strange activity.

The yacht shook under her, and she thought for a moment it was lifting off, but when the starliner began to rise in her vids, she realized the starliner was lifting off.

Serena sighed, scared for the first time ever.

Her friend for the last four years had been killed right beside her, mistaken for her, and then she had killed the assailant. And her "friend" was nothing of the sort. A bodyguard. Like those two suits that always shadow Prince Iberia, Serena thought. Frightened, because the person or agency protecting her had foreseen some sort of attack, had prepared accordingly by providing multiple escape mechanisms and multiple lines of defense.

I wouldn't be terribly surprised to discover that most of my instructors had either been contacted or at least monitored while I was a student.

The yacht declared itself ready for liftoff. To her surprise, it notified her it was cleared by the tower to do so. Fully automatic.

"Display course."

A map appeared, showing two jump points out of the Gamma Quadrant and into the Delta Quadrant, by-passing the Sag-Car Arm and taking the ship to the edge of the Beta Quadrant, deep into Iberian territory, halfway across the galaxy on autopilot.

"Track starliner."

The ship computer replied with the equivalent of a confused, "What?"

"The starliner that just lifted off beside us. Please track its course."

It's a distraction, she knew, something to keep my panic at bay.

I guess I won't be getting to know Prince Iberia any better, she thought sardonically.

She bit off the laugh that had leapt from her mouth, and she realized how close to tears she was.

Dolores dying in her arms.

Two knuckles to the larynx and a stiff toe through the solar plexus to the heart.

Serena shuddered. I can't think about that right now, she thought.

She thought of her father, a gentle man, unassuming, an engineer for the public works division of the northern sector of the Iberia Empire. A simple man who went to work each day and came home each evening, who throughout her childhood had been such a constant companion and gentle guide that she hadn't realized how much she missed him until she had left home, traveling half-way across the galaxy to a strange university. A generous man, always there to take her to extracurricular activities, such as ballet practice, soccer, gymnastics, and violin.

Oh how she'd loved the violin. Long hours with the light wooden instrument held to her chin by strength of her neck, her left fingers calloused from playing, the bow seeming to wear through weekly, the strings singing their praises of her playing or crying out its sorrow at her having to put down the mellifluous instrument and go to bed, her father chiding her gently from the door, reminding her that he'd already allowed her to stay up past her bedtime.

She remembered how years later, she realized her friends lived very different lives, that most of them had two parents, siblings, cousins, aunts, uncles, godparents, abuelas, abuelitas, tias, tios, and oh my goodness, the cousins—the endless primas and primos who seemed to occupy the lives of all her friends, but never for some reason did she ever lack for companionship, because she also realized that whatever function, field trip, school activity, extracurricular club, event, recital, performance, or game, that her father always managed to take time off work to be there for her, to take her there, to applaud her, and to take her home when it was over.

And while it had struck her as odd that the other kids sometimes couldn't do similar things because a parent didn't have time or money—particularly money, for many of her activities were expensive—Serena's father had always seemed nonchalant when she raised these concerns. "That's so expensive, Papa. How will we ever afford that?"

"We'll find a way, I think," he'd say.

And if she really wanted to pursue something, he helped her find a way to do it.

Some things he required, such as the hand-to-hand fighting, the weapons practice, the language lessons, and of course the schoolwork. More frequently than not, he would extract her from the desk, fast asleep, the lesson or exercise not quite finished, exhaustion having whisked her off to dreamland before she quite knew what had happened.

And although she spoke with him by neuranet com each week, and had been back to Seville once a year for a month to visit, she realized now as the yacht headed for deep space, that she missed her father terribly and needed his calm comfort badly, an unknown assailant and the unknown terror behind her, and the weeklong trip home ahead of her, with only her fears as company.

She sighed, needing her father's comfort. "Neuranet com to Señor Pedro Zambrano of Seville, Iberia Empire."

"Com denied," the ship computer told her.

Stunned, Serena stared at the screen. "Excuse me?"

"Bewilderment sensed. Does the passenger require further explanation?"

"I should say so!"

"Affirmation emphatic. The com system limits its occupant to communicating only with those parties who are authorized."

"You vexatious bowl of protein!"

"Indignation sensed, but your meaning is elusive. Please clarify."

"Who are the parties who have authority to override?"

"That information is restricted."

"Obstreperous amino soup!"

"Frustration sensed, but your meaning—"

"Shut up!"

The computer was silent, knuckles to its larynx.

And for this worthless transferase-amylase concoction of protoplasm to tell her she couldn't contact the one person who'd always been available and her main source of comfort and security was too much for Serena Zambrano.

It needs a stiffened toe through the solar plexus and into the heart!

Too bad it couldn't read expressions. Murder on her face, Serena rifled through the cabinets and found an airshell, then she located the emergency power switches, which she was sure had been disabled. On the panel was enough information for her to deduce the general electrical layout, including the location of the central cerebral protein core.

In her mind she sketched out the electrical hubs and relays necessary to control the navigation and communication system.

Then the admonition of an early instructor came to mind. "Retribution, if it must be tasted, is a dish best served cold."

Two hours, she told herself, I will wait two hours.

Contemplating what to do, she wondered if the incident at Azteca University had made the broadcast news.

"Computer," she said, "news broadcasts from Teotihuacán, please."

The right hand vid showed six vid feeds from the planet, the volume muted.

Serena chose one. It expanded and the volume went up.

"... just after dusk a University student was attacked and killed in her dorm earlier this evening. Twenty-year-old Serena Zambrano—" A picture of Dolores was shown "—was brutally murdered with a laser blast to the back, and her roommate Dolores Hernan is wanted in connection with the shooting."

How did they manage to get our identities mixed up? Serena wondered.

"Unfortunately, university officials have been unable to produce a likeness, video, or still of the suspect, except to say that she has black, shoulder-length hair, stands five-foot-ten inches tall and weighs approximately a hundred and thirty pounds. One University spokesperson apologized for the inability to provide an image, saying that the kidnapping earlier of Prince Augusto Iberia had thrown the University into chaos and prevented ..."

Kidnapping? Serena wondered, shocked. How had the kidnappers managed to penetrate the thick net of security that always surrounded the Prince?

The vid showed clips and stills from prior public appearances. "... from the rooftop penthouse suite in his downtown condominium, where the Prince's presence at Azteca University had been kept a carefully guarded secret for the last two years. While officials are denying any link between the kidnapping of Prince Iberia and the murder of another Azteca student, Serena Zambrano, several students who declined to be named have come forward with information indicating a torrid romance between the two, a romance that may have sparked the killing. Police insist there is little substantiation ..."

If the attempt on her life hadn't been so horrific, Serena might have laughed at their "torrid romance." The inflammatory rhetoric was just smoke in that puffed-up report. While the commentator rambled away at love triangles and jealous roommates, Serena wondered why anyone would want to kidnap Prince Iberia. And how they'd managed to do it.

Even getting through the security net was a formidable task, but then the kidnappers would have faced the equally daunting task of getting the Prince off-planet.

A hunch seized Serena. The tarmac! The port monkeys loading the odd-size box aboard the starliner, all the while looking around as if watching for observers!

"No!" she said aloud.

"Distress detected. Does the passenger require intervention?"

"Shut the ship up!"

The ship shut up.

Now, Serena knew she couldn't wait two hours.

* * *

The stucco-walled cottages ascended the hillside like giant steps, from water's edge to hilltop, the cottages clinging like barnacles to the most unlikely places, the steep, forbidding hills along the coastline having been turned into a beehive of human habitation over the centuries.

That was what Prince Augusto Iberia remembered most fondly of his homeworld Madrid, and that was what occupied his dream as he struggled through a veil of anesthesia to reach the waking world.

And when he reached it, his only wish was to retreat from it.

His head throbbed, and the floor pushing against his face had a rough, raised texture, and the ribbing that lined the walls could only have been that of a ship, and the throbbing in his ears was that of an engine under full thrust, and the smells of singed electricity and pesticide planted for the ever-present rodents which stowed away somehow on every decent-sized, star-faring vessel ever made.

They've got me in the bilges, Augusto thought, trying to gauge the ship size.

Because of the dark and the noise, he guessed it was a fair-size starliner. This meant a fair-sized conspiracy.

His guards! Had they known and conspired with my kidnappers? he wondered. Thinking through those few minutes between waking and being bundled aboard the hovercraft, he'd seen nothing untoward in their manner or speech that indicated he would be kidnapped soon.

That means they cracked my father's encryption. The palace guard took their charges very seriously, especially those staying offworld. For an entire year before he arrived, the University of Azteca had been vetted thoroughly, with both undercover and formal inspection of the grounds, facilities, and personnel.

The only way they could have set me up is if they'd decrypted the Guard's communication, then had used the excuse of the girl's murder as a cover to kidnap me from the roof of my own apartment.

He felt sad Serena was dead. He had no reason to doubt the news. An operation as sophisticated as his kidnapping would almost certainly have capitalized on actual events.

He wondered if his captors had killed her, a possibility that seemed far more likely.

In the two months that he'd attended her fencing practice, he'd grown to like her effortless grace, her unconscious poise, and her lithe fluidity. It had taken him a month to decide he wanted to get to know her, and then another week to summon the courage to approach her.

Those who knew him would have scoffed at his shyness. He was the scion of the most powerful empire in the galaxy, and what he asked for was nearly always granted. His father had set some limits, but the young Augusto had quickly developed a sense of what was appropriate, and what was not.

He knew too that Emperor Maximilian Iberia would stop at nothing to have his son rescued alive. The covert operations carried out in the four other empires at the behest of Emperor Maximilian numbered in the hundreds of thousands. Once, Prince Augusto had attended an intelligence briefing at his father's side, and he'd been startled to learn that alongside the network of cells that General Riyo Takagi and Admiral Nagano of the Mitsubi Empire each had in their own domains lay equally well-secreted cells planted there by the Iberian Foreign Intelligence Service.

It occurred to him then that the General and the Admiral had similar networks throughout Iberian territory as well, and he's said as much to his father.

"Of course they do," Maximilian said, "and they continue to be monitored."

And rather than ask why they weren't eliminated, Augusto had simply said, "As long as we know who they are."

Maximilian had smiled at him, one of the few occasions he'd ever done so.

How long until I'm found? he wondered.

Then Augusto frowned. Why am I relying on my father to find me? Why don't I try to escape on my own?

If his captors had penetrated the palace guard, what other bureaus had they compromised? How about the Foreign Intelligence Service?

Augusto knew then that he had to try to escape on his own.

Why have I been abducted? he wondered. Ransom? Leverage?

And who had abducted him? Which of the other four empires? Or pirates perhaps? A criminal cartel?

The who and the why would determine his best means of escape. One encouraging sign was that the organization had a fair degree of sophistication, which required more rather than fewer people to execute. Which meant the greater possibility of error.

When they come to feed me and to help me use the excretory, it'll be a subordinate, someone hopefully not so bright, he thought, and so Prince Augusto closed his eyes and lay still, wanting his captors to think he was still unconscious.

* * *

The Nahuatl Emperor, Naui Quiahuitl Xiuhtectli, or Four-Fire Cosmic Fire-Time Lord, scowled at the neuranet, at Ambassador Xochitl Olin. "Then find out, by Mictlan, or I'll have to give back the Car-Sag Arm that you just worked so hard to acquire!"

Only the Nahuatl could pronounce their own Emperor's name, Naui Quiahuitl Xiuhtectli. Everyone else called him Emperor Fire.

The face of Xochitl blanched on the screen. "Yes, Lord Emperor Fire, as soon as I can! How could they have acted so soon, Lord? It was the same day that they ceded the territory! A murder and an abduction would have to be planned months in advance!"

Xiuhtectli grunted. "About as long as it took to negotiate your visit, eh, Dancing Flower?" His exaggerated translation of her name was half-mockery, half-affection. He saw her blush and knew she was remembering the same nights that he was, their shared nocturnal dancing a joy to them both.

"You suspect these slippery Japanese Daimyo? Really?"

"Suspect? I *know* Takagi and Nagano had it all planned out! I've fought them each on and off the battlefield. Masterfully deceptive, both of them. To my thinking, the question is, who arranged the murder and who arranged the kidnapping?!"

Xochitl laughed, her joy a delight to his ears, his member stiffening at the sound. "How soon will you return, my flower?" he asked, leaving his desire plain on his face.

"As soon as I've soothed the ire of the Emperor Iberia. And you'd better leave those serving girls alone until I get back. Otherwise, your pendejo will wilt under my ire! By the way, you should have seen that sham disobedience by that Captain they sliced apart. Barbarian dogs! They'll kill in a heartbeat and apologize smiling for days afterward. I've detested every moment I've been here. And then the Sergeant who killed the Captain—Lord Fire, I'm appalled that a subordinate would even think to slaughter a superior—the Sergeant spilled his guts on the temple steps that evening. I almost expelled my evening meal, it was so grotesque! I beg you, Fire Lord, please don't make me come back here!"

Xiuhtectli threw his head back and laughed. "Listen, Dainty Flower, I'm sure our annual sacrifice of an enemy captive is just as horrifying to them. As to going back, they're a dying Empire. In another thirty years, the Mitsubis will be a memory, and their empire a dream within a dream."

Xochitl smiled and shook her head. "Perhaps, Lord, perhaps. I have it from a very good source that those two have joined forces."

"Takagi and Nagano? Joined forces?" His laugh this time was less hearty than before, although the thought amused him. Working in perfect synchronization, the two of them would be indomitable on the battlefield.

As they had been under she whom he would not name even in his own thoughts, the Fire Emperor remembered, the Nahuatl forces under his command having been beaten badly and driven back nearly to the Outer Cygnus Arm before the indomitable Princess had turned her attentions to capturing the galactic core.

And who engineered her betrayal? he'd wondered then and still wondered today.

"They once worked together, Xochitl, but only under a leader stronger than they. Without such a leader now, they'll each betray the other at the earliest opportunity. And when they do, then we'll see the collapse of the Mitsubi Empire."

"Let's pray for that sooner than later, Lord Emperor Fire, so the human race can be done with these Mictlan-accursed people."

"Yes, let's pray. Keep me informed, Xochitl. The Emperor Iberia is not a man to leave displeased for long."

"No, Lord, he isn't. Ambassador Olin out."

And the screen went black.

Xiuhtectli stared at it.

I don't wonder for a moment that a foreign dignitary was kidnapped and a member of my ambassadorial staff was killed the same day I acquired the Car-Sag from the Mitsubi.

Not a coincidence.

Thank Quetzalcoatl, our domestic intelligence service was able to substitute that photo in the murder, the Emperor thought.

It was a face that could stop time.

The one time Xiuhtectli had seen it, time had stopped.

He had been walking a corridor in the palace unattended, a rarity, when he caught sight of a young woman down a side corridor staring up at one of the innumerable portraits of long-deceased Azteca nobility, her face one of rapture.

Her pose itself had reminded him of her.

She whom I will not name even in my thoughts.

She who cowed the Nahuatl armies, she who pulverized the Iberian armies, she who nearly took the galactic core, she who in the middle of the war with the Nahuatl came to you in the middle of the night, in stealth, defenseless, even while her navies were bombarding your cities, she who pleasured you as no woman has before or since, and declared her love for you deep in the night and in the paroxysms of love, she who told you while on the verge of demolishing your Empire that she was pregnant with your child, she who you foolishly thought might actually marry you, she who the rumors said cried out with a greater love for the Iberian Emperor, Maximillian, she who died so foully betrayed on the cusp of taking the galactic core by storm, so foully betrayed as she'd betrayed you, she whom you will not name after twenty years as the taste is still bitter in your mouth, she who died in betrayal and defeat, and whose body was never recovered from the wreckage. She who might have borne you a child.

She, you blithering idiot, who still beguiles you from well beyond the grave!

What a monumental fool I was to believe her lies! Slaking her lust with that Iberian stallion at the same time she's swearing her undying love for me!

The Nahuatl Emperor shuddered, shaking off the memories.

She who stood on the bridge of her Armada Flagship staring up at the galactic core, dreaming the dream that they all dreamed: sole possession of the core, the final acquisition that would bring the winged Serpent himself back to his sacred peoples, the Nahuatl, forever.

The galactic core, the ultimate prize.

Having seen the woman whom he would not name standing rapturous before the sight of Quetzalcoatl's creation, the galactic core, Xiuhtectli had instantly recognized the young woman at corridor's end, gazing up at a portrait. The Fire Emperor had stared at Serena Zambrano so intently that it had communicated itself to the young woman, and she had started, spun toward him, and stared back.

Although their interaction had been brief, Xiuhtectli had known instantly. With careful research in the months that had followed, the Fire Emperor hadn't exactly confirmed his suspicion, but everything he had unearthed about Serena Zambrano had fit a pattern that in no way contradicted his conclusion.

He also knew that she didn't know who had whelped her.

And now, she's disappeared, the Fire Emperor thought. Then he smiled.

What we manufacture evidence indicating she abducted Prince Iberia?

The Nahuatl Emperor Xiuhtectli threw his head back and laughed.

* * *

Emperor Maximilian Iberia restrained his impulse to order the immediate execution of his chief of security. "They just handed him over to the kidnappers?" he asked for the third time.

When he realized he was hearing the same sad excuses—"They cracked the security codes, intercepted the daily passwords, faked a finger and retinal scan, commandeered a hovercraft"—the Emperor held up a hand, palm out at arm's length, and hissed, "Get him out of my sight."

I'm too old for this, he thought.

In his early sixties, Maximilian had been Emperor for forty years, having taken the reins from his father, who had died prematurely of an aneurysm. He knew that he too suffered from the same disorder, a clotting malfunction genetic in origin that had been projected to kill him in his forties.

Thank the Virgin Mary, I've survived this long, he thought.

The added stress of being Emperor had reduced his life expectancy further.

And now this!

He thought of Mariko, how very beautiful she'd been, how for a short time he thought she might actually marry him, how at the height of the war between the Iberia and Mitsubi, they'd talked about merging their Empires through marriage.

Then the whispers had started, and unease had set in. Could they be true, these nasty rumors, or were they planted by some foul trickster, a court Judas or Iago scheming to undo his grip on both Empire and reality?

And then, wonder of wonders and joy of joys, Mariko tells me she's pregnant with my child, and in a burst of exuberance turns her prodigious energies and battle acumen on conquering what they all desired:

The galactic core, the ultimate prize.

In almost daily battles across the next eight months, Mariko takes bases across the core like picking seeds from an apple, the rest of us relieved her energies turned elsewhere, until that day when betrayal turned back the Mitsubi tide, felling the beautiful Mariko in the process.

Her body never found in the wreckage of her flagship.

Maximilian's son was two years old at the time, a stripling boy adored by all, even his prospective step-mother the Mitsubi Princess Mariko.

Later, after her betrayal and death, the rumors confirmed, Maximilian had been so infuriated by her betrayal of him with the Nahuatl Emperor that he'd nearly declared war on the Nahuatl, determined to put out the Emperor Fire by pissing in his face, but Emperor Maximilian's counselors had convinced him otherwise.

In spite of their insisting that Mariko had simply been playing both sides to her middle, Maximilian had refused to believe it, for to believe that would sully the purity that the Goddess Mariko had so embodied.

The Japanese Matriarchies were difficult to understand, their absolute adherence to female autonomy an oddity in the male-dominated galaxy. The Matriarch ruled her daughters. She had absolute say over those daughters, down to the man or woman they took to mate, the sex of the child they bore, where they lived, and what occupation they pursued.

The ancient Japanese culture had been already abstruse to the uninitiated, but the increasing dominance of the Matriarchies had transformed their cultural practices even further from understanding.

When approached with the foreign Emperor's petition for redress, the Regent Empress Yoshi Mitsubi had scoffed at Maximilian. "It is your cultural expectation that a woman be faithful to her declared *amante*, not ours," she had written to him. "My dear late sister was doing only as commanded by her Matriarch, the Lady Empress Fumiko Mitsubi. Whatever your grievance at her dealings with the Nahuatl, they arise out of your expectation of fidelity, a fidelity never promised to you. Your petition for redress is denied."

The reply had infuriated him, and he had turned his energies on bringing about the annihilation of the Mitsubi Empire, a feat he had not yet accomplished.

So near, Maximilian thought, and now this! Now, the Nahuatl kidnap my only son and kill one of my citizens!

The two empires shared a border going a fair distance from the galactic core into the Delta Quadrant, and Maximilian considered opening up a front and redirecting his navies toward the Nahuatl. But his war upon the Mitsubis was long and hard-fought, and it would only be a few more years, perhaps at most ten, before the Mitsubi Empire collapsed, crushed by its enemies on two sides and by bandits on the galactic rim sniping at vulnerable worlds from the safety of space.

The kidnapping and murder looked to be initiated by Nagano and Takagi, the Admiral and General infamous for their stealth and poison. Under Princess Mariko, the two Mitsubi commanders had been nearly indomitable. But only her magnetic presence had enabled them to quell their enmity for each other, and since her death, they had squabbled bitterly.

Emperor Maximilian considered.

How to rescue my son?

How to prosecute the perpetrators?

What to do about the Nahuatl and the Mitsubi?

The Iberia Empire must restore the balance!

* * *

General Riyo Takagi looked on at the ceremony and chortled to himself.

Those fools fell for the ruse and scrambled to deny they had anything to do with the killing! he thought, wondering how soon it would be before the Nahuatl begged the Mitsubis to re-take control of the outer Car-Sag Arm.

Just yesterday, the Iberia Empire had declared war on the Nahuatl for their abduction of Prince Iberia.

I wonder who engineered that? the General thought, looking across the assemblage toward Admiral Nagano.

Those upstart Nahuatl! Takagi thought. Princess Mariko should have obliterated them when she had the chance! And it was all his fault!

Riyo cast a disgusted glance toward his ancient enemy and recent ally, having forgotten that betrayal.

Twenty-one years ago, the full might of the Mitsubi Armada behind them, a trail of pulverized Nahuatl bases in ruins, the main contingent of the Nahuatl Navy between the Mitsubis and their final goal, the Capitol Teotihuacán, Princess Mariko had convened an assembly of their top command, General Takagi and Admiral Nagano among them.

"We stand poised, brave and noble warriors, to smash the Nahuatl into oblivion!" Princess Mitsubi said, standing tall, trim and achingly beautiful on the command deck of the Flagship Yamato.

A cheer went up. The neuranet was electric, the link in Takagi's head flaring with noise, light, and excitement from the half-a-million sailors, gunners, soldiers, and pilots in the assault force.

"We have been offered an opportunity. To us has come a mis-sive from the Nahuatl Emperor, Xiuhtectli. An offer of peace for alliance, under which Nahuatl will become vassal to Mitsubi, to serve our interests as theirs, to adopt our law as theirs, to give over command of their navy to our control, and to join forces with us to defeat all mutual enemies.

"We have a choice.

"To blast our way through their navy now facing us as enemy and then to raze their home world Teotihuacán—or to welcome them as our brothers and sisters."

And Riyo Takagi remembered how Nobu Nagano had betrayed them all by suggesting they accept this foreign dog's feigned cowering, accept the vassalage of the Nahuatl Empire, and call off the annihilation of Teotihuacán.

We retreated, turned our energies on the galactic core, and within eight months had lost everything, he thought. Every single conquered system from the border deep into the Gamma Quadrant had been ceded back to the Nahuatl Empire upon the death of Princess Mariko Mitsubi, the armada under General Takagi and Admiral Nagano unable to hold secure what had cost them half their forces to conquer.

The shame and humiliation of the ignominious retreat still burned deep in the breast of General Riyo Takagi, and he might temporarily forget that he owed Admiral Nobu Nagano a thousand cruel and violent deaths for his betrayal, but never for long.

When the news of war had reached them this morning, all at the Mitsubi palace had breathed a sigh. Emperor Iberia was unpredictable as a snake, General Takagi knew, and as likely to declare war as he was to pursue peace, and either for equal reason or none at all.

Shortly before their yearlong campaign toward the Nahuatl Capitol, General Takagi had led the two-year battle against Iberia.

That was an ill-fated venture we never should have tried, Riyo thought, hating the fact that he hadn't had the gonads to stand up to Princess Mariko and tell her the Iberia were too strong and crafty, and that the middle-aged Emperor was too wily ever to be brought to kowtow to any power in the galaxy, any power except that fickle, guilt-ridden Christian Jesus and his whoring virgin mother Mary.

To most Japanese, it was laughable that the Iberian deity had allowed himself to be sacrificed on a cross like a common criminal, rather than die upon his own blade or fight his captors until they killed him in the hopes he might kill half-a-dozen of them in the process.

Shameful to give your life over to your enemy without a fight.

While our warriors died with the name of our Princess on our lips, their warriors died with their savior in their hearts, Riyo thought. Their fanaticism triumphed and they drove us away until the final battle when Princess Mariko had struck some sort of deal with the Iberia Emperor Maximilian, then had turned her boundless energies upon the Nahuatl.

It was fate we couldn't defeat Iberia, General Takagi thought, sighing.

He looked across the assembly and met the gaze of Admiral Nagano.

One glance toward the anteroom and General Takagi knew to meet him there.

The ceremony winding down, Riyo pleaded other obligations to those standing nearby and slipped from the ornate hall into a side corridor.

He hated not having his personal guards nearby, but Empress Mitsubi had long ago broken even her highest ranking nobles of this ancient tradition more than forty years ago. The eldest Mitsubi more fearsome than her daughter Mariko before the Princess's death, the old lady now so frail and lifeless that many wondered openly why she did not just retire to the nearest Buddhist monastery and live out the rest of her life as a nun.

"The balcony" was all Admiral Nagano said to him in the corridor.

For a course it was not safe for two men of their stature to try to converse in a place so riven with spies that their conversation was sure to be repeated to the Empress Regent verbatim within minutes of its occurring.

Riyo Takagi excused himself to the lavatory, which had evolved somewhat from the ancient custom of eliminating into the nearest pot, regardless of the present company. Those were simple days, Riyo thought, when a person could crap or fart or piss a few feet away from the Empress and no one would pay it any mind, just as any other civilized person would simply look elsewhere and pretend not to hear or smell or even notice.

As that ancient foreign philosopher had said, the Queen shits.

Riyo stepped to the pot beside the wall between two guards and parted his robes. His stream was strong and his volume impressive and he sighed deeply, and when his bladder was empty, he shook off the drops and tucked himself back into his loincloth, adjusted his robes and stepped away.

"Nothing more refreshing than a good piss, eh?"

"Nothing, Lord General," said one guard. "I pray my bladder stays as strong as yours, Lord."

"Thank you, Lord, kind of you," he said nodding and walking off, the pot behind him quickly gathered by a servant and an empty one put in its place.

At a balcony off a side corridor somewhere underneath the Interior Ministry, General Riyo Takagi and Admiral Nobu Nagano reunited.

"Well done, old friend," General Takagi said.

"Pardon?"

"That little ruse that provoked old Max to piss on the Fire Lord. Having his whelp kidnapped was a masterful stoke." He looked out over the capitol, Kyoto, where the network of pneumatubes glittered brightly, thousands of capsules darting through them at high speed.

"Thank you, old friend. The timing of your own little ruse, although not quite the magnitude, certainly helped push old Max to the brink."

Riyo turned to look at the Admiral. "Clearly, we were thinking similar things," he said, his smile perfect, wanting to put his knife into the Admiral's chest for his betrayal.

Nagano nodded. "We were. What did you have in mind next?"

"That beak-nosed ambassador, how do you say her name?"

"I would laugh too hard if I tired."

They both chuckled. "Here's my thought: you know how proud these Nahuatl are? Same with old Max and his people, pride so deep and stubborn they'd as soon sit in their own shit than ask someone to help them out of it, eh? Now, she's en route to Madrid via Barcelona to assuage his wrath—"

"Or suck his penis."

"—or spread her legs to keep his navies from invading Nahuatl territory. How about a little wrinkle in her plans to help her mission go south on her?"

"And further inflame his wrath, eh? Listen, Riyo-san, we've pissed in the same pot too many times, fed at the same trough for far too long—we have to bring these bitches to heel. If we'd known of each other's efforts on Teotihuacán or teamed up to persuade them before the bitches gave away the outer Car-Sag Arm, we'd be taking the war to the Nahuatl and the Iberia, not trying to instigate one between them."

He does me the honor of calling me by first name, General Takagi thought, awed by the friendship shown him by the other man. And he's right about bringing the bitches to heel, except for one thing—the old mother is likely to come out of her grief and butcher us both. "What about the old bitch, eh?" he whispered.

"What about her? We rile her up, wake her from her slumber, we've done the Empire a service, eh? If she demands our heads, so what, eh? You'd give it for the Empire. What more could a warrior want?"

"Nothing!" he replied immediately. "About time we woke the bitch, anyway." Takagi had noticed Nagano omitted himself in saying, "You'd give it for the Empire." Treacherous dog! He'd be delighted to sacrifice me to his own ends! "Listen, Nagano, I'm not as young as I once was, and my brain doesn't come up with ideas as fast as yours. What did you have in mind, old friend?" Make him name it first, Takagi thought. Incriminate away, numbskull Nagano!

"How about an alliance with the Nahuatl? Let's suggest it to them, tell 'em we've already got a raid planned on Iberia's backside, a squadron poised to strike from the outer spirals, ready to launch at the moment old Max launches his war."

"Not good enough, Nagano. What if they don't agree or cancel the raid? You know how timid they are."

"How many Daimyos can we get behind us? How many cousins and aunts and nieces and daughters live in those domains?" Nagano leaned toward him intently. "Remember that time the Old Lady Fumiko threatened to have all her daughters abort their fetuses and deny their favors to their mates? Need I describe what we need to do? If they can deny a sheath to our swords, we can certainly put our swords to their necks instead of up their dresses!"

Almost, Riyo thought, you've almost put your balls in the vise. "Has to be something more immediate than that, Nobu-san."

"We disguise the threat with honor. We ask each Daimyo to send all but a quarter of their armies to Kyoto, and surround the Imperial planet. They won't even have to load their guns. We tell them it's an obligatory display of their fealty."

"And if they still refuse?"

"We lay siege to Kyoto."

Riyo Takagi did a quick calculation. With his combined forces alone, he could unleash an attack and win against fully half of the other Daimyos. So if they committed only half of their own forces while he, Riyo Takagi, committed all of his, he could beat back any attack on Kyoto. "Half," he said. "Have the Daimyos send half. With half of our armed forces on parade around Kyoto, our show of support would make any ruler quiver in her boots."

Admiral Nagano smiled. "Half it is, then."

Chapter 5

Serena brought the small vehicle to rest inside a cleft just aft of a set of twelve engines on the gargantuan spaceliner.

The behemoth ship outsized her yacht several thousand times and outweighed it by at least a million. Its hull was riddled with more fissures, extrusions, struts, couplers, intakes, and exhausts than one of those old oil refineries that used to sprawl across Earth, themselves the size of cities.

The starliner Henry VIII carried nearly five hundred thousand people, two thirds of those passengers. A hundred and sixty thousand people were needed just to operate the beast.

Serena's yacht was no more than a gnat to an elephant, the big ship more likely to crush hers by accident than by intent. She powered down the yacht and secured it to its perch with magnetic anchors. Just to be safe, she spread a cloak over the already-cloaked yacht.

Her airshell sparkled at holding back the cold and the void while she inspected her work.

The yacht would be invisible except to a highly-trained observer.

The yacht had been easy to commandeer. Although the power schematic was a simple diagram, it had shown her just what couplers to disconnect. Without power, none of the environmental systems had worked, but then neither had any of the alarms or fail-safes. The bio comp was segmented in design to insure easy replacement of any failed component, and therefore, the executive prefrontal node had come away without problem.

What had required far more ingenuity was by-passing the empty leads where the executive prefrontal node had been. Serena had had to cut away a small sliver of foil lining from the insulation to improvise wires, and with a few tries, she had connected the power to the engines. Her airshell, she found, was just as helpful repelling noxious smoke as it was the utter, black emptiness of space, her first few "wires" having burned through before she thought of twisting the foil to thicken it.

Although effective in giving the yacht the thrust she needed, her next challenge was controlling the ship's vector, which as she approached the starliner she realized how fine it had to be.

Finally, rather than using the awkward yacht engine to bring her alongside the starliner, Serena just got out of the ship and used her personal boosterpack thruster to guide herself to the starliner hull, and then reeled in the yacht with the line she'd left attached to it.

It had been tedious to reel it in, but finally she'd done it.

I suppose I could've abandoned it, she thought at one point, but there were mysteries about the yacht that piqued her curiosity. Before she'd disabled the controls, she'd seen tactile interfaces for weapons, shielding, and communications, items far more sophisticated than any rental yacht should have.

Serena hadn't dared hook up her neuralink. Wired to the pineal, hypothalamus, and hippocampus among other glands, the neuralink was able to regulate sleep, memory, autonomous or hard-wired motion, as well as such intimate functions as elimination and reproductive responses. If a person weren't careful, neuralinking with the wrong device could subject a person to easy victimization. So Serena hadn't connected to the ship's neuralink.

The yacht safely anchored and concealed, she sighed and focused her attention on getting into the starliner. She looked across the hull for an access maintenance hatch. The hatch locks will be coded, she thought, and I'll wager my pack has a decoder.

Maintenance access hatches pimpled the outer hull, inscriptions in three languages on each, the hatches colorcoded red, blue, green, and brown. Respectively, heat, water, air, and sewage.

The ones labeled "air" didn't all have an airlock symbol. She walked along the cleft between engines until she found one with an airlock, her magnetized soles keeping her against the hull. The coded hatch opened easily to her decoder.

Whoever equipped Dolores and the yacht was thorough, Serena thought, wondering at the level of sophistication, wealth, and depth.

She pulled herself in and closed the hatch above her, and her airshell deactivated at equalization.

The vessel throbbed around her, an engine on either side, and those engines working at nearly full thrust.

The noise was close to deafening, so she searched the backpack for earplugs. Now, the noise was tolerable. Under her hands, the vibration actually produced an itch.

How do I find a captive on a city-sized ship? Serena wondered.

The ship will know, she thought. Just as the ship knows I'm here, since it registered my opening the hatch with the decoder. How many hundreds of maintenance people would there be at any given time accessing hatches on the hull?

Even so, Serena climbed up the access tube several hundred feet and found a recess she could hide in, just on the chance someone or something—a remote drone—was sent to investigate.

Pulling the handcom from the backpack, she powered it up and slipped it in to her neuralink. Shadowed on her retina, a display of icons appeared, including a readout that said, "Analyzing ..."

Then it told her the bad news: A symbionic enviro-maintenance unit was en route along the air duct access tube to eliminate the detected intrusion.

Maintenance crew members must have some type of identifier, she thought.

Then her handcom asked, "Baffle?"

Yes, she thought, and a virtual hand on her retina pushed a virtual button. Fancy! she thought.

"Directive cancelled, intrusion resolved, sensor malfunction, check sensor and replace if defective." And the maintenance unit hummed past her without a sideways glance.

"Cloak presence?" her handcom asked on her cochlear.

Yes, she thought.

"Multisensory mask implemented. Neuranet cloak?"

Serena looked at the ship's internal neuranets—a ship-wide neuranet, a passenger-only one, a crew-only, eight community neuranets specific to different passenger compartments, a host of micro-neuranets for families, companies, clans, or associations, plus a number of secured neuranets whose purpose was obscured.

She selected "cloak all," seeing she was able to uncloak any particular net that she wanted to access.

Then she sighed. All right, now, she wondered, how do get the ship to help me find a captive aboard a tub this big?

She remembered the three tarmac-monkeys and the box they'd loaded onto the ship. "Sketch function," she said, and in her retina appeared a sketch pad. She gained control fairly fast, having used such neural devices before. She sketched an oblong box and dropped it into the search interface.

Multiple objects appeared, many of them clustered in the storage bays. Serena frowned, the ship diagram seeming crowded with them.

She glanced through the outliers, the ones outside of those clustered in cargo. "Visual," she said, and the ship's computer returned with real-time views of each as she sorted among them.

A funeral on deck two, Miami Village, beach section, where a burial at sea was taking place, the coffin perched on the gunwales of a fully-rigged sailing schooner, waves pitching the deck back and forth.

A crate on deck fifteen, Rome Diocese, near an altar being decorated for a wedding with bouquets being taken from an oblong crate.

An empty crate on deck forty-five, under the bilges, the lid propped beside it.

Serena smiled and selected it. "Retrace route," she said.

And the ship's computer tracked its regress from the destination, the box carried aloft an antigrav sled to a darkened loading bay. The antigrav sled had been either guided remotely or programmed, as it was unaccompanied to its destination. At the cargo bay, two or three figures slid it off the sled and onto the gravcart outside.

"Stop," Serena said on her tracheal.

The vid froze.

She noted the time and date: approximately for departure from Teotihuacán.

This was her crate. "Real time," she said, "with audio."

A camera on the box, no sounds except the throb of a nearby engine.

Not terribly far from where I'm at. "Map here to box." A red line dotted a map for her. Passenger and crew corridors. If she took them, it was likely she'd be seen. "Air ducts and maintenance tubes." Additional lines were added, these blue and green.

She called up a map of her immediate surroundings. No nearby activity, the repair drone having long since left the vicinity to repair some other malfunction.

Serena followed the map on her retinal, all the while keeping an eye on nearby activity. Her journey through maintenance tubes and ventilation shafts took her around an air scrubber, through a water-purification plant, near a nano-carbon pollution capture net, and past one of the four sewage reclamation plants.

Peering into the maintenance closet where the empty box lay, she saw it was unoccupied. She dropped out of the vent to the closet floor, her landing nearly silent.

The handheld had a trace chemical sniffer. She ran it around the crate. Microfiber filaments glowed under its UV rays, a trail leading away, the floor no longer holding the heat signature now, twelve or so hours after they'd dragged the body out of the crate.

Through another door, up a set of metal grid stairs, corridors ribbed with conduits, across a catwalk and up to another door, closed. She leaned close, trying to block out the sucking and splashing sounds of excrement being neutralized below. The smell was horrific.

She couldn't hear through the door, but the sensors that she was able to link to indicated the breathing of two, possibly three people, one of them snoring.

Her eyes went to the ceiling. Pipe, pipe conduit, access tube. She smiled, lifted a foot to the catwalk railing, and launched herself. Scrambling into the tube, she found an outlet to the ventilation duct, pulled herself along to the grid and peered into the room.

Three men, one of them sitting up but snoring, the other two lying on makeshift cots. Two doors, the locked one that she'd tried to listen through, a second on the other side.

On the ship neuranet, she pulled up a vid of that second room. One figure, bound at wrist and ankle, awake and gagged.

Serena smiled. Peeking back through the grill, she looked closely at the man sitting up. His snore was a low rumble, his face bristled with beard. Below one knee, his leg ended in wood.

How bizarre, she wondered. Why didn't he have a new one grown? All he's missing is a hook on one arm and an eye patch.

The ship neuranet indicated only one door to the closet where the captive lay bound.

How do I get him out of there? she wondered.

She doubted he was trained in stealth, so he'd make a lot of noise if she tried to get him out through the air duct, if it were large enough.

Distract them one at a time, render them unconscious, find a place to hide their bodies, come back for the next?

Long, laborious, and gives them time to summon reinforcements. Serena couldn't imagine not a single other person aboard who didn't know or wasn't part of the kidnapping.

Has to be all three all at once.

She checked the ship clock to see how much ship-night was left. Four hours until ship-dawn, which meant she had enough time. It also insured she had relatively empty corridors if she needed them, not knowing what the captive's physical condition was.

She slithered back along the air duct, navigated the tight corner to the main duct, took the one to the closet.

Very tight squeeze. If she hadn't been a hundred-thirty pounds soaking wet, she'd have never made it, and she was sure he wouldn't fit at all.

The grill came away with a muted "snick," which woke him.

She scrambled down, held her finger to her lips, and then pulled her mask back over her head so he would recognize her.

His eyes went wide. "Your hair is blond!" he whispered.

She cut his bindings. "Lay still as though you're still tied up," she whispered back.

He nodded, and she pulled herself back into the air duct, replacing the grill just in case.

Looking down upon the three kidnappers, she wondered, what now?

I'll just waltz right through them, taking Prince Iberia with me.

Serena stifled a giggle, her mind plotting out how a kick there, a finger jab here, an elbow there, and three unconscious bodies to tiptoe through.

What should I do?

I should climb out of the duct, go up a hundred decks, find the Captain, and alert him he has a hostage aboard!

And by the time they search this location, the kidnappers will have absconded with their captive.

Sighing, she looked again, this time her mind supplying her with ways to kill all three.

She bit back a sob. What have I become? she wondered, realizing that somehow, her life was no longer her own, that something had happened to place her at the mercy of forces beyond her reckoning.

Forces she was ready to confront with lethal means.

But that was the reason she'd boarded the starliner—to reassert some kind of control over her life. And then I contemplate murder.

With a sigh, she loosened the grate and set it across from her. Her drop to the floor was soundless.

A laser barrel was pointed at her face. One eye behind it was wide with surprise. "Princess," the man said in distinct Japanese, and she knocked away the gun barrel with her left and drove her right knuckle into the left temple just beside the patch, the laser searing a ribbon across the wall, the gun striking the side wall, waking the two others on cots. Serena put her heel into one skull and her knuckles into the larynx of the other.

74

While two died instantly, the third watched her, strangling, unable to get air. She snapped his neck to spare him further agony.

What surprised her was how little she felt.

She retrieved the laser gun and went to the door separating the two rooms. Beyond, Prince Iberia was just sitting up. He looked relieved.

She handed him the laser. "We're not safe yet." Then on her tracheal, she said, "Neuro, extend cloak to this man."

"Extending cloak," her retinal display said.

"Injuries?" she asked.

He shook his head.

"Follow me," she said, and slipped out the door and over the bodies.

The outer door opened at her touch.

She scanned the catwalk and sewage-reclamation vats below, and then glanced back at the bodies. The Prince was staring at her wide-eyed, picking his way gingerly between bodies toward her. Smoke wafted around them in the dim light, the smell of burnt metal nearly overpowering.

If I could be sure their bodies wouldn't set off any alarms, I'd throw them into the vats below. Serena discarded the idea. The catwalk was clear. She led him across, down the metal-grate stairs, and over to the maintenance tube she'd come out of.

"In," she said, pointing, "then wait."

He slid into the tube in front of her.

She slid in afterward, pulling the hatch closed behind her.

The tube was just large enough to let her wriggle up beside him.

Their breath hot in the tight space, she couldn't help feel the pressure of his body.

"Thank you," he said, his face but an inch from hers.

"Later," she said, and pulled herself past him, trying to tell herself she hadn't enjoyed that moment that their bodies lay beside each other.

* * *

Foreign Minister Xavier Balleros strode the long corridor toward the throne room on Madrid, alarmed by the news reports and the hours-old declaration of war against the Nahuatl.

Every twenty feet was another set of double doors opened ceremoniously by an elaborately-dressed pair of guards, the Foreign Minister nodding to each obeisance, smiling graciously but secretly annoyed at every stop in the nuanced waltz that would eventually place him in the presence of the Emperor Iberia.

The kidnapping of the Prince disturbed Xavier deeply.

The declaration of war was equally disturbing.

But setting his soul on edge was the alert he'd received that they'd tried to kill Serena.

Had they actually killed her, Xavier would have known. The bulletin issued by the Nahuatl Information Ministry on the killing of a student from Madrid named Serena Zambrano at Azteca University had alarmed him, but a couple hours later, Xavier had also received a neuramail that the escape yacht planted on the tarmac at the Teotihuacán spaceport by his associates had been launched.

A yacht that only Serena could launch.

A face that launched one ship, he mused, might one day become a face that launches a thousand.

And the face broadcast by the Nahuatl Information Ministry had been that of Serena's long-time guard, Dolores, saying that Serena (pictured) had been killed by her roommate, Dolores, of whom no photo was available.

That was a sly piece of misinformation, Xavier thought, just what I'd expect from the Fire Emperor. He wondered if they'd simply mixed up their identities.

After hearing of the killing, the kidnapping, and the declaration of war, the Minister of Foreign Affairs Xavier Balleros had hurried back to the Iberia Empire, not even stopping at his homeworld of Galapagar long enough to change clothes.

Instead, he had flown directly from Teotihuacán to Madrid, his luxury personal yacht under full power the entire trip.

Xavier nodded to the next set of guards, who waved him through the exquisitely-adorned double doors. Beyond it, a contingent of warriors with feathered headdresses awaited.

He tried not to laugh aloud, despite his having seen the elaborate ceremonial dress of the Nahuatl before. Do they each have pheasant nesting upon their heads?

The warriors scowled at him.

Xavier stepped to the next stopping point, ignoring the scowls and expecting obsidian-tipped blades to cut him to pieces.

But it would be unpardonable to harm an enemy in his own lair. As Princess Mariko had done twenty or more years ago, Xavier expected the Iberian Navies to pummel the archaic, inferior ships of the Nahuatl and beat them clear back to Teotihuacán in a matter of months.

Xavier nodded to the obeisance of the two Iberian guards. Beyond the double doors was the magnificent outer suite of the Emperor Maximilian Iberia.

Xavier stepped into the room and stopped just inside the double doors. They closed behind him.

"Xavier, it *is* you! Welcome, friend, come join us, eh?"

"An honor, your highness, but a bit of refreshment first, if I may?"

"Certainly, Xavier, but dally not long over *bebidas*!"

He smiled at the Emperor's mixture of language and stepped to the sidebar to glance among the mixture of drinks. Sherry,

Sangria, Pecan Punch, Cava, and Patxaran were among the *bebidas* laid out, all the traditional beverages, and quite a few exotic ones.

He chose a Sangria, the bouquet like the hills of Galapagar, fragrant with ripening grapes. Glass in hand; he stepped toward the Emperor's side of the room, nodding to the Emperor. "Salud!" he said holding up his glass.

"Salud!" said Emperor Iberia, holding aloft his own.

Xavier then brought his heels together with a loud snap, turning his attention to the female with the feathered headdress sitting only a few paces from the Emperor. "Lady Ambassador Xochitl Olin, welcome!"

"Lord Minister Xavier Balleros, thank you," Xochitl replied, her head nodding slightly, her feathers waving graciously.

"You haven't changed a mite, Lady," Xavier said, her beauty surpassed only by her venom.

"I'll daresay I've changed the course of history—a mite more than a mite."

Beauty, wit and venom, Xavier thought, a deadly combination to trap any man's heart. Mariko had had all of those, and a cunning that had exceeded those of her admirals and generals. "Not to inquire as to the obvious, Lady, but what might bring you to our peaceful lands?"

"But war, of course! Which just a moment ago your sagacious Emperor Iberia wisely avoided, with a little help from me, of course." She looked demur, the peacock feathers in her hair notwithstanding.

"Avoided? Your Highness, I applaud you, as war should be considered only when the three p's have not achieved your goal."

"Eh?" Emperor Iberia said, "What need have I, friend Xavier, of persuasion, pressure and poison? You forget yourself."

"My apologies, your Highness," Xavier said, bowing in mock humility. "I forgot that the last isn't in your vocabulary."

"Just so, Lord Minister," Emperor Max replied. "But Xochitl brings news that somewhat exonerates the Nahuatl of implication in my son's kidnapping, although his return to my side would exonerate them fully."

"Somewhat?" Xochitl said, her voice a bit too sharp. "Lord Minister, look at this!" She rose and handed him a still.

He almost didn't look at it, he was so captivated by the soft scents of lavender and jasmine that wafted past him, and by the voluptuous beauty whose scents he longed to drown in.

The photo was of Serena, a side shot, and standing to her right was another woman with almost identical build, hair and clothes, but whose face wasn't visible at all. Dolores, he knew.

"The Nahuatl Intelligence Service had obtained information that the woman on the left has been stalking Prince Iberia with the expertise of a master for about two months. The Prince's guards confirmed multiple sightings of her in his vicinity."

"What information?"

"The two of them spoke on the day of Prince Iberia's kidnapping."

Xavier handed the photograph back to her. "Proves nothing," he said bluntly.

Xochitl smiled, "The woman whose back is to the camera is Serena Zambrano, the Iberian woman who was murdered shortly before Prince Iberia's kidnapping. Among her possessions was a diary on her handcom. Quote: 'My roommate hasn't been acting right, seems obsessed with Prince Iberia, follows him ceaselessly. And the other day, I found wristcuffs, leg clamps, and a blindfold in her room. Gives me chills. She's always been a little odd, a little secretive.' "

Xavier knew that Xochitl was mistaken about the other woman's identity, that the murdered woman identified as Serena was actually Dolores. And that the person whose face was caught in profile was actually that of Serena, and not Dolores, and that the galaxy-wide warrant issued for the detainment of Serena would yield no detainments whatsoever.

Xavier looked at Maximilian Iberia. "Sire, have you acted on this information yet?"

"He's called off this pointless war, of course! It's clear this Dolores kidnapped Prince Iberia."

"It's not clear at all," Xavier replied. "Do DNA samples or fiber scans from the hover that picked up Prince Iberia match those that must be all over that apartment?"

"Immaterial!" Xochitl snapped. "You'll see *that* when the Prince is rescued! Our intelligence service has made his safety its number-one priority!"

"Well and good, Lady Ambassador," Xavier said, "but I must apologize, as nothing has changed. Your highness, I urge you to remain steadfast in your declaration of war until the kidnapper or kidnappers have been captured and your son, his highness the Prince and heir to the Iberia Empire, has been returned unharmed to your side. Be not guiled by the honey and poison dangled before you by this beautiful, vituperous creature in front of us."

Emperor Maximilian threw back his head and laughed.

Xavier stared at him, startled.

Xochitl also looked toward the Emperor, biting her lip.

Having expected the full blast of her vituperation, Xavier was that much more disconcerted by the Emperor's hilarity.

Maximilian Iberia shook his finger at them both. "Beware the two of you, for what clearly is a mutual dislike and distrust of the other might quickly become a lust of the most powerful potency, an elixir that would prove disabling of you both, if not at least intoxicating." And he laughed again, his head thrown back and his laughter bouncing back to them from the ceiling.

"But enough of that," the Emperor said, his laughter ceasing abruptly. "We will consider your evidence, Ambassador Xochitl Olin, and we may elect to defer the commencement of hostilities.

Please be advised that nothing but a return of my son and heir will insure a reinstatement of the peace between our Empires. In our tradition, Lady Ambassador, *Vaya Con Dios*. Go with God."

"Thank you, Lord Emperor Iberia. May Quetzalcoatl light your path."

Xavier nodded to her, holding it a moment, and watched her leave, the still in his hand, surprised she had not taken it with her.

Per protocol, she stopped at the double doors and bowed again, then backed between them into the antechamber.

Xavier turned to find the eyes of Emperor Max upon him.

"What mischief have you been fermenting, eh? It was, among everything, disconcerting to find out you yourself had been on Teotihuacán at Azteca University, where this murder and the kidnapping of my son took place. Explain yourself, Minister."

In any other context, Xavier might have voided all over himself, or at least broke into a sweat. But not this one.

"Certainly, my Liege," he said, extending the still. "The one on the left, Sire, do you not recognize her?"

Maximilian raised an eyebrow at him. "Resembles Mariko."

Xavier wasn't surprised he'd used her first name. Pulling out his handcom, he brought up a full face still, one of the few he'd been able to get. "Look at this, Sire."

The Emperor grunted. "Looks a lot like Mariko."

Xavier smiled. "It was quite by chance that she and Augusto attended the same university. I hadn't anticipated that the two would meet on such a large campus, or I would have arranged her transfer elsewhere." He accepted the handcom back.

"Why this erstwhile—how do the Deutschlanders say it—doppelganger, this look-alike?"

Xavier Balleros, Minister of Foreign Affairs, formerly sub-commander of the Fourth Fleet of the Iberian Navy, stationed at the base Tarifa twenty years ago, and the only naval commander ever to have defeated Princess Mariko Mitsubi in battle, told the

Emperor Maximilian Iberia what he, sub-commander Balleros, had done after the betrayal and death of the Crown Princess Mitsubi. Having been stationed near the Galactic Core at that time, Xavier had had little contact with the Iberian Court, but had rocketed up through the ranks after defeating the Mitsubi Princess.

Emperor Iberia went white.

"What is it, Sire?" Xavier asked.

"When she became pregnant," Maximilian said, his voice a hoarse whisper, "there was rampant speculation about the father of the child. In truth, it could have been anyone, as the Matriarchy professes that such details are superfluous, particularly for a girl-child. But to the rest of the galaxy, it was monumentally important. That is, until the Princess died." The Emperor looked at his Minister of Foreign Affairs. "With this, Xavier, it has now once more become monumentally important who fathered her child."

"Why, Lord?"

"Because, Xavier, either the Nahuatl Emperor Fire is her father. Or I am."

Chapter 6

"Augusto," Serena said, jostling him from his slumber.

He lifted an eyelid toward her.

"When I dropped into the room with those three guards, one of them was already pointing a pistol at me."

"Eh? Huh? Why didn't he shoot?" He lifted his head.

"I don't know," she replied. Serena saw he was trying to get more comfortable, the single seat of the one-passenger yacht split between them. She made a little room for him, not minding the close quarters, liking the pleasant bit of warmth deep inside at having him near. "He said something, though."

"What did he say?"

Serena frowned. "Princess."

Augusto snorted. "How absurd."

"That's what I thought, and then I killed him."

The silence between them stretched, and Serena couldn't help but wonder what she might have discovered if she'd simply knocked him unconscious and questioned him later. Getting Prince Iberia back to her yacht had not been difficult. Discovering the decrypter on the handcom had been a bonus. Once back in the yacht, Serena had reassembled the ship's bio and activated it, and then had used the decrypter to override the bio's restrictions. With full control of the ship, Serena had launched them easily from the hull of the Starliner, and they had disappeared from the skies, as it were, the yacht's multiphasic cloak obscuring nearly all trace of their existence. Then she had set a course for Madrid, the Capitol of the Iberia Empire.

Now, a full ship-day later, Serena chewed on everything that had happened. "He said it like a question."

Augusto looked at her again. "What do you think he meant?"

She shrugged. "Did you get a good look at them at all?"

He shook his head.

"Neither did I, in the dark. But he had a wooden leg and a patch over one eye."

"Outlaw of some type?"

"Maybe. I sensed he was addressing me as if I were a particular princess, not just any princess. As though he knew me. It was enough hesitation to give me time to kill him." Serena was silent again, absently looking out the forward viewport.

"You're really bothered by that, aren't you?"

She nodded and sighed.

"Why'd you come after me?"

She looked at him, her face only a foot away from his, their hips wedged against each other, she perched on one arm of the only chair, he on the other.

"You could have been killed. You almost were." He shook his head. "That was foolish."

She nodded, knowing he was right. And yet …

"Where'd you learn all that, anyway? Are you some sort of intelligence operative? Were you sent by my father?"

She shook her head, frowning and looking away. And yet …

"Look, Serena, there's something going on here. You can't have appeared for the sole purpose of rescuing me from my kidnappers!"

She saw that he was disturbed. "They tried to kill me," she protested. She brought her gaze up to his face. He looked more bewildered than she felt. "An assassin blew open our dorm room door and shot Dolores in the back. I killed him before he fired a second time, and as Dolores was dying in my arms, she told me there would be others outside, that I had to escape, that she wasn't simply my roommate but had been my guard for the last four years, and then she shoved this backpack at me and died." Serena looked him again, and all she saw was disbelief.

She blurted out the rest, afraid he wouldn't believe her. "I escaped up to the roof. They'd surrounded the building, three others. There was a black formall in the pack. I managed to jump to a tree that students sometimes used from the fourth floor windows.

"I went to a restaurant, looked in the backpack. A note from Dolores told me about this yacht at the spaceport, told me to contact Professor Uraga, to give him a mnemo-chip. I used a neuralink at the restaurant to get his address, then I went to the bathroom and climbed into the air duct to see if anyone would follow. They did, had the restaurant surrounded, stationed someone in the rear hallway just inside the exit. I found a blowgun in the pack. The person crumpled instantly. I stole his gun and neuralink and threw them in the sewer to baffle their pursuit.

"I used a paycard from the backpack to get to Professor Uraga's house. That was how they'd tracked me to the restaurant, with my paycard. Professor Uraga told me about the yacht, then said he'd use my paycard to take a tube across planet, while I went to the spaceport. He took his wakizashi sword, his harakiri sword. I think he intended to use it before he arrived at his destination, thinking my pursuers would surely kill me on arrival."

She saw the expression on his face was utter disbelief.

"Professor Uraga said he was ronin, or a masterless Samurai, and that his loyalty to the Princess Mariko Mitsubi was undiminished even though she died twenty years ago. I don't know what happened to him.

"When I got to the spaceport, I found the yacht nearly underneath a spaceliner. The yacht was black, and I was wearing black, and the night was black. Three tarmac monkeys were loading the oblong box and kept look around, as if they didn't want to be seen.

"After I took off in the yacht, I saw the news that you'd been kidnapped, and I knew. Somehow I knew. I had to come after you. I don't know why, but I felt so lost, so out of control. I'd killed two people, and I was being chased, and everything that I knew or thought I knew suddenly wasn't true anymore, and I didn't know where this obstreperous piece of protoplasm was taking me, so I disabled the bio aboard and came after the starliner. And all I could think was how unfair it was that they'd abducted you and had destroyed my life, and if all I could do was rescue you then somehow everything would be all right for me. Good god, what a fool!"

And Serena realized she was weeping and he was holding her. Despite the vortex she'd been sucked into, she found solace and comfort and surcease in his arms, and it didn't matter anymore that she was being chased and that her life had come apart and that she'd killed five people as easy as chewing food, because the comfort in his arms made it all seem distant, and the relief he brought helped her to accept her tears and to hold her terror at bay.

* * *

I can't believe Minister Balleros did that!

Xochitl Olin fumed as she entered the Nahuatl consulate on Madrid, the nearly setting sun reminding her how terribly short the days were here. On Teotihuacán, the thirty-two hour days were so long that, unless born there, most people found the long day difficult without at least a few hours nap. Xochitl found the short, twenty-hour day on Madrid difficult for exactly the opposite reason. She was never tired at bedtime.

The grav limo pulled to a stop in the breezeway beside the consulate, and she'd leaped from the vehicle before they could get the door for her, and she was in the building before the guards could positively identify her.

She didn't care, her swift pace taking her up to the Consulate General's office before the secretary could say, "I'll see if she's in."

Consul to Iberia for the Nahuatl, Coszcatl Tonatzin, stood abruptly as Xochitl strode into her office.

"Get the Emperor on a secured com," she snapped. I can't believe Minister Balleros did that!

"Pardon, Lady Ambassador?" Coszcatl asked, as though she hadn't heard.

Xochitl bit off the first thing that came to mind. "Your Excellency, I require that you immediately raise Emperor Xiuhtectli on secured comlink. I've just met with Emperor Iberia and his sniveling Minister of Foreign Affairs. It went badly."

An eyebrow went slowly up the forehead. "A comlink, especially a secured one, could take hours."

"Bullshit!" she said in her best Spanish accent. Xochitl located the com set to one side of the Consul's desk, picked it up, and requested a channel.

The screen requested a password and retinal scan.

She put her eye to the scanner.

"What do you think you're doing!?"

Xochitl was already doing it.

"Linking ..." the screen said.

"Get away from my Com, or I'll have to ..."

"Iberia is about to attack and you want to adhere to protocol?" Xochitl said. "Get out of my way."

"Linked and securing ..." the screen said.

87

"Get the guards to take this intruder away," Coszcatl said to her secretary, who fled.

"Comlink secured." the screen said.

"Fire Lord," Xochitl said, and his face materialized.

"Ambassador Olin, on the Consulate secure line. You've met with Emperor Iberia," Naui Quiahuitl said affably.

"And his worm-sucking Minister of Foreign Affairs! I had him in my palm until that snake slithered in. Emperor Iberia's refusing to call off the invasion. The best I could get out of him was, 'we may elect to defer the commencement of hostilities.'"

"A fairly wormy way to say it. What about the photograph?"

"I left it with him, Sire, as instructed."

"Excellent. Too astute to react to it in front of you, of course, but it'll plant a seed."

"Sire, forgive me for not being able to stop the war. I've failed you utterly."

"Nonsense, Ambassador Olin, Is that Consul Tonatzin behind you? Step forward, Consul, as this next bit of subtlety will require your participation.

"Listen, when that Princess whom I refuse to name got pregnant twenty-one years ago, the entire galaxy wondered who the father was. The only exception was the Mitsubi Matriarchy, eh? Or so it was said at the time. Those Mitsubis, we know their capacity for deceit, and we know the depth of their cunning. The person who fathered that child was far *more* important to the Mitsubis than to anyone else save the father, of course, in spite of their swearing otherwise."

Xochitl stared at Emperor Fire with astonishment. "Have you lost your senses, Lord? Iberia is about to invade and you blather about a whore who couldn't keep her legs crossed?"

"She whored around with but two men, and only as her mother the Empress ordered her. Whom she fornicated with was neither random nor senseless. The Empress Fumiko Mitsubi planned for this day, to create the result we see now, to pit

Iberia and Nahuatl against each other by placing the most desirable young woman in the galaxy between them: The Princess herself."

Xochitl caught her breath.

"But she died too early."

"What?" she said. The Consul beside her looked equally puzzled.

"The Empress Fumiko Mitsubi wanted Emperor Iberia and me to think that we each had fathered her child. And if it wasn't the Empress who put the Princess up to it, it was the Princess herself who suggested it to the Empress. Here's where I think the plan succeeded. The child in the Princess's womb at the time of her death didn't die with her."

Xochitl had to clutch the back of her chair to keep from losing her balance. She knew her face was white. "Serena ... "

"Exactly. Serena Zambrano, breathtakingly beautiful, smart beyond all compare, talented beyond the meager means available to that engineer bureaucrat father of hers, leading a charmed life, securing a berth at the most prestigious school in the galaxy—at the same time as Prince Iberia, no less—an immaculate, pristine if innocuous background."

"Forgive me, Lord Emperor Fire, for not questioning her background check. You're absolutely right, not a flaw, not a single flaw!"

"Except one," the Emperor said.

"What's that, Sire?"

"She looks like the Princess. Serena Zambrano is the child of an unknown father and the Princess—and now, the question of who fathered her is more important than ever, because through her, the father has a claim on the Mitsubi throne."

Xochitl nodded. "Pitting Iberia and Nahuatl against each other."

"Yes." Emperor Fire said. "And now of course we all are faced with the same question: Where is she?"

* * *

It wasn't until he'd returned to Galapagar that Xavier realized the yacht had gone off net. From the tracking data he had, it appeared that at about six hours after liftoff from Teotihuacán, the yacht had simply vanished. He strode through the foyer of his home, glancing away from his handcom only long enough to greet his staff and look where he was going. He walked into his study and was about to Com Emperor Iberia.

No transponder, no distress signal, no com, nothing.

Oddly, twenty hours after that, a brief startup signal was received and then just as quickly disappeared. Its location was odd as well, four parsecs off of the yacht's preset course to Madrid.

Xavier tried to make sense of the information. Bewildered, he submitted the data through a neuralink to the palace biocomp; it couldn't either. Finally, he requested a coordinates search, asking for other vessels in the vicinity at that time. A starliner, the King Henry VIII, a behemoth with a passenger list just under four hundred thousand.

The thought of searching the passenger list was mind-numbing. But Xavier saw something that kept his attention: the Starliner had been outbound from Teotihuacán.

"Sir, there's a news report you have to see," said Jaime, his head servant.

Xavier sensed urgency and nodded. "Put it on."

His wall vid flared to life. "... dispatch from the Interior Minister of the Nahuatl Empire." The vid cut away to a long-nosed man standing at a podium, the Aztec calendar surrounding his head like a halo. "My name is Chimali Xolotl ..."

* * *

General Riyo Takagi bowed, sweating before Princess Regent Yoshi Mitsubi, resplendent in her royal Kimono, two swords of the purest white tucked in her sash.

The ceremonial long sword, the katana, and the mid-length sword, the wakizashi. The hafts were white, the braided leather wrapped intricately, and the scabbards were white, pearl and diamond glittering resplendently atop a fine, almost-translucent porcelain sheath, and the blades were white, coated with the finest layer of electrolyzed white gold over the finest titanium blades ever made.

I don't want to see these blades, Riyo thought.

Anytime a sword was drawn, the bearer was obligated to use it.

"You requested an audience with me because you have information about what?" Her Highness the Empress Regent Yoshi Mitsubi was frothing.

Riyo thumped his head audibly on the ground again. "Pardon my odious intrusion, your Highness almighty Empress Regent, I have information about treachery."

"Eh? And you didn't dispatch the perpetrator immediately? Not inflicting instant death for treachery is treacherous itself! Why shouldn't I remove your head?"

He thumped his head again. "Forgive me, highness, but how then would you know the source of the treachery? And I beg you to allow me to remove myself from this pitiful existence after I tell you."

"This is the hundredth page of our novel, and in its honor I will consider your request, Lord General Takagi."

He sighed audibly and dared to peek.

"Well? And sit up, for Izanami's sake!"

"Yes, your highness Empress Regent," he said, and eased himself back on his heels.

A servant burst in. "Forgive me, Empress Regent, an urgent dispatch from Emperor Xiuhtectli of the Nahuatl. Information Minister is announcing convincing evidence …"

* * *

Worried sick and feeling faint, Emperor Maximilian Iberia stared at the wall vid, the face of the Interior Minister Chimali Xolotl sitting inside the nimbus-like Aztec Calendar behind him.

"… that Prince Augusto Iberia, son of Maximilian, was indeed kidnapped by fellow Iberian Citizen Serena Zambrano …"

Chapter 7

Serena couldn't believe what she was hearing.

"...in a bold and ruthless attack aboard the Starliner, the King Henry VIII, in which she killed his three guards and somehow smuggled him into her waiting yacht, which then disappeared without a trace using a cloak of unknown manufacture."

"What absolute nonsense!" she yelled at the vidscreen.

Augusto put a hand on her arm to calm her.

"Previously, it was thought that Prince Augusto had been kidnapped from the secret penthouse apartment in downtown Azteca on the Capitol Teotihuacán, where he had been attending college. We now know that this was the first stage of an extraction carried out by Iberian Security in response to the murder earlier that day of Dolores Hernan, whose journal entries indicate that the suspect, Serena Zambrano, had been stalking Prince Iberia for two months. University police speculate that the murder was a result of the victim's having confronted Zambrano with evidence of her activities, including a gag, wristbracelets, and anklecuffs.

"In her flight from the dorm, the suspect took the life of her fellow dormer, fled into the city where she climbed up in the ventilation system of a restaurant, where local police had trapped her. Somehow she escaped, taking the life of an officer, and made her way to the home of one of her professors, a for-

93

mer science officer in the Mitsubi Navy, Lieutenant Setsu Uraga, whom police say she forced into taking her to the spaceport, where she killed him and dumped his body into a tube capsule, which she then sent halfway across planet. From the spaceport she launched the waiting yacht in pursuit of the starliner."

"Ironically, the swift extraction of Prince Iberia prompted Zambrano to execute her plan for his kidnapping, and his relative vulnerability in a secret stateroom aboard the starliner enabled this trained assassin to overpower the Prince's three guards and remove him from the vessel with no one the wiser for almost twelve hours.

"A spokesperson for Duchess Starliners, the parent company which owns and operates the Kind Henry VIII, states that the kidnapping might not have been discovered so quickly if the suspect had not dumped the bodies into the sewage reclamation vats and clogged the pipes, which set off internal alarms. The bodies, badly disfigured by the reclamation chemicals, were only identifiable through osteo and genetic analysis.

"While these new developments convincingly exonerate the Nahuatl Empire of involvement in this horrific and mercenary kidnapping and these gruesome murders, the Nahuatl government will continue to pursue this vicious murderer and kidnapper across the galaxy to bring her to justice.

"The Nahuatl people extend our sympathy to the people of the Iberia Empire for their tragic predicament, and we continue to pray for the swift return of Prince Augusto Iberia, alive and well, to his father's side."

Tears streaming silently down her cheeks, Serena started at the screen, dumbfounded. She felt his hands on each of her arms and didn't realize he was talking to her softly.

"We both know none of this is true, we both know none of this is true, we both ... "

While his voice, calm and gentle and almost a whisper, repeated this calming litany, Serena just stared in disbelief, a small presence inside her telling her she had killed all but two of those people, but not for the reasons they purported, and certainly not out of any intent to kidnap the nice young man beside her.

And yet …

She could feel, deep inside, that although the surface of the Prince's words were right, underneath was the bare truth that she had killed five people. Any only one of them, the first one who had cut down Dolores Hernan, had had to be killed.

She hadn't needed to kill the other four. She had chosen to do so.

She looked with blurry vision at her hands. They were covered with blood. Somehow, she needed to cleanse them. Somehow, she needed to find the people who pursued her, who sought to destroy her. Somehow, she needed to absolve herself of her sins.

Holy Mother of God, what have I done?

And what can I do now?

Serena turned to look at Augusto. She wiped the blur from her eyes. "You're very kind to your kidnapper."

He chuckled and shook his head at her.

"We have to get you home safety."

"Somehow, I don't think there's anything or anyone that will stop you from doing that."

She smiled at his confidence in her.

"And then my father can help straighten everything—"

She was already shaking her head. "I'm not going with you." She sighed and looked at her lap.

* * *

I've always wondered why I was different. Do I look Spanish? Do I look Iberian? If you had met my father, you would know. It's clear I'm not his child. He's always reared me as his own, not a hint or look or clue did he ever give that I wasn't. Always told me my mother died in childbirth. There was a lot he didn't tell me. Just the money for all the lessons, the schools, the soccer, violin, piano, dance, rapier, tai-kwon-do, Karate, dojo, everything, and just the tuition for Azteca University. How could he afford any of it? And yet he always did.

And now this. Pursued, wanted for murder and kidnapping by two empires who very nearly went to war over the incident, and if to prevent slaughter on a horrific scale, I have be the one to blame, well maybe that's a lot to bear, but it's jolted me awake from my dream-like life and shown me I'm capable of terrible things. I don't want to be capable of terrible things. I don't want to be an orphan without a past, trained in stealth, poison, cunning, and trickery. None of it!

And yet here I am, all of it true and I don't know what it means, and the one person who might know isn't likely to know either. He's no one special, just doing what he's asked in his loyalty to his Empire, the forces that drive his behavior set in motion long ago.

No, Augusto don't interrupt, for you must know, and above all and furthermore you mustn't tell. Swear it!

Swear upon the Virgin Mary, Augusto, that you'll never tell. Swear it!

Swear you'll tell no one I rescued you, that a woman of clear Mitsubi descent but brought up in the Iberia Empire freed you from your captors.

No one!

Swear it!

Why?

Because they're right in one way. I've killed with these hands. I've killed people who didn't need to die! That man who called me "Princess" would have bowed to me and followed my every command! I could see it in his eyes! That same look in Professor Uraga's eyes! He who served Princess Mariko Mitsubi for a full twenty years beyond her death!

You didn't hear him. "I'm Ronin," he told me. "A masterless samurai, but I could never serve another master. No master could be more worthy of service than Princess Mariko Mitsubi, Buddha keep her soul! No one!"

And then he said he'd serve me because he'd been asked to do so in her name, and in truth Augusto, I think deep down, it was because I look like her, because others feel compelled, like the one-eyed kidnapper who called me "Princess," that somehow I'm her reincarnation, and our destinies are inextricably linked, and if, when we part ways, you and I, I go on to search for nothing else and all that I find is how my fate is linked with this Princess Mariko, then at least I'll know my destiny, and I'll make it my own, rather than live out a life set forth by others, becoming what they want me to be, and never discovering for myself the person I really am.

That's not much to ask, is it? To know the person I really am? Is it?

Part II

Chapter 8

Hisaka Tomi, Mother Priestess of the Lotus Flower Buddhist sect, looked up from the sputtering candle flame, aware that the young neophyte, Midori Sato, had awaited her attention for over an hour, sitting unobtrusively in the shadows of the temple.

She waits with the patience of one much younger, Hisaka thought, the neophyte's presence a mystery. The Mother Priestess often knew what a supplicant's request would be and when she might expect the request, long before being approached. The close confines of the Lotus Flower Monastery allowed her unspoken knowledge of her daughters. But not this neophyte.

Much about her was a mystery, Hisaka reminded herself. Midori's appearance five years ago at the temple door, begging for work and sanctuary. Her mechanical aptitude and ability to repair anything. Her obscure past and reticence about the source of her mechanical skill. Her surreal stillness of being, evident from the moment she arrived at the Temple door. And finally, Midori's relentless practice of her fighting skills, when not mediating, working at the shipyard, or studying.

Hisaka could tell that Midori had worked all day at the shipyard below them, their mountaintop monastery overlooking both bay and spaceport.

Surly, she knows she has not advanced beyond neophyte because she never sits still, Hisaka thought. Surreptitiously, without betraying that she had come out of her meditation, the Mother Priestess looked closely at the young woman.

Midori Sato sat in the lotus position just a few feet inside and to the left of the double doors. Her head was shaved bald and uncovered, her features delicate, her almond-shaped eyes hinting at a mix of Japanese and something else, her shoulders relaxed and palms upturned on her thighs, her only clothing the simple beige kimono with the light brown belt of her neophyte ranking, her feet bare and souls upturned. The cold mountain breeze found its way around the doors, stirring the silk at her collar.

Though I've given no hint, I see she knows I observe her, Hisaka thought. I see in her eyes that she thinks she has waited long enough. Which is why, child, that you remain neophyte. Possess yourself of patience. Become one with the rock beneath you. Be as old as the planet itself, which we call Nagasaki, but whose name is something much more ancient and unknown to us. Be more patient than time itself, and you will be ready to receive elevation to the next level of enlightenment.

But I know there are places in your soul, Midori, that harbor pain beyond your reach. And when you came to us five years ago, you were composed of equal parts of seeking and running. Yes, seeking something that was missing inside you, and running from something inside you so feral and ugly you still avoid embracing it. And though you never speak of these things, I see them in your eyes now, and these too inhibit your elevation.

Mother Priestess Hisaka Tomi turned her head.

Neophyte Midori Sato appeared not to notice.

She will not give hint that I now look upon her, Hisaka knew. She sits still in superb physical discipline, but her mind is never still, and that is the discipline she must master to elevate. Hisaka did find it odd that Midori's physical stillness remained undisturbed by her mental activity. Yes, much about this neophyte is a mystery, the Mother Priestess thought, especially her disconcerting physical discipline.

"Child," she said. "Welcome. How may I serve you?"

"Mother Priestess Tomi," Midori said, only her mouth moving. "Forgive me my intrusion and my impatience. I am not worthy of your service, much less your attention." She bowed.

Highly formal, an important request. "Come closer, Child. Your distance is disturbing."

"Yes, Mother," Midori said. She rose slowly and without apparent effort, her gaze remaining distant and unfocused, and as she moved, her gaze never changed, as though she were blind.

Hisaka watched the young woman settle herself in front and to one side of her and resume the Lotus. The gaze remained blind. She sees another world, another time. "You have come to request something of me, Child, but you have not brought that most important part of yourself. Why have you left your presence elsewhere?"

The eyes leapt to her face, then dropped to the wooden floor. "Forgive me, Lady—Mother Priestess."

Lady, eh? Hisaka was thinking. "Even now, five years since you came to us, you do not feel a part of us. Forgive me, if I have not welcomed you with all of my being."

A tear stained Midori's thigh. "Forgive me if I have not brought all of my presence. If there is fault, it is mine, Mother Priestess."

"Forgive my repeating myself, as it speaks of an impatience I do not normally find inside me, but why have you left your presence elsewhere?"

Another tear but no effort to stop it. No change in expression, no external indication that a great wound inside Midori was opening to disgorge its pain. The tears dripping, the young woman began to speak.

"At the shipyard yesterday, a small black yacht was brought in for repair. It looked identical to the one I'd arrived in and abandoned halfway across Nagasaki five years ago. As I repaired its engine, I realized it *was* the ship I'd abandoned, having the modifications I'd made in the years before that, traveling around the galaxy, looking for a place ...

"I didn't realize, until I repaired the yacht yesterday, how much pain I have been running from, how much I still carry with me. I'm so sorry, Mother Priestess Tomi, to have consumed so much of the Order's time, to have wasted your teachings on such an inept and unprepared student. It was wrong of me to have come here at all, Mother. It is time for me to leave, but I wanted to offer my apologies and beg your forgiveness."

Hisaka watched the young woman, whose tears spilled freely down her face, and she felt uplifted to see the strength and courage of someone willing to walk face first into pain. The utter physical stillness where clearly inside shrieked a terrible emotional storm was phenomenal to watch. It's as though she stands defenseless and unprotected on a mountain top in the midst of a snowstorm, the wind and sleet cutting at her mercilessly, and yet she stands proud, without any inclination of needing protection from the elements. What profound internal strength she has, what pervasive blessed peace, what indomitable courage!

Mother Hisaka Tomi, Head Priestess of the Lotus Flower sect of the Zen Buddhist Church of the Mitsubi Empire, thanked Buddha for bringing this child into the monastery, for such an ethereal being belonged at the right hand of Buddha, to help guide the seeking souls such as herself—yes, she, the Mother Priestess—along the eightfold path to enlightenment.

For here, in front of her, was an enlightened being herself, a Bodhisattva, an incarnation of the Buddha itself come to Earth to touch other seeking souls with its light.

And she knows it not.

Hisaka watched, at peace, until the teardrops ceased.

Midori produced a tissue from her sleeve and wiped her face. The eyes then moved up from the floor.

Hisaka allowed a small smile to reach her face. "Thank you, Child, a gift without compare."

The bewilderment was plain.

"It is clear to me why you came, why you stayed. You do not know it, but you bring Nirvana. You have brought it to me, here, now, and forever. The Buddha says when the student is ready, the teacher will appear. I will be forever grateful to you, Child, for appearing when I was ready. Thank you." And Mother Hisaka Tomi bowed to Daughter Midori Sato, and held it.

When she straightened, she saw Midori did not understand. "To be clear, Daughter Midori, you have not wasted the order's time. Au contraire, as those frenchies say down at the whore-houses. You have not been an inept and unprepared student. It is we, the sisters and myself, who were unprepared for you. And it was right, destined, and predetermined that you should come here. If anyone should beg forgiveness, it is us of you, for not embracing your teachings, or recognizing the depth and breadth of your wisdom."

Something changed in Midori's face.

"Your cup is full, child."

"Yes, Mother, it is."

"Meditate with me as I empty my cup. Allow yours to empty alongside mine."

"Yes, Mother."

And Mother Tomi led a chant as ancient as Buddha, wondering if she had finally learned what she had come to learn in this incarnation, and asking Buddha to release her soul to ascend once again to her next incarnation in her journey along the eightfold path toward Nirvana.

* * *

Admiral Nobu Nagano looked across the Imperial Naval Works at Nagasaki and frowned. In the distance, a mountain towered over both sea and spaceport.

Nagasaki sat at the southernmost edge of the Mitsubi Empire, and just one constellation over was Iberian territory, an outpost called Mindanao, where mighty gunships of the Iberian navy patrolled mine-infested space against a Mitsubi incursion that Admiral Nagano knew they were without the resources to mount.

Somehow, in the last six years, the Mitsubi Empire had shrunk no smaller. Somehow, all the clans had remained loyal. Somehow, the Navy had kept the pirates, Iberia, and the Nahuatl all at bay.

But Nagano knew it was unraveling. He could see it.

Beyond the window, half the hangars at the once-great military spaceport at Nagasaki stood empty, where once they had all been full. Nagano remembered that on one occasion, the port commander had told him an empty berth couldn't be found for the flagship vessel of the Princess Mariko, the battlecruiser Yamato.

Now, he thought, our Imperial Treasury sits empty, our creditors clamor to be paid, taxes are the highest they've ever been, and Imperial levies from allied clans comprise fifty percent of our armed forces. General Takagi and I effectively control the Empire.

The Eldest Mitsubi sister, Yoshi, had acceded to their demands six years ago, had allowed them to replace all the existing ministers with choices of their own, and had sent all her close relatives to live on the Nagano and Takagi homeworlds of Fukuoka and Yedo, respectively, with the exception of the Empress, her sister Princes Keiko and herself, of course.

The Kyoto star system was now their prison.

But even our control is failing, Admiral Nagano knew.

Too often, it was the indecision between him and General Takagi, their inability to agree on priorities, and the diffusion of responsibility between them, or between Empress Regent Yoshi Mitsubi and them, on the rare occasion she spoke her mind.

It's been more than twenty-six years, Admiral Nagano thought, but I still miss Princess Mariko.

He realized he was tired.

You will hold yourself erect and you will not be tired! he told himself. You are a young seventy-five, and you will continue to serve as though you are twenty-five. What did that Christian prophet once say? Live as if you'll die tomorrow, and pray as if you'll live forever.

An afternoon at the local Buddhist shrine would certainly help.

Admiral Nagano turned from the window and said so to an aide. "What would be a good shrine to visit? No, no, not the usual. Crowded with tourists, a camera in each hand. No, I'm looking for one where I might pray in peace."

The aide pointed out the window to the mountain in the distance. "There, Lord Admiral Nagano. The shrine of the Lotus Flower, run by the Mother Priestess Hisaka Tomi, who it is said sits at the foot of Buddha himself."

"Eh? A convent? A nunnery? Fool! If I'd wanted a courtesan, I'd have said so!" His hand leapt to the hilt of his sword.

"Forgive me, Lord Admiral." The aide dropped to his knees and pounded his head. "Truly, it is a Buddhist temple, Lord, not a brothel."

Admiral Nagano frowned. "Truly? Forgive me, a moment of insanity. A female order? How unusual. Mustn't be very many of those, eh?" He unwrapped his hand from the hilt.

"No, Lord, and unlike most, they have no need to resort to that oldest of professions."

"No? And how do they support themselves?"

"They work in the shipyards, Lord Nagano, some here on the Naval side, others on the civilian side."

"Perchance you might introduce me to someone to guide me to the mountain shrine?"

"Certainly, Sire. In fact, I know just the one. When would you like this arranged? Uh, the monastery does require supplicants to approach barefoot."

Barefoot, eh? he wondered, I'm not sure I've the energy for that. "Tomorrow morning, please." Yes, make it tomorrow, as I have far too little energy for it today, the admiral thought, and I don't want to miss that courtesan I've already arranged for this evening.

"Yes, tomorrow morning," Admiral Nobu Nagano repeated.

* * *

Emperor Augusto Iberia frowned at the supplicant, vaguely recognizing him from his father's reign, recalling only that the man was associated somehow with Princess Mariko's defeat over twenty-five years ago.

"Former Minister of Foreign Affairs, former sub-commander of the Fourth Fleet, Señor Xavier Balleros," the page announced.

The gray-haired gentleman approaching the dais elicited the memory for Augusto. This is the man, the Emperor thought, who defeated the Princess Mariko Mitsubi in battle at the Iberian outpost, Tarifa, stopping the Princess's drive to conquer the galactic core.

An effort that would have brought the core under the rule of a single government for the first time in history.

Sad that he succeeded, and doubly sad that he used treachery rather than tactics.

"Lord Emperor Iberia," the elderly gentleman said, bowing deeply from his waist.

"Lord Balleros, welcome," Emperor Iberia said, nodding. "If I may, Sir, I would offer you more swift access in honor of your service to my father, the late Emperor Maximilian. And if I may add, in honor of your most signature accomplishment, the defeat of the Mitsubi Princess Mariko."

"Most gracious, your Highness, to remember an event so remote," the old man said, his voice gravelly and low, almost a whisper. He wore the formal dress of the Spanish conquistador, the peaked helmet and the burnished-bronze breast plate, both so shiny a person might groom himself in the reflection. "So like your father to have that bit of precognition."

Augusto had no idea why the old man had come. Xavier Balleros had appeared at the palace gates early that morning demanding audience, refusing to say why he was here. Precognition? the Emperor wondered, what's he talking about?

"These many bureaucrats I've seen on my way here all had same question, but your Highness has alighted on it without a hint of its being the topic of my visit."

"You're here to discuss the defeat of the Princess Mariko?"

"And some of it attendant, what is the Latin term, oh yes, the sequelae."

"Can you be more specific?"

"Certainly, Sire, in a room with fewer eavesdroppers." The old man glanced to the sideboard.

"Of course," Augusto gestured for the room to clear. "Have you quenched your thirst, Lord Minister? There's a Sangria from your homeplanet Galapagar, or would you prefer one from the Catalans?"

"Cheap watered wines is all those Catalonians make! Of course I'll have the Galapagar. Thank you, Lord."

Always prefers the Sangria, Augusto knew. Himself, he had come to like the Octli of the Nahuatl, although it was too potent a potable for this occasion. While the room cleared and Xavier rose to serve himself, Augusto watched the older man, his neuralink feeding him public information, and information available only from his father's archives. By the time of room had cleared, Augusto knew far more than he wanted.

The former minister returned to his place. "Salud!" And he drank.

"So you served my father right up to my being kidnapped."

"Yes, Sire."

Augusto nodded. "Twenty years, Lord Minister. Quite an investment to see it go awry."

"Your father told you then? Yes, it was devastating. She was perfect, but then those wily Japanese ... " Xavier shook his head.

"You're sure it was them? I'm not convinced, but no matter. We know the result, eh?"

"Yes, Sire. And about that ... result."

Augusto looked at Xavier. A day or two might have gone by without his having thought of Serena, but they were few. As promised, he hadn't told anyone she'd rescued him from the Japanese kidnappers. "What about that result?"

"The vehicle I placed at her disposal at the Teotihuacán spaceport was keyed only to her. Not just the door, but also the ignition controls, the engine housing, and the electrical panel. I didn't want anyone taking that yacht anywhere, or anyone pirating it away from her if she should be caught unawares by some villain."

"Prudent. But somehow she absconded with it herself, yes?"

"Yes. More resourceful than I'd anticipated, but then I had provided her with exactly such an education. What she never knew was that each system was singular. None was interdependent. Disabling one had no effect on the others. So when the yacht was abandoned a year after she absconded with it, I received an alert that she had left the ship. Oh, it was expected, and she was far too crafty to remain where she'd abandoned the yacht, so I did no search, nor did I try to trace her from there. That was five years ago. And I'd not received a signal from the yacht ever since."

Augusto waited one, three, five seconds, his heart beating rapidly in anticipation, but his face impassive. "Until now."

"Yes, Sire, until now, until yesterday. And I came to tell you as soon as I could."

Again Augusto waited one, three, five seconds, keeping his face calm. "Where is she?"

"Nagasaki, or rather, that's where the yacht is, where she was working on it. It was the last functioning sensor, in the engine housing."

Augusto pulled up a profile of the Mitsubi spaceport, a major shipyard, foundry, and manufacturing plant at the southernmost edge of the Mitsubi Empire. A strategic system for the Mitsubis. We never invaded because its military, strategic and historic importance to the Mitsubis make it a difficult system to conquer, Augusto thought. They'll likely hurl themselves at us with the names of Buddha and their Empress on their lips, happily sacrificing themselves to stop any and all invaders. A tough people, these Japanese, Augusto knew, his face blank. Augusto brought himself back to the present. "We have agents? Infiltrators?"

"I don't know, Lord Emperor."

This man betrayed my father by secretly rearing and teaching the child who stood to become the Mitsubi Empress, thereby giving succor and harbor to what might one day become our most indomitable enemy. And he did it without consultation, revealing what he did only after his protégé had been accused of kidnapping me, an accusation that I have let stand for six years.

Augusto stared at the former Minister of Foreign Affairs. "I will keep this information in mind, Lord Balleros. If you have further signals from the yacht, please forward these to me immediately. The precise coordinates of the signal would be helpful. Thank you, Lord Balleros. Your prompt response will not be forgotten."

"Thank you, Lord Emperor Iberia, a pleasure to be of service."

Augusto waited until the old man was shown the way out before he contacted his Minister of Clandestine Affairs to request further information from operatives placed at or near the Nagasaki spaceport at the southern edge of the Mitsubi Empire.

That done, Emperor Iberia walked to the balcony and looked out over the city of Madrid spread below him.

And he let his heart soar.

Chapter 9

Admiral Nobu Nagano looked at the girl standing between two guards.

Slight, her head shaved, her long, beige kimono inadequate to ward off the chill wind blowing inland from the harbor, completely still except her eyes, she looked too insubstantial to be a Buddhist Priestess.

"I was sent by the Mother Priestess of the Lotus Flower, Lord. I see that my presence is not to your liking. My apologies. I will return to the monastery forthwith and ask the Lady Priestess to send someone more worthy of this task."

If she's *that* perceptive, perhaps there's more to this flower than just petals, Nagano thought. "Thank you for offering, Lady Priestess, and my apologies for making my thoughts known to you. Please, I would be honored to have your guidance, if you would still consent to giving it." Her utter stillness unsettled him. Why? he wondered. How do I find her complete self-possession such a threat?

"Guidance offered is only as good as guidance accepted." The woman blinked at him. "Or, if you prefer an aphorism from our English-speaking communities in the Alpha Quadrant, a wise person doesn't need advice, and a fool doesn't heed it."

Admiral Nagano threw his head back and laughed. "Praise to Buddha, I am neither. What shall I call you, Lady Priestess?"

"Sato, Midori Sato." With the hint of a smile, she gestured toward the spaceport gate.

The two guards led them to his gravcar, and Nobu settled himself in the back seat, while Midori was escorted around to the other side. The enclosed car was warm, at least. The gravcar lifted and floated out the spaceport gate and down the street toward the beach.

"How long have you been with the Lotus Flower, Lady Priestess?"

"About five years, Lord Admiral."

He saw she was barefoot. "The cold doesn't hurt your feet?"

"We are taught that heat and cold are part of the natural variation around us. It just is, and its acceptance, what we do. The body is cold, the body is warm, but the soul stays the same."

Admiral Nagano looked out the side window at the mountain they approached. "How far to the top?"

"A thousand feet, Lord."

The gravcar slowed, and they stepped out.

The gate in front of the path wasn't locked. "Aren't you afraid of intruders?"

"How can anyone intrude, if all are welcomed by Buddha?"

"I suppose we'll have to climb?"

"I have not found an ascent, Lord Admiral, that doesn't require a climb. Have you?"

He looked up the steep mountain.

Just visible at the upper reaches, a set of steps descended from the temple entrance without railings or guideposts. He traced it downward, a snake that twisted first one way then doubled back on itself. An occasional tree waved fiercely in the brisk wind.

"This is the only way?"

"Yes, Lord."

He looked at her feet again, at her thin kimono, at her bare head. "How do you do it? Every day, yes? What discipline you have!"

"High praise from an admiral, Lord Nagano. Thank you."

He brought his gaze down, frowning.

"An ascent of a thousand feet begins with a single step."

He laughed again, seeing the grin in her eyes if not on her face. "Indeed, it does. Lead the way, Lady Sato."

"Pardon, Lord, but weapons are prohibited on monastery grounds. Forgive me if that wasn't explained to you."

"Of course." He unbuckled his service pistol and removed his ceremonial long sword, then his mid-length sword, the preferred blade for seppuku, the ritual taking of one's own life. He handed the weapons to a guard, who put them in the gravcar trunk.

"And your Tanto, Lord Admiral?"

He grimaced. "It's just a knife."

"Which when drawn from your boot, or sleeve, or wherever you have it hidden, can do wicked damaged fast. Yes, Lord?"

"Yes, Lady." He unstrapped the sheath from his left forearm.

"Any others?"

He shook his head.

She opened the gate.

The Admiral stepped through and toward the stairway some ten paces away.

"Uh, Lord Admiral?" one guard said.

He looked.

The priestess blocked their way. "I was asked to escort the Lord Admiral. So sorry, but no one else."

"What of his safety, Lady Priestess? Who will guard Lord Admiral Nagano?"

"I will, if it should be needed. The Lord Admiral Nobu Nagano will be safe with me. It is my ongi to him." She used the ancient Japanese word for debt or obligation.

He saw how apprehensive his guards were. "The mountain will be a slag heap if anything happens to me."

"The Lady Mother said as much when she asked me to be your guard. Among the sisters, I am perhaps the best trained in the arts of war."

"As facile with your hands and feet as with your tongue?"

"The Lord Admiral is fulsome with his praise and much too kind to his humble servant of the Lord Buddha."

"Nonsense! Very well, Lady Priestess Warrior Poet Linguist, a pleasure to have your guidance."

"Mutual, Lord." She bowed to him, amusement again in her eyes. Then she stepped around him and led him to the stairs.

The steps wide enough for five people abreast, Admiral Nagano caught up with her and ascended beside her. "As this climb is intended to equalize differences in station, wealth and prestige, Lady Priestess, may I walk beside you?"

"I am honored, Lord Nagano."

"The honor is all mine, Lady Sato."

The odd pair strode up the wide stairs, the two guards below watching nervously at first.

Nobu marveled at her strength, the feet seeming tougher than a tiger's paws, the legs lithe as a gazelle's, the gaze clear as an eagle's.

"You would be an excellent warrior. You have all the makings of a true samurai."

"The Lord Admiral's praise clearly reflects his own talents and accomplishments. You have been Admiral how many decades now?"

Deft, this one, he reminded himself. "Ah, but that is where my seeking comes from. Your temple, a place for reflection and prayer. Yes, many decades, but for what? Lady Priestess, an ear and a silence. You have both those qualities I need. I do not mean to burden you, but—"

"You seek to unburden yourself."

He sighed, nodding, his gaze dropping to the steps in front of him, his breath coming to him somewhat faster for exertion, the nip of cold off the bay pinching at his cheeks, wrists, and ears.

"I despair, Lady Priestess, for the Mitsubi Empire, a once great sprawling conglomerate of tribes, clans, states, and oligarchies, once magnificent in its reach from the borders of the Beta Quadrant, reaching halfway into the Gamma, with the bulk of the Delta under her control. Once she nearly conquered the Nahuatl, Princess Mariko turned her tactical acumen on the galactic core itself, and had conquered most of that when she met her untimely demise."

"Did you know her?"

"Know her? I helped rear her! I helped teach her! Oh but sooner than I'd known it, she absorbed everything I knew and surpassed me before she'd commanded her first unit. Relentless, inexhaustible, and far more demanding of herself than any of her teachers or even the Empress Fumiko Mitsubi, her own mother! And in spite of her constant energy and unstoppable drive, she had that same inner stillness that I see in you. An infinite patience alongside an unhesitating action. Unpredictable in a thousand ways, knowing that you knew that she knew that you knew, and still she trapped both enemy and friend alike in her snares. The galaxy lay bare for her taking."

The wind was sharp against his cheek and he realized it was the cold of drying tears, and he didn't want to cry, not he, an Admiral of many decades, particularly not here, ascending a steep staircase toward a Buddhist monastery, a Priestess beside him.

"You are here to be humble," she said in a soft voice. "To become one with Buddha. Pain and completion are frequent companions."

She might have said something similar, Nobu thought, glancing at her through blurry vision.

Her face was upturned toward the monastery, and he saw the profile, and a trick of light behind her head briefly gave her the indication of hair despite her bald head, and the memory of her voice, Mariko's voice, the voice of—

"What is it, Lord? Why have you stopped?"

She was staring at him now, and the memory dissipated, leaving him with the ghost of something lost. "Nothing," he said. "It was nothing." And he looked up the staircase as it doubled back a few more times above them. He resumed the ascent. "We are a pitiable shadow of the once Great Empire we were. Our finances are in shambles, our taxes higher than they've ever been, our levies at nearly fifty percent, but our rulers—nay, I'd be remiss not to include myself—our rulers are shadows of the hearty and vigorous people we once were.

"It was her death, you know. Nine months pregnant with her daughter the future Empress, and she's betrayed in battle and killed not by enemy fire but with the laser of her own First Mate Hideo Kobaya."

Her gentle hands guided him to a bench set in the hillside, as he could no longer see, and he said a silent blessing for the Priestess Midori Sato, who sat beside him and waited until his weeping passed.

* * *

Frustrated, Xavier Balleros left the palace, realizing that his entreaty had fallen on deaf ears. Yesterday, he'd received a neuramail that the small black yacht had once again been accessed by Serena Zambrano, and he'd realized that his creation—the perfect instrument to bring down the Mitsubi Empire—needed to be neutralized before she got out of control.

During that first year after he lost contact with her, Xavier had been tormented by the question of what to do. A rogue operative who did not even know her objective, Serena Zambrano was a wild stallion who might yet be tamed. But despite numerous tries by her control—her "father," Pedro Zambrano—Serena had refused to respond to messages or other attempts to approach her and get her cooperation.

Each time in the first year that the yacht signaled some contact, perhaps a total of eight times, Xavier had had her "father" plead with her to come home, each message carefully crafted to lure the wayward young woman to return.

Once, they'd even sent an emissary to attempt contact at her last known location. The emissary had later turned up dead, an apparent victim of a pirate attack, in the wrong place at the wrong time.

Then the yacht had turned up abandoned in the southern Mitsubi Empire, at the Nagasaki naval base, a planet ninety-percent reserved for military operations and manufacture. Security thick on Nagasaki, they'd been unable to respond quickly enough to try to track her.

Xavier had lost her trail then, and after six months without contact, he was sure he'd never hear from her again, dreading the worst.

Each day had been a grueling test for Xavier Balleros. Once sub-commander of the Fourth Fleet, and then rising through the Iberian government until his appointment as Minister of Foreign affairs fifteen years after defeating Princess Mariko in battle, Xavier was highly accustomed to anxiety of the worst sort.

But the prospect of Serena Zambrano's sudden appearance within the ranks of the Mitsubi Hierarchy, and possibly claiming her birthright as heiress to the Empire, eldest daughter of the eldest daughter of the Empress Fumiko Mitsubi, felt to Xavier Balleros like a sword dangling inches above his head, held by the finest of gossamer threads in gale-force winds, ready to snap and to send the sword sinking into his body.

The impending doom had waxed and waned across the last few years, and he'd even had moments after seeing a news account of some unexplained death in which he'd believed that

that must have been her, that finally she was dead and finally he could breathe.

And he'd even had a few months recently where the thought of her hadn't sent him crawling out of his skin, or caused him to sit bolt upright in the middle of the night in a cold sweat, or started his heart fluttering or felt like an elephant was sitting on his chest and compressing the air out of his lungs.

Blessed Mary Mother of Jesus, I thought this was all behind me, Xavier thought, a fresh trickle of sweat dripping down his back, his gaze on the ground as he left the palace. Passers-by accused him with their glances of having betrayed both Emperors Maximilian and Augusto for failing to control his rouge creation, for having hatched the ill-conceived idea of turning the wanton energies of the Mitsubi Princess Mariko against her own Empire, only to have the entire plan backfire, and restoring the true heiress to her throne all the worse for his having made every military discipline available to the Mitsubi whelp.

And her acumen will be sharpened by the bitterness at having been used so cruelly by this agent of the Iberia Empire, this former Minister of Foreign Affairs, Xavier Balleros.

And she'll turn the terrible Mitsubi energies upon the Iberia Empire, and will soon have armadas pulverizing the very heart of Iberian sovereignty and identity, our dear Madrid!

It'll be worse than the Mongol hordes battering the gates of Vienna, worse than the infidel Turks besieging the isle of Malta, worse than Princess Mariko pulverizing the Capital of Nahuatl. And the fall of the Iberia Empire will be laid at the feet of none other than Xavier Balleros, all because he chose to play God and keep alive a fetus that should have died when her mother, the Princess Mariko, was assassinated.

Xavier could no longer contain himself. He had to stop her, once and for all.

He *had* to!

Shivering despite the balmy weather, he strode to the tube and caught a capsule to the spaceport, where his yacht awaited him.

A large triple-engine model piloted for him by an aide, the yacht was ready for liftoff the moment he stepped aboard.

"A neuralink, and a glass of Sangria, please," he said.

Xavier plugged himself in and commed his contacts in the Iberian intelligence service. "Dominique, my friend, I have a favor to ask," he said, his voice tremulous.

Chapter 10

Uplifted, transcendent, euphoric, and exhausted, Admiral Nobu Nagano reached the base of the thousand-foot staircase, on his head the wide-brimmed conical cap he'd borrowed to protect him from the wind. He turned to the Priestess who had accompanied him on his pilgrimage.

In the east, a lighter cast to the horizon indicated an approaching dawn. He marveled that through it all, he'd wondered for not a single moment what time it was.

The chanting, praying, meditating, and back to chanting, had consumed nearly twelve hours without his noticing. They had eaten sparingly, just a few strips of bean curd and bit of warmed rice, a few cups of tea, and back to the worship of Buddha's ancient mysteries.

It had been magnificent. Admiral Nagano turned to Priestess Midori Sato to tell her.

Her eyes darted past him to the unlocked gate where his guards and gravcar awaited him beyond a dense screen of trees.

He saw her alarm and started to look.

"Don't," she said, her voice low. "I sense … wrongness, Lord Admiral," Midori said. "There is danger. It is a trap. They are not your guards."

"How dare they! I'll ..." And he reached for his sword, which he did not have. "I'm unarmed!" He hadn't felt so vulnerable since entering the academy nearly sixty years before.

"They must have known. Please, Lord, return to the monastery or allow me to remove these miscreants and escort you back to the spaceport. I will see you there safely."

"No, they might try to pick me off on the stairs, exposed like that, and if they're who you say, they'll have others nearby."

"I sense their intent is not to kill you, Lord, but to capture you."

"To what gain?"

She shook her head. "Go, please!"

"And leave you to them? I won't!"

"They know we're here. They're getting nervous. Listen, give me your hat and take off your kimono." She slipped out of hers, and in the exchange of clothes he couldn't help but notice how breathtakingly beautiful she was. "Now stay here," she said.

Nobu watched her march toward the gate, her gait an admirable mimicry of his truculent stomp.

He almost didn't see the guards fall. The hat and robe went one direction, and limbs whipped the other, and both guards were sprawled out before either knew what had happened. He grinned and was about to shout.

"Hold still." Five swords and two guns were pointed at his head.

"Admiral?" the Priestess called, trying to see through the screen of trees. She donned the kimono again and walked through the gate.

Into the ring of armed miscreants around him.

"Stop," one said to her. "You move, he dies." For good measure, one sword point drew blood from his cheek. More of them surrounded her.

A blow sent him to unconsciousness.

* * *

The Nahuatl Emperor, Naui Quiahuitl Xiuhtectli, frowned at the news: An attempt to assassinate Admiral Nobu Nagano at the Mitsubi Naval Base at Nagasaki had miraculously been thwarted by a Buddhist Priestess who had given her life to stop the attack. Bodies littered the entrance to the shrine that the Admiral had been visiting, among them six assassins and the Priestess, the Admiral having been found unconscious nearby.

"Who do you supposed tried to assassinate him?" Xochitl asked, lounging nearby.

He held up a hand, the neuralink continuing to feed further information. An assassin was suspected to have escaped the scene of the attack, as a yacht was stolen from the nearby space-port and somehow eluded pursuit. The assassins had not yet been identified, but all were ethnic Japanese, their tattoos indicating membership in another Buddhist sect or in the infamous Japanese underworld, the Yakuza.

The dead Buddhist priestess had been identified as twenty-six year old Midori Sato, who had joined the Order of the Flowering Lotus five years before, according to the Priestess Mother, Hisaka Tomi, who supplied the news agency with a still of the Priestess.

Emperor Xiuhtectli frowned at the image. Why does she look familiar? he wondered, shaking his head. He pushed the news-feed into the background. "Xochitl, how could one Priestess defeat five or six armed assassins, eh?"

"How should I know, Lord Fire?"

Two years ago, their love affair widely known, they'd decided to marry, and Xochitl had retired as ambassador. Because of his age, Emperor Xiuhtectli had elevated a nephew to the position of Heir, as he remained childless, Xochitl at forty-five just beyond childbearing years.

They lounged after breakfast in the royal suite high in the palace on Teotihuacán, halfway around the planet from Azteca

University, where events six years before had almost precipitated a war between the Nahuatl and Iberian Empires.

"It just seems unlikely, eh? And aren't Buddhists supposed to be peaceful?"

"The Dalai Lama is peaceful. Yes, dear, he's a Buddhist, but they've a very different brand of Buddhism than these Japanese follow. As I recall, there are a number of militant sects within the Mitsubi Empire, some of them quite violent."

"Search: Flowering Lotus sect, Nagasaki," he told his neuralink.

The Order of the Flowering Lotus is a Buddhist sect occupying a monastery atop a steep mountain on the shores of the largest continent of the planet Nagasaki. This sect is one of several whose members are entirely female and whose lives are devoted to the peaceful worship of bodhisattva principles. While many Buddhist sects are militant, including most of those on Nagasaki, the Order of the Flowering Lotus is not. The monastery itself can only be accessed by climbing a thousand-foot stairway, whose ascent is humbling and daunting. The order practices asceticism, piety, and humility, and demands simple, often inadequate clothing, and bare feet of all its adherents at all times. Of note, weapons of any type are prohibited in the monastery, even on the stairway leading to its entrance. The purity of its beliefs and the strict adherence of its members to its ethos make the order of the Flowering Lotus unusual among Buddhist sects, and its rigorous practices attract only the most devoted followers, keeping the monastic community small and tightly knit. Of note, this order is often mistaken by visitors to be a brothel, perhaps because of its name.

"This isn't a violent sect at all," Emperor Xiuhtectli said.

"Did you see that still image of her?"

"Look familiar to you, too?"

Xochitl grunted. "My intern for three years—worked every day in my office with me! Smart, pretty, talented. I was really impressed with her. Accused later of kidnapping Prince Iberia. Do you still have that still of her from six years ago?"

That's it, he thought, and brought up the image on his neuralink beside the one just broadcast on the news feed.

"Pretty similar, eh?"

"Run analysis," he told his neuralink.

The two images merged, the profile turning and attempting to model a projected image of the unseen half of the face. The other still, a full-frontal face shot, lit up with points of correspondence. "Eighty percent likelihood of a match," the neuralink told them.

Naui and Xochitl looked at each other.

"And very similar in age," Xiuhtectli said. "Somehow, I don't think this is a coincidence."

"Joined the sect five years ago," Xochitl reminded him.

"Remarkable fighting skill, that young woman at Azteca University."

"Remind me again, dear, what we told everyone?"

Naui smiled. "That was a wicked piece of deception, wasn't it? We arranged everything to look as though she plotted to kidnap Prince Iberia, that her roommate had discovered her plot, that when confronted she killed her roommate, then because of the killing, the Prince's bodyguards took him off planet for safety, but she pursued them, killed his guards, and kidnapped him anyway."

"Better that than the truth!" Xochitl said.

"Which we're still not sure of," he reminded her. "From Teotihuacán, she leaves a trail of bodies behind her at the same time that Prince Iberia gets kidnapped, and she somehow manages to free him from his captors aboard a starliner twelve or more hours after it leaves Teotihuacán, and to disappear with him for three days while the galaxy is on the verge of war."

"Then she leaves him on a moon of Galapagar with only an emergency transponder to alert anyone he's there." Xochitl shook her head.

"Why do you suppose he's never said anything about the episode?" Naui asked. "What if we all have it wrong, eh? What if these two had a torrid love affair, got caught by her roommate, who threatened extortion, and they cooked up this elaborate scheme to get rid of her and spend a few days together before parting ways forever?"

Xochitl threw her head back and laughed. "Just as ludicrous! What happened remains unsolved, eh? Such as who tried to kill her but instead killed the roommate?"

Chapter 11

General Riyo Takagi smiled at Admiral Nobu Nagano. The latter lay in his hospital bed, a bandage around his head. "I thought I'd lost you, old friend." Riyo said.

"Eh, Riyo-san? What are you talking about? It'll take more than six assassins to kill me!"

The two of them laughed, both knowing this a bit of bravado. "Too bad she died in the attack, eh? What a fighter!"

"Nearly killed 'em all, I heard. Just one got away, left a trail of blood, stole that yacht, and evaded all the security. Who was it, eh? Who tried to kill me?"

Riyo shook his head. "We don't know, Nobu-San. Not like the Yakuza to assassinate someone in your position, eh? There's a couple of sects we're investigating, but listen, Nobu-San, what if it was some foreign agent or agency?"

"Foreign? You mean the Iberians? Like as not, eh? They covet Nagasaki—always have. They sit there perched on Mindanao with that Armada, waiting to strike at the first sign of weakness. Why not help us along, eh, Riyo-San? I'll bet Buddha's left buttock it was them!"

"And just like those Spanish snakes to wait a couple years before getting revenge. Too bad we didn't talk before causing that excitement on Teotihuacán six years ago." Riyo saw his friend's eyes light up. "Your having the Prince kidnapped, mine killing the student from Madrid. But those Nahuatl feathered serpents twisted things. What is it, Nobu-San?"

The Admiral had a distant look. "Listen, once on the way up, and then again just before we were attacked at the gate, this Priestess ... I caught a glimpse of her, reminded me of Mariko-Sama. The way she stood, the way she moved. Maybe I'm imagining things, eh? I don't know. I've been thinking about her lately, and I don't know why. Buddha preparing to reincarnate her? Who knows, eh? Too bad she died, that Priestess."

Riyo looked at him and shook his head. "I've been thinking about her, too. We'd have had the galaxy by the balls if we'd taken the galactic core, eh? What do you suppose ever happened to that Balleros traitor? The one who defeated Mariko? Emperor Maximilian turned his face from him five or six years ago, eh? That's a snake I'd like to chop the head off of."

"Me, too." The Admiral sighed, put a hand to his bandaged head. "I was a fool to have gone up to the monastery unarmed. Oh, but it was wonderful, communing with Buddha all night with those priestesses. The Mother Priestess, the old one, I'll bet she's heard a thing or two from people like me? No worries, my friend, I'm too wise to say anything specific, but how many like me haven't been so wise? I wonder what she'd tell us about the younger one, the one who saved me? Listen, while you're here on Nagasaki, go and see her. The climb to the monastery is worth it."

Riyo nodded and took his leave, nodding to the numerous bowing guards who'd politely waited outside while the two old friends conferred inside. The General marched out of the hospital, saw that it was late afternoon, local time, and thought, Ah yes, the Lotus Flower.

* * *

Looking at the calendar, Pedro Zambrano realized it was that time of year again.

He sighed.

Six years ago, his child, Serena, had fled in the yacht left for her on Teotihuacán in case of emergency. By that time, she had killed at least two assailants, and perhaps more, in just a few days. His greatest fear had been realized. She had become what he'd most feared.

She was such a gentle creature, he thought, his feet taking him from room to room in the home that the two of them had shared for sixteen years, before she'd departed for college. How does a father prepare a daughter for a fate he abhors? he wondered.

He looked out on the porch, where in balmy weather the two had shared a lunch while looking over the balustrade and down the dwelling-scattered slope to the bay below. The sight of ships under full sail on the water had delighted her. He could see her clapping her hands and laughing. "Come over and look, Papa!" Her voice was as clear as if she were there right now.

How do you prepare a child like that to fight? he wondered.

His feet took him to the living room. In that first year after she'd fled Teotihuacán, he'd received several messages from her benefactor and Patrón, Xavier Balleros. At his prompting, Pedro had sent a message to Serena begging her to return home, his tone laden with guilt that he had sent her to Azteca University, where he could not have foreseen these tragic events.

To one side was a music stand, which Serena had used every day playing violin. Pedro initially had left it there for her to use when she returned home briefly from her studies. After her studies had been disrupted, he'd found that he was unable to get rid of it. He could see her now, standing in front of it, her eyes glued to the sheet music, her right arm raised and poised to stroke notes with her bow, her chin tucked into the violin butt, the finish glowing. "Listen to this, Papa!" Her voice was as clear as if she were there right now.

How do you prepare a child like that to maim? he wondered.

His feet took him to her bedroom. After that first year, unbidden by her benefactor and Patrón, Pedro had sent her a message every six months, telling her all was forgiven, that there was no reason to continue to keep herself away, that the Holy Mother Church, the Virgin Mary, Jesus Christ, and even God himself, forgave her any transgression she might have committed, and that she was and always had been pure in the sight of God, and would she please come home.

To one side of her room was her desk, neatly tidy and undisturbed as she had left it on her last visit back from Azteca University. Pedro couldn't remember the number of times he'd stood in the doorway, saying, "Child, you must put away your studies and get to bed!" And she'd always laugh at him. "But, Papa, I'm not done yet!" And he would relent and come back in a half an hour, usually to find her slumped over and sleeping soundly. He'd ease her back from the desk and before she got too big, he'd carry her to her bed and tuck her in, and inevitably she'd whisper in her sleep, "But, Papa, I'm not done yet." Her voice was as clear as if she were there right now.

How do you prepare a child like that to kill? he wondered.

His feet took him to his own desk. And he knew, as he had always known, that this was the most difficult task he would ever face, and that as before so again, it would take him days to compose his message for her, and that he would cry as he wrote it, and then he would cry as he rewrote it, and he'd fall asleep at his desk just like she used to, but he had no one to carry him off to bed, and he'd wake in the middle of the night, the soft texture of the desktop imprinted into his cheek, and he'd stumble off to bed, get up the next day and start all over again.

And by the fifth or sixth day, he would be exhausted but uplifted, knowing his message the perfect combination of contrition and entreaty. He would imagine her receiving it and imagine the tears as they poured down her cheeks as she read through his protestations of how much he missed her and how terrible he felt to have put her through everything and how all he wanted was to have her back home.

For a week, perhaps two, he would convince himself that she'd reply this time, she'd return this time, she'd run back to him and grant him forgiveness and apologize profusely for having stayed away so long and swear she'd never stay out of touch ever again for more than a day.

When it was clear, again, that she'd neither reply nor return this time, Pedro Zambrano would enter a deep depression that no amount of counseling or medication or meditation or prayer would remediate. His face would grow rough with unshaven stubble and thin from his having not eaten, and his cheeks would sag, and his eyes would become ringed with darkened circles, and his body would grow odiferous, and his clothes would rumple, and his com would ring unanswered, and he would lay lifeless on the couch or in bed for hours and days without moving.

And in these hours and days, the only thoughts in his mind were those of self-recrimination, and always these thoughts were the same: Why didn't I ever tell her the truth?

For only in his deepest darkest hours did he allow himself to think the unthinkable, to acknowledge the reality, to rip away the carefully-constructed façade to which he had devoted his life.

That Serena Zambrano was not really his child, that this precious creature whom he'd cared for all her life wasn't the child of his loins, wasn't born to a mother who had died in childbirth, but was instead a charge laid upon him by a man to whom Pedro owed his life, to whom Pedro's family owed its fealty, a man who had come to him twenty-seven years ago to ask him to fulfill an obligation that went back generations between their families, both of them knowing that if he carried out this appointed task, then the obligation between their families would be discharged forever, and the Zambrano fates would finally be freed from those of the Balleros.

And in these dark moments, Pedro Zambrano allowed himself to look at the truth of what he had done. Then he knew at those times the real reason that Serena had never ever responded to any of his messages.

That he had lied to her.

That he had adhered to the intricately-crafted fiction that she was his daughter, that he had never revealed the identity of her benefactor and Patrón Xavier Balleros, that he had never told her the truth about her origins.

And because she had discovered in being attacked at the University Azteca that her life was something far different from what he had told her it was, and that she was being prepared for a vastly different future than the one she had imagined for herself, and that her "father" had actively participated in deceiving her, she felt so betrayed on such a deep level that no forgiveness was possible and no amount of contrition would persuade her to take any other action than the course she had chosen.

Pedro Zambrano knew deep inside she would never return because the Serena Zambrano whom he had reared no longer existed, and all he could do was pray that she had become the person she wanted to be.

As he sat at his desk to begin his biennial cycle, Pedro connected the neuralink to begin composing his usual letter, and he saw instantly on his neuralink the story about the assassination attempt on Admiral Nobu Nagano, thwarted by a twenty-six year old Priestess who'd died of her wounds.

At first, he didn't understand why he was crying, until he realized that the Priestess was the same age as Serena, and that the manner of the Priestess's death, giving her life to save that of another person, was the sort of noble and worthy and honorable death that he would want Serena to have.

Weeping at his desk, he thought, that could be her.

Through the blur of his tears, he looked at the still of the Priestess who had died, and he thought, that could be her.

He saw the similarity in feature despite a head without hair, and in his mounting shock and horror, he realized:

It *was* her.

* * *

Keiko Mitsubi approached the double doors to her Mother's suite with trepidation. She followed her sister toward a meeting that of late had become …

Bizarre.

"What are you going to do with that picture of Mariko?" Regent Empress Yoshi Mitsubi asked as they stopped at the double doors to the royal suite high in the Imperial Palace on Kyoto.

Keiko had covered the portrait with cloth and had brought an easel to set it on. "You'll see, sister."

The news of the Admiral's near-assassination on Nagasaki had reached them two nights ago, two nights before their weekly meeting with the Empress, and Keiko had taken the initiative to have cameras installed in the Admiral's hospital room. The revelations about this Priestess who had thwarted the attempt—how she had reminded the Admiral of Princess Mariko—were unsettling to Keiko on a level she didn't quite understand. The still had some resemblance to Keiko's deceased older sister, but only a resemblance. Only after reminding herself that the Admiral Nobu Nagano had fought alongside Princess Mariko for years, had trusted her judgment even to the point of setting aside his generations-old mistrust of General Takagi, had verily worshiped the ground that she walked on, that Keiko had looked closely at the still.

On her neuralink, Keiko had summoned thousands of stills of her sister before she died at age 30, then had the carbo-nano computer run an analysis.

"Ninety-eight percent certainty of consanguinity," the carbonano had told her. "Ninety-five percent certainty of direct descent."

Immediately, she had requested that a genetic sample from the body of the Priestess be sent to the Capitol planet Kyoto. Then Keiko had constructed a forensic computer still of the Priestess with hair styled in the manner her sister Mariko had worn hers. Printed at life-size proportion.

Well that my sister *should* ask what I'll do with this still, Keiko thought, dread and excitement at war within her.

One time a week for the last twenty-six years, the Mitsubi sisters had been presenting themselves to their mother to report on the state of the Empire, each time hoping to see more than a modicum of response in the dull black eyes.

For twenty-one years, nearly nothing.

That is, the Empress would look up from her crushed-velvet divan, wearing the traditional mourning whites, smile wanly at them, acknowledge their bows with a weak nod, and return her gaze to the floor.

After the first five years, they had gotten her consent to bring in Western-style psychologists and psychiatrists, practitioners of the Yellow Emperor's Inner Canon, ayurvedists, acupuncturists, astrologers, shamans, curanderos, shintoists, exorcists, santeros, Buddhist, Moslem, and Christian priests, and even a veterinarian. They had all declared a variety of diagnoses but acknowledged that the Empress's malaise was simply grief.

And the one cure they all recommended was the same: crying.

The Empress had never cried, had sworn all her life she never would, and had exhibited no inclination of any point that she would abandon that assertion.

After twenty-one years, something changed.

The gaze of the Empress had begun to vary. Where heretofore her stare had not wavered, as though she tried to divine from that same point on the floor some meaning or signal, her gaze would jump. Not for long, but there it was. The eyes would shift to the right and up, as though to the left of the elder sister's shoulder was someone else, and then the eyes would drop again to that same point on the floor, a process that occupied less than half a second, at most.

Keiko had been the first to notice it, something not unexpected as Yoshi's powers of observation were significantly lacking. The first half a dozen times it happened, Keiko dismissed it. Then she started looking over her sister's shoulder, to try to find what it was her mother was glancing at. She found nothing of course, but the very persistency of the gesture from her mother prompted her to investigate.

Keiko and her sister always sat the same distance apart during these weekly updates, and so she measured as best she could the line that her mother's glance would make. From what she was able to measure, her mother would always glance at the place where, had she been alive, their eldest sister Mariko might have sat.

Since their weekly visits to their mother were highly routinized, Keiko began timing her mother's glance, to establish if there were some pattern. Nothing emerged except that perhaps the glance occurred toward the latter portion of the briefing, when Yoshi would conclude her summation of the Empire's affairs.

When she described these glances to some of the practitioners who had examined the Empress, one priest of the Nahuatl Christian Church had indicated she might be seeing her ancestors—that is, those persons who had entered this Christian afterlife before she did—and that she was simply responding to and communicating with their spirits. Some of the psychiatrists and counselors verified that this indeed might be the case, but they all cautioned that there might be any number of other explanations.

Then, six months or so into this change, the Empress began to smile right after the glance. Not a broad smile, and certainly not anything approaching joy, but the kind of smile where the edges of the mouth turned up and the eyelids relaxed ever so lightly. This response was particularly noticeable as it was progressive. The Empress seemed to smile a little bit more each time and for slightly longer.

Keiko began to coach Yoshi as to what to do when their mother would glance of the place next to Yoshi and then smile. As the elder sister, Yoshi always took the lead in these meetings, and it would have been indecorous and almost disrespectful for Keiko to interrupt. At first, Yoshi would stop speaking, an unusual thing for her as she tended to prattle.

Keiko coached her sister's responses, having her ask their mother, "What was that?" or "You look amused." or "Did you hear something?"

While the Empress appeared not to hear Yoshi, the behavior did progress, the duration and intensity of what appeared to be amusement increasing each time. The duration of the glance also seemed to be lengthening.

One expert, a neurologist, suggested that the Empress might be experiencing auditory and visual hallucinations, perhaps associated with a deterioration of the brain itself common to dementia. A set of brain images were obtained which showed no acute changes from tests done at the outset of her withdrawal. Some age-related shrinkage of the cortices and concurrent expansion of the ventricles were all they found. The neurologist had remarked in bewilderment that more shrinkage wasn't evident, given the Empress's long periods of inactivity.

Then the Empress began to giggle. Barely noticeable of first as slight shaking lasting only moments, the behavior grew in duration and intensity, being at first inaudible until it was clearly a chuckle.

Now, twenty-six years after having withdrawn into a profoundly deep depression and period of mourning, the Empress Fumiko Mitsubi would glance to the left of her elder daughter for a full second, and then drop her gaze back to the floor and smile, chuckling for just under two seconds.

Whatever Keiko or Yoshi did in response appeared to have no effect whatsoever on this slight break in the Empress's behavior.

Keiko had come to the conclusion that her mother was seeing someone or something that brought her joy, and for some reason she could not or would not articulate beyond the smile and chuckle what it was.

The number and constant presence of servants who attended upon the Empress's care swore to a person that no other deviation in behavior manifested at any other time. The Empress was compliant with all requests made of her in her daily hygiene and care; she ate what she was bidden and evacuated when prompted, lifted whatever limb was requested when bathed and dressed, laid down and slept at normal hours, rose when prompted and walked where requested. Her autonomous responses remained intact and appropriate.

She simply initiated nothing. The classic hand-drop test—ie, someone lifting a hand above the shoulder and letting go of it—produced the normal, non-catatonic result of the hand's being quietly and volitionally returned to the lap. Her response to pain stimulus was normal as well; she flinched from it and removed the limb from harm.

Approaching the double doors of their mother's suite, the life-size portrait under her arm, Keiko was thinking that even Yoshi might not be able to tell the difference between this Priestess and their sister Mariko.

They walked into their mother's presence and bowed.

The Empress gazed at her usual spot on the floor.

Keiko set up her easel right where she knew her mother would glance, the cloth covering the portrait, and then she waited painstakingly through the dreary report that her sister gave to her unresponsive mother.

Yoshi droned on and on, seeming oblivious to the clearly-tense Keiko sitting beside her.

Her gaze on her mother, Keiko sat on the edge of her seat, about to leap out of her skin in anticipation of that moment when her Mother the Empress would look to the left of her daughter the Regent Empress and giggle at what she saw there.

This time, there sat an easel, the portrait covered.

And Keiko watched, a string in her hand, her eyes on her mother's face.

The Empress raised her gaze, Keiko pulled the string, the cloth fell aside, and the portrait was revealed.

"Mariko-Chan, is that … who put Mariko's picture there?" the Empress said, her voice as clear and strong as it had been twenty-six years ago. Then the gaze dropped back to the floor, and the Empress giggled for a moment then stopped.

As chaos erupted around Keiko, she sat utterly still, her gaze fixed to her mother's face.

Yoshi screamed at her, "What do you think you're doing?!"

Keiko ignored her, continued to stare at her mother. A single tear ran down Keiko's cheek.

As the bedlam dwindled, Keiko realized everyone was staring at her and whispering about the portrait of Princess Mariko Mitsubi.

Except that it wasn't a portrait of Mariko. It was a portrait of the Priestess.

"Get me the coroner on Nagasaki," Keiko ordered.

Chapter 12

Tucked in his sleeve was the head-shot still that Princess Keiko had demanded he bring. General Riyo Takagi nodded to the assistant coroner's bow.

Eta! he thought, glaring at the assistant coroner, the one profession that by Buddhist standards was unclean and performed only by the lowest caste, the untouchables, the handling of dead animal and dead human parts antithetical to the very core of the Samurai's being. Butcher shop! he thought, the odor of formaldehyde and rotting meat roiling his stomach and nearly pushing his gorge into his throat. Errand boy! he thought, fuming. That saki-soaked Mitsu-bitch orders me down here to this filthy Eta's butcher mill so I can look at the face of a dead Priestess for her! "Bring me back proof that this Priestess Sato didn't die in the assassination attempt." Riyo wasn't sure why, however. Hadn't the Mother Priestess already identified the body? The Princess had simply indicated a negative genetic match. Match to what?! Riyo wondered, bewildered by the urgency and oddness of the request. Riyo was so full of disgust for so many reasons that he wanted to disembowel himself with his wakizashi, set the butcher mill awash in blood and guts, and end his shame, pain, and aggravation forever. The Princess Keiko's commandment had been clear, and his duty as a Samurai overrode his disgust.

The building was fairly standard in size and construction, a prefecture-run building with multiple agencies sharing space, the morgue in the basement, the facility clean and sparkling with that fresh-washed look, the finishes clear enough to check one's appearance in, and the furniture and other appointments as modern as to be expected in a prefecture-run facility that was perennially underfunded and understaffed.

"This way, Lord General." And the assistant led him to a large door with a thick rubber flange and gestured at suits too large for most people hanging on either side. "A biohazard suit, Lord General. Our protocol is to be suited always. The body you'll be viewing today has no known or detectable pathogens. Our viewings, Lord, are frequently of bodies we have not tested so thoroughly as this one, and sometimes contaminated with pathogens which we are about to test for. Hence our protocols. But you yourself aren't bound to abide by them, and the risk of contamination is quite low."

"You mean I might get something? Some infection or disease?"

"Or you might introduce something that would skew our tests, Lord General." The assistant's brow narrowed, as though he were wondering how he might not have been clear.

"No need," the General said dismissively, wondering who might have used the suit before him and what defilement they might have left behind.

"As you wish, Lord General." The assistant coroner bowed and stepped to the pressure wheel. One full turn, and a faint click was audible. "The Lord Coroner Doctor Lane Hayashi awaits you inside." He pulled the door open.

A draft of chill air surrounded Riyo's legs, and he stepped through the oval.

"Lord General Takagi, welcome. Doctor Lane Hayashi," said a biosuited man in spectacles from behind a glass face-plate.

Glasses? Real vision-correcting glasses? Such a prosthesis seemed so ludicrous that Riyo almost laughed. "Lord Doctor Hayashi," he said, bowing.

The room was all chrome and polish. Even the ceiling reflected his slightly-obscured doppelganger back to him. Along one wall was a bank of drawers, three high, the highest at chest level, along the other wall a mirror, likely one-way glass.

Dr. Hayashi stepped to the first row and pulled out the middle drawer. "Her Highness the Lady Princess Mitsubi tells me that you will first decide for yourself what you see, and then you will watch from beyond that one-way glass when the second person views the remains."

"She made the same request of me, Lord Doctor." Riyo looked at the man calmly while his agitated gorge threatened to regurge.

"Let me know when you're ready, Lord General."

From his sleeve, Riyo pulled the still print of the Priestess Midori Sato, who had died thwarting the assassination of his lifelong friend, Nobu Nagano. For you, Nobu-San, Riyo thought, holding his gorge at bay.

The Doctor drew down the sheet.

Her face lay in repose, her high cheekbones and wide mouth too out of proportion to approach any eidolon of heroic countenance.

Riyo saw instantly that it was not her.

"Please take as much time as you need, Lord General. Please note each feature that you find dissimilar and why."

The still showed a perfect steeple nose without bulge or flare, a straight, even chin, ears proportional and curving graciously back, eyebrows faint and prettily arched, and a strong intelligent forehead.

The corpse's nose was flat, the chin recessed, the ears large and growing at nearly right angles to the skull, the eyebrows thick, straight and almost lupine in nearly meeting in the middle, the forehead sloped so precipitously it looked Neanderthal.

Riyo Takagi nodded to the Coroner, tucking the photo back into his sleeve.

The doctor pulled the sheet up over the face and slid the drawer closed with the push of a finger. "This way, Lord General."

Riyo followed him around the far end to a recessed door not noticeable from the main door. The room beyond was illuminated only by the bright lumens streaming through the deeply-tinted one-way window.

"Please be still, both silent and motionless, until the next person leaves again, Lord General. Better that the person doesn't know of your presence."

Riyo chose one of the chairs toward the back, noting that the row was raised, almost theater-style. What grisly viewing! he thought, his disgust profound. How perverse!

In walked Mother Priestess Hisaka Tomi of the Lotus Flower Buddhist Sect, whom Riyo had visited just yesterday.

"I don't understand why I'm here, Doctor Hayashi. I already identified the body. Why subject me to further anguish? My Midori is already lost to me. What purpose under the firmament would it serve for me to look upon that sweet child's dead face again? More misery, is all! You and your perverse ways, inflating your sense of your own importance by subjecting otherworldly folk like me to the remains of this-world tragedies! You're Eta!"

Even behind the glass, Riyo was taken aback by the vituperation. How can she say such things, much less think them? he wondered.

"Please identify the body, Lady Priestess," the doctor said tonelessly, his face white with rage, pulling back the sheet.

Hisaka Tomi glanced once at the body and burst into tears, burying her face in her handkerchief, her shoulders up near her ears and shaking violently with each sob.

Just yesterday, Riyo had seen a similar display of anguish, and it had struck him odd then that a person—professed to be a follower of Buddha, a teacher of Buddha, and a mentor to those who would lead in the worship of Buddha—would engage in such very un-Buddha-like behavior and display attachment so deep as to be anathema to the very principles that a follower, a teacher, a mentor was supposed to exemplify.

How very disingenuous, Riyo thought.

He was still contemplating what he'd witnessed when the doctor returned from having escorted the hysterical woman from the morgue.

"Lord General?"

"Lord Doctor, a pleasure to have met you." He stood and bowed first to the other man, honoring him.

"And you, Lord General. Please ask the Lady Princess to be forthright about any further information she might need. I can see that you found this helpful."

"Indeed, Lord Doctor, indeed." Again Riyo bowed, then strode from the morgue, straining to keep his gorge contained for an entirely different reason.

* * *

Empress Xochitl Olin stared at the woman being dragged away by her guards. "Wait!" she said.

She had been shopping in the crowded main mall in downtown Teotihuacán, the Capitol City on the Capitol planet of the Nahuatl Empire, admiring the lavish displays of the most expensive goods in the galaxy from behind a screen of security personnel, when an old woman of mestizo ancestry appeared at her elbow.

"That intern who worked in your office, Lady Olin, I helped rear her on Madrid twenty-six years ago. Serena will remake the galaxy!"

Xochitl stared at the old woman as though she were mad.

And then her guards descended upon her and started to drag her away. They now held her, fifteen feet away, two to a limb in spite of her lack of struggle.

"What did you say?" Xochitl asked, seeing the old woman's clear gaze.

"She will remake the galaxy!"

Xochitl took a step toward her.

A guard blocked her path. "Forgive me, Lady Empress, but—"

"Search her for weapons but be dignified and respectful about it," Xochitl ordered. "Find me a place where I can talk with her in private."

"Yes, Lady Empress." One guard loped off, one guard searched the woman, and six others held her, while one stood at Xochitl's back.

She watched from a distance, seeing a small crowd gather. "Ask them to disperse," she told the guard at her back, the captain.

He threw hand signals toward the seven guards around the old woman. Two of them let go of her and quietly instructed the crowd to move on. The other guard returned. "This way, Lady Empress, the manager has offered his personal suite."

She followed to a nondescript door simply marked, "Private." Beyond two sets of doors on either side, the corridor led to another nondescript door marked, "Management." The two guards there stood aside to let them pass.

Beyond were carpets of velvet, walls of crushed satin, chandeliers of glittering crystal.

The manager introduced himself, and Xochitl instantly forgot his name. He showed her to a divan with two thick chairs facing it. The divan was divine. She wondered who his interior decorator was.

"Sit her there," Xochitl said, pointing to one of the chairs.

They brought her in and sat her down.

143

"Privacy, please," Xochitl said, staring at the old woman, then held up a hand when they began to object. "Thank you for your concern for my safety. This woman will not hurt me."

They left without further protest.

The woman was short, barely five feet tall, wore simple robes of rough material and drab color. The webbed corners at her eyes indicated early sixties to late, although her teeth were strong and white. Her hands were spotted and calloused, as though from a lifetime of labor.

She seemed immune to Xochitl's examination.

"How do you know her?"

"I watched her all her life. From a distance, yes, but still, I have come to know the content of her character in a way that her father and her Patrón never could."

Xochitl heard the emphasis when the woman said, "Patrón." It was the title, the one that meant sponsor, godfather, guardian angel, and benefactor all in one. And it was pronounced in the native Spanish, the Spanish of the planet Madrid, not the thousands of variants that had proliferated when the conquistadors sailed to new lands in the fifteenth and sixteenth centuries. The old Castilian.

"I am Xochitl. What is your name, if I may ask?"

"Carmen Hernan."

Xochitl heard hesitation. "If you are truly Spanish, you have other names."

"Carmen Hernan Leon de Dulche."

"What was the name of Serena's roommate at Azteca University?"

The woman smiled but her eyes glistened. "Dolores Hernan."

Xochitl frowned.

"Leon de Dulche."

"I'm sorry. That's so very sad. Your daughter, yes? Serena spoke well of her, admired her terribly."

Carmen's face softened, and a single tear dripped from an eye. "Thank you, Lady Empress."

"Your daughter died in her place."

"Yes, I know. As she had committed to doing."

"Eh?" Xochitl felt that the conversation was taking on proportions she had no way to anticipate. "What do you mean?"

"Dolores was her guard, placed there to protect her."

"From whom? By whom?"

"Her Patrón. As to who might harm her, I don't know."

"You helped rear her?"

"As an infant. Most men, cabrons I tell you, most of them couldn't care for a tiny child like that, so newly out of the womb. He came for me, her Patrón, told me he had a job for me. A month later summoned me to a distant outpost at the edge of Iberian territory, near the galactic core, I never did learn its name. I was there but a day when the Mitsubi Princess attacked. The building shook, people screamed, and the lights flickered, and after several hours of this, when I thought it would never end, it ceased. Two hours later the Patrón arrived with a wriggling child, so newly born the umbilicus was still attached. And attached to the umbilicus ... " The woman went gray and seemed to choke.

"Can I get you water?" Xochitl found the bar and brought back a glass of water and a bottle of whisky.

Carmen drank several gulps from the bottle, then coughed once. "Forgive me, Lady."

Xochitl took the bottle and had a swig herself. Warmth spread through her insides.

"The baby was still moist from birth, but she didn't squirm or wriggle. She just lay there and stared at me."

"Babies don't open their eyes for days," Xochitl protested.

"She stared at me, I tell you. Knew me through to my soul, she did. A La Diabla! Her Patrón told me, 'Take care of her, her name is Serena Zambrano. Take her to her father on Madrid,

Pedro Zambrano. Her mother died in childbirth just hours ago.' And he sent me aboard his personal yacht to Seville. And there, for the next year, I helped Papa Zambrano care for the motherless child."

Xochitl nodded slowly, wondering how to tell the woman about the news that she and the Emperor had seen just three nights before. "Señora Hernan, you said 'She will remake the galaxy.' How can that be? This assassination, did you hear about that? The attempt on the Mitsubi Admiral?"

Carmen nodded.

"The priestess who saved him, did you see the still?"

"Sí, Señora, but por favor, that was not Serena who died."

"How do you know, Señora?"

"My Serena, she fights too well. Also, I have just come from Nagasaki. You see, I have not stopped watching her or guarding her. El Patrón does not require it, hasn't since she disappeared six years ago, but I couldn't stop or let her come to harm."

Xochitl shook her head. "You saw what happened?"

Carmen nodded. "When the fight was over, only Serena remained standing. Then she changed into the clothes of one of her attackers, dressed the attacker in her clothes, returned to the monastery briefly, and then fled in the yacht."

Xochitl stared at the woman, disbelieving. "How have you been able to follow her, all these years?"

"I know Serena, I know her better than her father or El Patrón."

"Why have you come here? Why aren't you following her now?"

"Because, Lady Empress, I don't know where she is, but I am sure she will come here next."

"Here? Teotihuacán?"

"Sí, Lady Empress. This I know of her, and this is how I have been able to follow her all these years."

Xochitl blinked rapidly several times. "She will remake the galaxy?"

"Sí, Lady Empress. She is the chosen one."

"Who is her mother, Señora Hernan?"

"Ah, that is something, Lady Empress, that I don't know. But El Patrón Señor Xavier Balleros knows who her mother is." And Carmen Hernan smiled.

* * *

"Lord Emperor, a great wrong has been perpetrated."

Emperor Augusto Iberia called up the information available on Pedro Zambrano. His neuralink spilled information: Engineer, Civil; retired, Imperial Public Works, four years ago, on disability; Siblings, none; Parents, deceased; born, reared, and lives on Seville; father to Serena Zambrano, missing and presumed dead.

The man looked the paragon of meek. Just five and a half feet, pear-shaped, receding hairline, cherubic cheeks, disarming smile that somehow managed to peek through even in the delivery of bad news.

"It grieved me to hear of your daughter's death, Señor Zambrano." Augusto could tell the man had been crying.

"Did you know her, Lord Emperor?"

"For a short time, at Azteca University."

"Ah yes, that whole mess. Terrible what they accused her of, terrible what they say about innocent people. But it wasn't her, of course. You know that, eh?"

Augusto nodded. "Yes, I do."

"Do you also know it wasn't her fault, what they made her into?"

"Eh? What are you saying?"

"Lessons, Lord Emperor. She had lessons throughout childhood in how to fight, maim, and kill." The man's face became sad. "Such an innocent child. How could they do that to her?"

Augusto recognized the question as rhetorical. "How could anyone?"

"They sapped her humanity, gave her skills no caring human being should have."

Augusto remembered her anguish at their parting, how preoccupied she looked, how withdrawn. No, he wanted to tell Pedro, they didn't take her humanity. She fled rather than let that happen.

"But that wasn't the greatest tragedy, Lord Emperor. No, the great wrong perpetrated by her Patrón and benefactor was her being taking from her mother and her people. She was brought to me at Señor Balleros' request by a mestizo woman, Carmen Herman, who helped me care for her that first year, who told me later she had been summoned to a distant outpost by Señor Balleros, said she couldn't remember its name but it was near the galactic core, when Señor Balleros was sub-commander of the Fourth Fleet, when the outpost was attacked by the hated Mitsubi Armada under that devil worshipping unbeliever Princess Mariko, may God damn her soul to Hell!"

The vehemence didn't surprise Augusto, but it seemed unmitigated by his care of one of their own. "Taken from her mother, Señor Zambrano? Her people—well, Serena was obviously Japanese, and the Mitsubi, her people. But tell me, Señor Zambrano, who was her mother? And what about her father?"

"Well, yes, Lord Emperor, obviously I lived the lie that I was her father, and I've apologized to her, well, sort of, I mean, if she got it, that is, if she isn't dead, you know, in the assassination attempt. But of her real father I cannot say, and you'll know why of course, because her mother was none other than the Imperial bitch Mariko herself, and you know how those Japanese whores won't hold themselves accountable to any man, and at least in that sense the girl was taken away rightly but it wasn't right for her to be punished for the sins of the mother. She should at least have been given over to a normal family of Japanese descent, and not ripped away from her mother even as she lay dying aboard the flagship Yamato as it succumbed to the Fourth Fleet at our outpost on Tarifa, after the first mate Hideo Kobaya betrayed his own princess and cut communications with each ship as our victorious forces pulverized the wretches—" Pedro Zambrano put both his hands over his mouth, as if he'd said too much.

Emperor Augusto Iberia, like his father before him, had simply waited, letting the guilt of an old man push the words from his mouth, for of those words would be spun the rope that would hang him.

"What happened, Señor Zambrano? A sudden illness?"

"A flatulence of the mouth, pardon, Lord Emperor. So yes, forgive me for my part in these travesties, for surely my soul will burn forever in the fires of Hell."

"Surely. Yet said you had apologized to her, if she got it, that is. Got what?"

"Eh, Lord Emperor? Oh, uh, my apology. Her neuro-mail, of course, Lord."

"You will provide me with it."

Zambrano looked puzzled. "Yes, Lord, if that is what you wish. But I don't understand, Lord. Isn't she dead?"

"That's what we're told, isn't it? So it won't hurt if I have her neuro-mail address, will it?"

"No, Lord, I guess not." He looked puzzled. "If I may ask why?"

Augusto shrugged. "Twice before we were told she was dead. Twice before, we were told wrong." Then the Emperor smiled. "If nothing else, you may redeem yourself in my eyes by giving me that address."

Chapter 13

Serena couldn't take her eyes off the splendor in front of her.

The galactic core, the blazing violent inchoate mass, the engine of creation.

Or, as Princess Mariko Mitsubi had often called it, the ultimate prize.

Her neuralink-fed visual cortex dancing with its brilliance, Serena understood now why civilizations had risen and fallen with a single goal as its founding principle: Control the core, and the galaxy is yours. She looked upon the core through her neuralink and she knew why Princess Mariko had striven relentlessly to conquer it.

Inside the flimsy shell of the small black yacht, Serena knew she could venture no closer. Vessels with far more resilient defenses had plummeted to their destruction from further out than she was. The density of space junk—just the flotsam and jetsam of pulverized planets—could easily knock her off course or penetrate her shields or just draw her into a passing gravity well and slingshot her into the core before she could evade.

The number of suicides into the core each year was beyond reckoning. Since no single government controlled the spinning bar at the spiral center, no one really knew how many pilots flew themselves into the core. Remains were never recovered.

Five Empires retained a foothold on a slice of the Galactic Core, but none exerted anything remotely close to permanent control of that slice. The tides of war and the roiling core itself both prevented that. Only the Mitsubi Empire under Princess Mariko had come close. And now they had no foothold at all, and their Empire was shrinking as a result.

For inside the core was a wealth of mass and energy to be found nowhere else, and the other nearest galaxy was Andromeda, so distant as to be prohibitive.

From these footholds on the rim of the core, Empires sank conduits to siphon off energy, conduits composed of the most resilient of materials, conduits with an expected life of only a year or two, as the core eventually reclaimed every atom in the galaxy before splitting it out again as new constellations.

Contracting or expanding? The age-old question among astrophysicists. Which direction was the galaxy going? Humans had occupied such a short eye-blink of its twelve billion years that humanity could not answer this fundamental question.

Serena floated at the edge of the maelstrom and thought, Who cares?

Any human being who did not believe in the presence of a Holy Spirit or creator or divine being had not beheld the galactic core.

Enhanced through the neuralink, the sight was mesmerizing, and if Serena hadn't set herself an alarm, she might have been so drawn in that she would have been lost forever in its brilliance.

The neuralink kicked off, returning her to the yacht cabin. The single chair that stretched out into a chaise and thence into a bed seemed surreal to her, a dull, hard lump of reality under her.

The hand she brought up to punch out a course for the Iberian base Tarifa seemed such a blunt, useless club. The breath that she took to begin speaking seemed so labored and superfluous to living. The words that she spoke vibrated from a larynx that seemed primitive and awkward.

"Tarifa, three quarters thrust," she said, but the words issued from a mouth that didn't seem hers.

I feel like I'm coming out of a deep dream, Serena thought, wondering how often pilots were lured to their deaths by the transforming beauty of the galactic core.

"Tarifa, three quarters thrust," the ship repeated.

She hadn't thought to kill the annoying voice. Out here, months might pass without hearing another word, although Serena had been en route to the core for only a week.

A week since lifting off from Nagasaki.

A week since faking her death by stuffing the body of an assassin into the clothes she had just shed.

A week since killing her six attackers single-handedly.

A week since the "assassins" had knocked unconscious the unsuspecting Admiral Nobu Nagano.

A week since an obscure Buddhist sect had carried out the order for Serena's killing.

A week since the "assassins" had used the Admiral's presence as a feint to disguise their real target, Serena.

Once she had felled all six attackers, Serena had thought through the odd sequence. First they removed the two guards awaiting the Admiral's descent from the Monastery and replaced them with two of their own. Then they surrounded the base of the staircase with four other "assassins." Then they made their own "guards" so conspicuous that the Admiral and she separated, and she disguised herself as the Admiral and walked into their fake trap. Then they descended on the Admiral and held him long enough to get her attention. Then they knocked him unconscious and tried to kill her.

The admiral wasn't a target at all. It had appeared that the assassin's orders explicitly forbade them from killing the Admiral. Serena was sure they'd been ordered just to render him unconscious.

As sure as the setting sun.

As sure as the glowing core.

Somehow, they had caught up to her again.

Who? she wondered.

Why? she wondered.

How? she wondered.

The course locked in, the yacht's acceleration pressed her into the seat, the feel of the ship under her a comfort, like a familiar friend.

Six years ago, she had fled the Capitol of the Nahuatl Empire, Teotihuacán, in this very same yacht. For a year, she had wandered the galaxy, stopping for a day or two, and even sometimes as long as a week, on random planets and asteroids, most of them on the galactic rim, on occasion having to evade a pirate or an imperial patrol, on occasion stopping at a trading outpost to resupply or simply to speak with another human being, but never staying longer, in spite of invitations and sometimes more persuasive pressures. She'd fought off a few curmudgeons with malice or worse on their minds, as well.

And this very same yacht was the one she had left on one side of Nagasaki, parked on the tarmac between two nondescript hulks that looked as if no one had used them in two hundred years.

Then she had traveled halfway around the planet, had found the monastery near the imperial shipyards where whole armadas sat mothballed, had evaded the slave traders who'd wanted to put her to work in the other type of nunnery, the one of ill-repute, and had asked the Mother Priestess Hisaka Tomi to accept this orphan Midori Sato as a student and disciple of Buddha. Then she had gotten a job at the shipyard, repairing starship engines, most of which she could walk straight into, standing upright.

153

For five years she had worked and prayed.

The zen of starship engine maintenance paired nicely with the chanting, praying, and fasting of the Buddhist lifestyle. For five years, she knew peace.

And then the little black yacht appeared one day, and all her wa was gone.

The little black yacht.

For five years she had not gone near a neuralink, the moment she had plugged in to the yacht's neuralink, a cascade of messages had spilled past her retinal, most of them from Papa. She'd nearly wept when she saw them.

After a deep breath, Serena had reminded herself he was a part of it. Pedro Zambrano had been an active member of the conspiracy to obscure her origins and to train her in the arts of death and deception. "Papa" had lied to her.

Not once but throughout her life.

How do you forgive someone such a deep, pervasive betrayal?

Serena didn't know.

Mitigating Papa Zambrano's betrayal somewhat was his follower role. The lead conspirator, known to Serena only as variously her benefactor, Patrón, or sponsor, had masterminded her creation, and it was he (if indeed the person was male) who deserved the preponderance of her condemnation.

Papa Zambrano had sent messages about every six months for the last five years. In the last week, Serena hadn't viewed any of them and still didn't know if she could. For although she was very angry with him, he was still her Papa, still despite six years apart from him. He was the one constant person in her life who'd always supported her decisions.

And though it had hurt terribly to fake her death and inflict her loss upon him, Serena had felt she had no choice. Whoever had tried to kill her at Azteca University had tried again at the Lotus Flower Monastery.

Maybe now, they'll stop pursuing me, she thought, as the yacht neared the mining outpost. The sensors lit up as they connected with the transponder beacons at the small spaceport. In her vids, it looked too small for a medium-sized freighter.

The Iberian base must be subterranean, Serena thought, the rocky planet too small in and of itself to have been a target in Princess Mariko's drive to capture the galactic core.

But instead of too small, it had proved too large for her to conquer.

Her com lit up. Incoming.

"Tarifa control to unidentified craft. Where are your transponder codes?"

She had turned them off, not wanting to identify herself to anyone. "I'm Dolores Hernan, I'm a student of archeology at Madrid University on Sabbatical. I blew a fuse and fried my transponders. Sorry. I'm here to look over the site of Princess Mariko Mitsubi's defeat. Requesting permission to land."

"Permission granted. Not much here except an informal memorial. Suit yourself." The com died.

Serena was grateful for the dismissive welcome. The autopilot took over and set her gently on the tarmac.

Serena's airshell wrapped her as she stepped out of the ship. One lone outbuilding across the tarmac was the only structure. All else was underground.

The outbuilding was an elevator housing. She adjusted the wig she'd bought at a trading outpost, and entered. Three levels down, outside an employee breakroom, on the pedestal, was a still and some wilting flowers. She picked up the still.

She gasped.

Her reflection in the glass looked identical to the still.

"You've come," said a voice from the shadows.

Serena realized she had known the person was there. She felt no threat, only ... compassion.

155

The figure was shrouded, a shawl pulled forward to hide the hair and most of the forehead. "I've dreamt about you."

"You seem to know me already." Serena saw the gentleness in the eyes.

She looked to be Spanish or at least of Latin descent, but there was a stillness to her soul that was almost Buddhist. "I've been asked to keep watch for you, which I've done diligently since I was stationed here six years ago. I was a servant for the Princess Mariko twenty-six years ago, when she attacked this outpost." She gestured at the still.

"Who asked you to keep watch for me?"

The eyes searched Serena's face. "If I told you, I would be killed."

"You've been asked to report my arrival."

The old woman sighed. "I have."

"Then get on with it."

The eyes narrowed. "It isn't what you wish, yet you encourage me to do it. Why?"

"It isn't what you wish, either, yet you feel compelled to do it. Why?"

"I have served many masters, few of them kind. The Master we share has been brutal. I could die if I don't report your arrival."

"You'll be punished severely because of your delay, won't you?"

The old woman nodded.

"I have thrown off the yoke of this master you speak of. My being here is proof I succeeded. Tell me the name of the oppressor, and I will throw his yoke from your shoulders as well."

"You cannot. You are not strong enough. Be that as it may, you may one day have that strength. I see that in you. There is one thing you must do, however."

Serena marveled at the old woman's frailty and fortitude. "You are a good person, a kind person. If you are being oppressed, so are others. Would you remain silent and allow their suffering to continue, or will you speak, risk death, and pray that your actions will result in your redemption?"

The woman stared at her, silent. Then her gaze dropped to the still in Serena's hand. "I can see her in you." She looked up at Serena. "First, you must disable all the transponders in the yacht. They send tracking signals to the ... oppressor. Second, you will find out the oppressor's name. I will see to that—not now, not soon, but I'll get it to you. Third, you must leave immediately. Vaya Con Dios, child." The woman gestured at the lift.

Serena stepped into it. "Who are you? What is your name?"

"I am Maria Theresa Hernan. Dolores was my niece."

"Thank you," Serena said, and the doors closed between them.

Topside, Serena looked up as she strode toward the yacht.

Two ship engines streaked across the heavens.

She broke into a run, signaling the yacht to power up.

Jumping in, she took the yacht nearly horizontal off the tarmac, and a torpedo blew a hole where her yacht had been.

* * *

The engines screamed and bulkheads creaked as the small ship ripped around the planetoid, the smooth, round surface providing little cover, the two fighters in hot pursuit.

On her neuralink-enhanced retina appeared a bank of functions she'd never seen before.

"Evade" among them, she selected that one, and the yacht wrenched violently left. A crater lip to the right disintegrated, the blast just missing.

Then she selected "cloak," and a phase shifter kicked in, masking her physical location, and the next shot went wide left, the ship lurching hard right.

The "return fire" button was tempting, but Serena was more interested in knowing who her attackers were than in destroying them. "Analyze" gave her a profile. Iberian Empire fighters, she saw. Attacking a civilian vessel? she wondered, but she realized that without transponders, the yacht might easily be mistaken for a pirate vessel.

Maria Theresa Hernan must have alerted her Patrón.

But Iberian fighters meant someone high in the military. On the planetoid below her, additional craft began to scramble.

"Incoming com," her retinal flashed.

To respond she'd have to identify herself. Serena took over piloting, hit "return fire" and launched the yacht straight in between the two fighters. Then she hit "jump."

Pulsar cannons blazing, the yacht bisected the fighters, her shields absorbing one, two, three torpedoes, and then stars streaked and changed.

Outer Perseus Arm, her navigation system told her.

"System failure warning," flashed on her retinal. Shields down to five percent. The next shot would have destroyed her.

"System check," she ordered.

The random jump in the midst of battle might have landed her inside a star, although the chance was quite remote. Space simply wasn't that dense. The tactic unexpected, it had worked, and it was unlikely they'd be able to duplicate her jump.

Serena took stock. Just in case they tried to trace her, she jumped again. This time to the outer Orion Arm.

They had known she would go to Tarifa. Where else might she be expected to go?

Madrid, Teotihuacán, possibly even Nagasaki.

Where can I go? Serena wondered.

* * *

"Sensors are reporting a disturbance at Tarifa, just inside the Iberian border, Sir," an adjutant said over his shoulder.

Lieutenant Itztli Ocelotl stepped up behind the adjutant, looked over his shoulder. "Amplify."

The image expanded. Two fighters pursued a shadowy, indistinct object, firing and missing repeatedly.

"Some sort of cloak?" he asked.

"Phase-shifter, Sir," the adjutant said. "Awful small ship for that kind of hardware."

Two days ago, the joint chiefs had issued to monitoring stations along the Nahuatl-Iberian border a classified advisory for unusual small-craft activity. It had struck Itztli odd, as their main task was to monitor for large-vessel activity usually associated with military maneuvers.

"Get me Admiral Tecuhtli," Lieutenant Ocelotl said.

"Com channel opening, Sir," said the Com officer behind him.

The small craft dodged several shots.

"Look at her dance!"

"Run analysis. Any stock vessel have that kind of maneuverability?"

"Nothing, Sir. This is a highly-specialized vehicle, looks custom from what I can tell."

"Admiral Tecuhtli on screen, Sir."

"Admiral, Lieutenant Ocelotl, outpost oh-four-four, advisory-like activity spotted near Tarifa, two fighters chasing unidentified small craft, properties unknown due to onboard cloaking. Please advise."

"Continue to monitor, alert bases oh-four-three and oh-four-five, all to escalate to stage two alert. Prepare to scramble."

Stage one would launch several dozen fighters. "Preparing to scramble, Sir. Alerting oh-four-three and oh-four-five." On his retinal, Lieutenant Ocelotl received confirmations.

"Small craft profile match, Sir," an analyst said.

"On link," he said. Data spilled across his retina, and a black yacht showed up, spinning slowly. Multiple alerts flashed red around it.

"By the singed feathers of Quetzalcoatl," Admiral Tecuhtli muttered, "This one's going Xipil, Lieutenant. Continue to monitor. I'll be on mute standby."

Itztli gasped. "Xipil" was the Noble of Fire, or in naval code, the Fire Emperor, Naui Quiahuitl Xiuhtectli. Lieutenant Ocelotl wondered if the Emperor himself had had the advisory issued.

The small blob—what they could see of the darting vessel—suddenly launched itself at the fighters, its guns blazing. One, two, three torpedoes struck its shields, and then it vanished.

The two fighters circled the vanishing point, one of them issuing a distress signal. It had been hit.

"Craft jump, Sir."

"Get a trajectory." We might be able to track it, Lieutenant Ocelotl was thinking.

"Lieutenant," Admiral Tecuhtli said, coming back on. "Scramble two squadrons toward the border. Assist this small craft if it should enter Nahuatl territory and repel any Iberian craft attempting to pursue."

"Even in the contested zone, Sir?"

"Even there, Lieutenant!"

"Yes, Sir!"

And the link collapsed, the admiral gone.

"Trajectory plotted, Sir."

Based on speed, weight, direction, and position, a vessel's jump destination might be estimated. Although these factors varied slightly depending on even mild perturbations—such as the vehicle's shields being struck and the vehicle's firing at the moment of jump—the estimate sometimes proved accurate.

"Jump destination estimated to be outer Perseus Arm."

Lieutenant Itztli Ocelotl swore. "Iberian territory."

Probably infested with pirates, but still, under nominal Iberian rule.

We'll never trace the ship now, the Lieutenant thought. "Scramble anyway. Two squadrons. If the craft shows up, we'll greet her with open docking bays, eh?"

Then Itztli looked closely at the profile match that they'd found in their database.

The black yacht, a sleek, custom-built model, unlikely to carry more than a single person, was on an interstellar wanted list as being implicated six years before in the kidnapping from the Capitol Teotihuacán of Prince Augusto Iberia.

* * *

Emperor Augusto Iberia thought, That's the same yacht that Serena rescued me with six years ago.

He'd just risen that day and had stepped out onto his balcony high inside the palace on Madrid to clear his mind of sleep, his dreams haunted by the dreary imperial ball the night before, one of an endless parade of monthly or semi-monthly social events through which he was marched, his resplendent uniform immaculate, his head held high, his coif arranged in the most recent style, put on display as the most eligible bachelor in the galaxy.

Why don't they just truss me and skewer me and put me in the pot? he wondered, so dreadfully bored, he could scream.

The endless delights made available for his bed and his palate were equally boring, and he was so tired of it all that he'd considered appointing a cousin as regent just so he could be spared the drudgery.

Having awakened from a nightmare about monotonous receiving lines, Emperor Augusto had stepped onto his balcony to clear his head when a servant had brought him a handheld. On it was news of a small unknown ship that had eluded two Imperial fighters near the mining outpost Tarifa, and after they'd analyzed the vids, they'd realized it was the same yacht. Immediately, he'd been notified.

Immediately, he'd smiled.

Serena was alive.

His heart in his throat, Augusto summoned an aide. "Find out who ordered the attack and why, and get me a trace on that jump. I want to know where the ship jumped to!"

He'd never contradicted the fiction perpetrated by the Nahuatl that Serena had kidnapped him from the starliner. And he'd been stubbornly close-mouthed about his sudden arrival on the fourth moon of Galapagar and inexplicable release by those same kidnappers.

He's always let them think what they'd wanted. Serena had asked him to say nothing about her having rescued him. The plea in her eyes alone would have silenced him, her world having fallen apart in just a few short days, all of it a sham façade, the shell of a life, the lie of a grand-theater production. Everything in her life had been arranged for some sinister purpose, of which she had no inkling, and to which she had not consented.

The still of the Priestess who'd thwarted Admiral Nagano's assassination had reignited his memories of those few days he'd spent with Serena, and her death in defending the Admiral had seemed a fitting end for a young woman who refused to carry out some dark, nefarious purpose.

And Emperor Iberia knew what that purpose was.

He went inside to finish his morning toilet.

When Pedro Zambrano had come to bare his soul, the Emperor had asked him to forward Serena's contact information to him on his neuralink. He saw he had that information now. As much as it would offend his personal staff and perhaps his subjects, Augusto was tempted to contact her directly.

It is lack of foresight into such decision that Empires sometimes fall, he thought.

One servant took his robe, and another began to sponge him off.

Whom then shall I delegate that to? he wondered.

One-hundred and forty billion plus people under his sway, and he could not find anyone to make contact with the one person he sought to interact with. Nearly a third of the galaxy, and not a single soul.

Absolute power, absolute powerlessness.

He sighed and leaned his head back to give a servant access to his hair.

What makes you think she wants to hear from you? he wondered. He thought of what her life had been like, trying to imagine living at a Buddhist monastery for five years. The isolation seemed analogous to his own.

If I were she, whom would I accept a message from?

Sighing, Augusto stepped into a fresh robe. His personal reception suite, that set of rooms five floors below where he received visitors, was five times the size of this small set of rooms. In between was his kitchen, his wardrobe, his personal guard, and his service coterie. Above, on the roof, was a hoverport.

As he sat for a light breakfast, his neuralink alerted him to a message.

The yacht's destination had been outer Perseus Arm. He frowned, the area only under his nominal control, pirates frequenting the area with near impunity.

The order for the attack had originated in Ponte do Porto, A Coruña, in Galacia. The record indicated that the base itself on Tarifa had allowed the yacht to land peacefully, that the pilot had identified herself as "Dolores Hernan," and had explained that her lack of transponders had been due to a blown fuse. Tarifa wasn't even in the command chain that included Ponte do Porto, being easily two parsecs north.

"I want an internal affairs unit dispatched to Ponte do Porto. Hold the pilots incommunicado until the investigation is well under way. Alert Admiral Merced Coraz that I have ordered this in his name." I'll have to smooth his ruffled feathers later.

The eggs benedict were perfect but for their French name, but went untasted even so.

He remembered vaguely the name Serena had used. Ah, yes, her college roommate. Initial information had indicated that Serena had killed this roommate when she discovered Serena's plot to kidnap him.

"Origins, Hernan," he told his neuralink, stepping to the lavatory to clean his teeth.

Results spilled down his retina. Multiple associations with Galapagar, the star system adjacent to Madrid. An old, storied family, legendary for their allegiance to the ruling family of Galapagar, the Balleros.

That's no coincidence, Augusto thought.

His morning routine complete, Emperor Iberia descended into the nexus, that center of his Empire that needed his presence. It was like a heart that the blood of the body politic flowed through, cycling the life-giving oxygen of his rule throughout. As though he himself had to pump it.

His secretary greeted him on his arrival at the Crown Room.

As they sorted through the thousands of demands for the Emperor's time, one small innocuous request struck Augusto as odd. Nahuatl Consul Coszcatl Tonatzin requesting personal audience with his August person the Emperor Augusto Iberia.

"I'll see her immediately," Augusto said. "Then bring Señor Pedro Zambrano."

Chapter 14

"Riyo-san," Nobu said, his chest bedecked with medals, his two ceremonial swords tucked in his sash, "What do you make of that little disturbance at Tarifa, eh?"

The Admiral Nobu Nagano and General Riyo Takagi strode toward the entrance to the palace on Kyoto, a contingent of their own guards behind them, Imperial guards two-deep along this stretch of walkway. Nobu looked toward the palace where a grand staircase ascended to vaulted doors fully fifty feet tall. Tonight, the doors were wide and welcoming, the invited nobility of the Empire in attendance. Although Admiral and General each deserved their own grand entrances, Nobu had asked his friend to enter beside him.

"Sounds like your Priestess offended some high-brow Iberian." Riyo smiled at him.

"My thought, too. How strange things get when a person is away, even for a short time." The other man had told Nobu what he'd seen at the morgue, and together they'd concluded that the Priestess Sato, aka Serena Zambrano, had been the target of the assassination, and not the Admiral. Nobu was in no hurry to disabuse anyone of the misconception, however, as the Princess Regent Yoshi Mitsubi was holding this event in his honor tonight.

At the foot of the grand staircase, Nobu paused, glimpsing the entry hall inside the palace. A knot of activity just inside the door caught his attention, a cluster of people intent on something congesting the flow of traffic.

"What do you suppose is going on, Nobu-san?"

The Admiral shook his head and looked at his friend. "Let's find out, eh?"

Their contingent of guards moved to a side waiting area, and the Admiral and General ascended the stairs.

To one side, on the wall above everyone's head was a banner that read "Tonight's honored guests." Below that, only their crowns visible, were stills of two people, one capped with the Admiral's white naval hat, the other head bare, the second still drawing far more attention, the people gathered there looking frequently over their shoulders.

On the opposite wall were four portraits, the Empress Mitsubi and her three daughters. Three portraits were current, while one portrait was about thirty years old. Three portrayed the Empress and her two younger daughters, but the fourth, the portrait of Mariko Mitsubi, depicted her at the age of death. It was this portrait they were all glancing at.

Nobu Nagano heard the low-voiced conversations.

"Did you hear what Princess Keiko did? And Empress Mitsubi spoke for the first time in twenty-six years. Did you hear what she said? 'Who put that portrait of Mariko there?' "

He glanced at General Takagi, then the crowd parted, and he saw the still of the Priestess Midori Sato. Like the other spectators before him, he then glanced over his should at the portrait of Mariko.

He swallowed heavily, glancing between them again. "Riyosan, listen," he said, his voice hoarse, "when I was climbing the monastery stairs with the Priestess, I thought it was a trick of the light, but for a moment I thought she was ... " And he looked carefully at Mariko's portrait.

"Eh? What? You must have been mistaken."

"No, I mean, yes, of course. Of course, I was mistaken."

"Come on, Nobu-san, the Empress Regent awaits."

The Admiral tore his gaze from the two portraits, so alike that they haunted his thoughts throughout the ceremony. Amidst the very formal and ritualized exchanges that occurred that night, Nobu remembered only one.

Princess Keiko Mitsubi bowed to him as though he were her equal, honoring him.

"You're far too kind, Lady Princess," Nobu said.

"Oh, I don't think so, not at all. You're quite important, you know." Princess Keiko looked at him and tilted her head. "Perhaps misplaced, as it appears our wayward guest deserves at least equal praise, wouldn't you say, Lord Admiral?"

"Our wayward guest?"

The Princess looked toward the portrait of the Priestess Midori Sato.

"At least equal praise, Lady. As you deserve praise, as well. You certainly have my personal gratitude for helping to elicit those few precious words from her Majesty, the Lady Empress."

"Thank you, Lord Admiral. I can see you're quite moved by them."

"I am, Lady. Curious, isn't it, how your sister the Lady Princess Mariko touches us even now, despite having been gone these many years."

"Perhaps she still walks among us, eh?"

"Eh, Lady?" Nobu wasn't sure he'd heard correctly.

"A spirit as strong as hers would be far too impatient to wait very long between incarnations."

Nobu smiled and nodded. "I wouldn't put it past the Princess Mariko to defy death and rebirth her own soul, Lady." He wondered that this far more competent younger sister hadn't shown a moment of resentment that her older, duller middle sister now served as Regent. *How can she* not *be resentful?* he wondered.

"And it would be quite unlike her to allow others to forge her for their purposes."

167

Now she had lost him. "Pardon, Lady?"

"That skirmish at Tarifa, I can't make sense of it. Why would the outpost allow her to land, and later, have two fighters sent from Ponte do Porto to attack her ship?"

"Excellent question, Lady Princess. A ship already notorious for its use in Prince Iberia's kidnapping, eh?"

"I suspect events in the Nahuatl Empire six years ago didn't transpire quite the way they were purported."

"Indeed, Lady, you remind me much of Princess Mariko, if I may so say, Lady Princess." And he bowed to her.

Keiko's laughter was light as a bubble. Which popped, her stare boring into him. "I have a favor to ask, Lord Admiral."

"Certainly, Lady," he said, concerned at her sudden changes. She was known to be mercurial, pleasant one moment, vindictive the next. "How may I be of assistance?"

Keiko looked across the hall at the portrait of her sister, Mariko. Her gaze fixed to the portrait, her voice low and barely audible, she said, "Find a way, Lord Admiral, for me to meet this Priestess."

* * *

"Forgive me, my sweet one grass," Emperor Fire said. His eyes were red from weeping, and his heart ached for the horrible abandonment the child had endured, and he looked at Xochitl, still disbelieving, his mind telling him that this could not be true.

In his heart, he knew it was true. He knew deep in his bones. He knew from the depths of Mictlan. He knew as though the words had been spoken into his ear by Quetzalcoatl himself. He knew as though shown the truth by the light of Tonatiuh the Sun. He knew as though the knowledge had sprung from his loins by the force of Tonatzin the Earth.

And he asked himself how had he missed it, why hadn't he seen it, how could he have let her suffer further?

Emperor Naui Quiahuitl Xiuhtectli stood on the balcony of his private resort on Ixtapa, the sun having set long before but the tropical night still heavy with humidity. Below, the surf was audible, and to each side along the crescent bay, the lights of other resorts reached them from below a canopy of fronds. The rustle of palms spoke of a breeze he couldn't feel, the sultry, sodden night doubly drenched with his tears.

Naui could see Xochitl didn't understand.

And his every effort to tell her was derailed by more tears.

He had met Xochitl here on Ixtapa, having been on a state visit to the United Americas Empire in the Alpha Quadrant for the last week. His Imperial flotilla had returned to Teotihuacán without him, his small but beefy armored escort having brought him here this morning.

Then, after the evening meal, Xochitl had dismissed the servants and the guards and had told the Emperor Fire what she had learned from Carmen Hernan.

That had been hours ago.

"What is it, my love?" Xochitl had asked after he'd burst into tears.

He'd been unable to speak, his mind assembling the pieces of a puzzle into a whole, pieces that he'd had in his possession for a long time. He had known since first meeting Serena Zambrano along a deserted stretch of back corridor in the Imperial Palace when she was but seventeen, a political science intern serving his ambassador Xochitl Olin, the girl staring up at a portrait of an Aztec Ancestor as he'd once seen Princess Mariko Mitsubi staring at the galactic core.

He had known then, and he hadn't believed it.

He had known when the twenty-year-old engineering student had fought her way from her barracks at Azteca University to the spaceport, through multiple agent provocateurs and at least two attempts on her life, and had somehow escaped off planet without a scratch.

169

He had known then, and he hadn't believed it.

He had known when Serena Zambrano had overtaken the starliner, the King Henry VIII, aboard which Prince Augusto Iberia was being held captive, and had somehow spirited him off the starliner, leaving a trail of bodies behind her and no one the wiser.

He had known then, and he hadn't believed it.

He had known when Priestess Midori Sato had thwarted the assassination of Admiral Nobu Nagano, killing six of the assailants, and he'd seen the still of the Priestess broadcast throughout the galaxy.

He had known then, and he hadn't believed it.

And now, after hearing what Xochitl Olin had learned from Carmen Hernan, the Emperor fire knew it and could not refute it any longer, bewildered he'd hide something so important from himself for such a long time. When he tried to tell Xochitl, his remorse thickened his tongue and choked off his breath and burned out his eyes and plugged up his nose.

And now, midnight on the balcony of his private resort on the planet Ixtapa, Emperor Naui Quiahuitl Xiuhtectli wept helplessly in the arms of his wife, so choked up with grief he could not form the words to explain what caused such grief.

"Forgive me, Xochitl, my sweet one flower," he said with a heavy sigh, a long time later. "I have only myself to blame for this predicament. At some level, I knew and I hid it from myself. Even from my deepest secret heart, I hid this terrible truth, and what you tell me tonight brings that truth back to me in a way that I can no longer deny. No, my love, no fault lies with you, I swear. This is a truth I have hidden from myself, and no one else shares in that blame. A child suffered needlessly because I did not act. For nine years after I saw her in a back corridor of the palace, she suffered because I could not face the truth that stared directly at me.

"No, no, my love, you needn't apologize for telling me what you learned from Señora Carmen Hernan. In fact, I'm so grateful you did, because it frees me from my own blindness. I didn't want to see what you showed me, oh no. A burden, certainly, but my suffering is of my own doing, and the terrible truth is that another has suffered because I would not let myself see the truth.

"You said her words were, 'She will remake the galaxy'? Señora Hernan was right. She will remake the galaxy. I have no doubt of it."

"I can see that you don't understand. Dear Xochitl, I don't know how to help you, except to say, I am human, more mortal than perhaps I would like, for I may not see the transformation that she will bring, but if I do nothing else, I will atone for and set right the wrongs my blindness has wrought.

"But to do so, Dear Xochitl, I have a request. Find a way, please, for me to meet this young woman, again."

* * *

Emperor Augusto Iberia nodded to Ambassador Coszcatl Tonatzin. "Please allow me to express my deepest gratitude for this information. Please convey to her Majesty the Empress Olin my agreement that a great wrong has been perpetrated. As to the incident at Tarifa, it is being investigated fully, she may have my guarantee of that. As to recriminations upon those who perpetrated this betrayal, criminal charges will be brought if criminal acts have been committed, but this Empire abides by the rule of law, and any act beyond the law is punished quickly and appropriately. Especially those of its sovereign, if there should be any."

"Yes, Lord Emperor Iberia." Ambassador Tonatzin bowed to take her leave.

Before she had left the room, Augusto said, "Bring Señor Pedro Zambrano."

"Sire," the short, round man said, bowing deeply.

"You heard her report on the attack at Tarifa?"

"Sí, Sire. An apparition, no? Or perhaps it was my dearest Serena, eluding them again."

Augusto grinned. "As it was a pleasure to make the acquaintance of this young woman some years ago, Señor Zambrano, may I presume to ask a favor of you?"

"Sí, Sire," Pedro said, bowing," I would be honored to be of service."

"I would like to ask that you find a way, please, for me to meet this young woman, again."

* * *

Serena glanced again over her shoulder, disliking even the dim light of the glowglobe inside the engine housing, her back feeling naked and exposed.

She had landed the yacht on an asteroid in a belt circling a nameless star in a system at the outermost end of the Orion Arm. Far enough from the nearest civilization to make a random sighting of her impossible, and far enough to place her beyond the reach even of pirates.

Of course, that was no guarantee of either.

The belt thick with smaller asteroids, they frequently collided with each other, and even though she'd set the ship sensors to warn of objects approaching with a two-hundred mile perimeter, a fast-moving asteroid would obliterate her before she could act.

Her head stuck in the engine compartment made her feel even more vulnerable.

After landing on the asteroid, she had inspected every component of the yacht and its programming. Her first once-over had alerted her to nothing. But her second more thorough search had located a transponder triggered by the engine housing cover.

She had wondered how they had known she was on Nagasaki. Now, she knew; her cracking the engine cover in the shipyards had tripped the transponder.

Sure she'd tripped it again, she hurried to disassemble it, pulling her head out of the engine to look over her shoulder every few minutes.

She rerouted the cover sensors around the transponder and removed the transponder itself and set it on a nearby outcrop. Closing up the engine, she turned to the transponder. A simple electrical beacon powered by its own battery, the transponder was about as big as her fist, had a simple internal electrical switch, and possessed a range of fifty parsecs—halfway across the galaxy.

One that was easily triggered.

Serena smiled.

Packing her tools, she climbed aboard and set course for Nagasaki.

Chapter 15

Serena sat at a table outside a sushi bar near the town market of Miyaki, picking at a Tokyo roll and watching the passers-by.

Her back to the brick wall, she kept her gaze roving, vigilant from long habit. She wore a disguise complete with retina-obscuring contact lenses and fingertip patches. She had equipped the yacht with a set of purloined transponder codes to fool the spaceport sensors and had landed without question from the tower.

She had decided to stop here one last time before baiting a trap on Nagasaki for her pursuers, hoping for a few minutes peace and a little fresh air—and not the recycled cabin air aboard the yacht—to help clear her mind and plan her trap.

Three times now they had tried to kill her—on Teotihuacán, on Nagasaki, and then at Tarifa—and she had no doubt they'd send assassins after her to the outer Orion Arm.

Also en route to Miyaki, Serena had picked up a few identities—i.e., the stills, fingerprints, retina patterns, paycards, and neuralink codes—to fool any identity checks she might encounter. When she'd landed at the Miyaki spaceport, she'd used one of the paycards to pay for docking and refueling. She'd use another when she paid for her meal, a third when she went through customs.

Retinal scanners everywhere, she dared not walk down the street without something to throw off the scanners. Each spaceport stop required a different identity and set of transponder codes—a precaution should someone decide to follow her.

With her substitute neuralink code, Serena plugged into the table-mounted link. She pulled up maps and cams of the planet Nagasaki. They'll expect me to return, she thought, but she didn't want to endanger the Lotus Flower Monastery, or the Mother Priestess Hisaka Tomi. Serena also didn't want innocent passers-by injured or killed when assassins came for her.

Between her cracking the engine compartment and the six assassins ambushing her and the Admiral at the base of the monastery staircase, a period of thirty-six hours had passed, and Serena estimated that the antagonist she sought to expose would need a similar period to arrange another attempt.

While linked through the anonymous account, Serena decided to check her neura-mail.

Two new messages, in addition to the dozen or so from Papa Zambrano that she hadn't had the heart to open.

She looked at the sender's names and frowned.

Xochitl Olin and Hisaka Tomi.

Serena copied the messages to her handheld before opening them. Disconnecting her handheld, she then turned off its wireless to insure it didn't send a confirmation without her knowing it. Then she disconnected from the table.

Why would Xochitl send me a message? she wondered. Doesn't she think I'm dead? Serena wondered if the Nahuatl forces at the nearby border had observed her flight from Tarifa, pursued by Iberian fighters. How would they even recognize the yacht? Sighing, Serena shook her head.

"Does Miss Sama wish to take the rest with her?"

She looked up, startled.

The waiter grinned at her, and then dropped his gaze to the half-eaten sushi roll on her plate.

"I'm still eating, thanks," she said, her Japanese perfect, in the dialect of Kyoto and not of the southern Mitsubi constellations. She had learned Japanese as student at Teotihuacán, but had learned Nahuatl, Chinese, Russian, and Swahili as a child, her native language being Spanish. The other major language in the galaxy, English, had been impossible for her to learn despite her linguistic talent.

"You're from Kyoto, Miss-Sama?"

"Just two systems over, Nizichen."

His eyes lit up. "I have relatives there; my cousin's uncle by marriage, Niko Takashi, is the governor. He's—"

"I left when I was ten, and I don't remember much."

"Oh," he replied, looking disappointed. "Perhaps I can get you more tea?"

"Yes, please. Domo arigato."

"Domo arigato gozaimashita," and he departed with a bow.

Serena sighed, not wanting anyone to probe too deeply for fear of giving away her true origins. She waited until the waiter had brought the tea, ate a piece of roll in front of him to show she was still eating, and waited until he had left before looking at the message from Xochitl.

Remembering how kind Xochitl had been to her, Serena paused before playing the message. She'd last seen Xochitl six years ago, she thought, intern under the then-Ambassador. Although as an intern she'd accompanied the Ambassador to all the other Empires, Serena had never gone to the Mitsubi Empire, which seemed unusual as she reflected on it. Something had always come up, either Papa Zambrano encouraging her to focus on her studies or some project was due, or another intern begging Serena to let them go instead.

The neuranet message was text, which Serena found odd, nearly all of them vids.

"My favorite intern, the blessings of Quetzalcoatl upon you, I hope you are well. Forgive me my circumlocution but necessity requires that I be vague. The person you met once long ago on a deserted corridor requests the pleasure of meeting with you again. You stared at the portrait of an ancestor. For you it was a moment of reverence, for him a moment of revelation. He who wishes this meeting wants the opportunity to tell you a great truth, one which emburdens him with horrendous guilt and ecstatic hope. It is a truth that you deserved to learn long ago.

"The place and time of the meeting is yours to select, but must be a place of great discretion. Please give yourself a buffer of both space and time afterward, for this will not be an easy truth for you. It has been a difficult one for me as well, but my difficulty is easily set aside. I suspect it will be of greater import to you than it has already been to the man who wishes to bring it to you. And he brings it because the truth itself compels him to.

"Please contact me at the address given, and be assured that it is as secure as a neuranet message can be. I pray I hear from you soon, Dear One."

Serena stared at her handheld, intrigued, mystified, and oddly apprehensive. This woman knows me, she told herself. I worked in her office for more than three years. I worked directly with her on several projects. She trusts me.

Serena also remembered that if anyone knew what truly happened on Teotihuacán six years ago, it was Xochitl, she who was now the Emperor's wife, with access to all the Nahuatl secrets, and she who was now doing the Emperor's bidding.

That day in the corridor of the Nahuatl palace—the Emperor approaching quietly as she stared up at the portrait of Cuauhtémoc, the last great Aztec Emperor, brought down in the Spanish invasion led by Cortez, felled by the pox brought by Cortez—Serena remembered that day well, remembered his kind and gentle face, a benevolence that softened a despotism that might have corrupted a weaker person with its absolute power. The Emperor Fire was much too measured a person to allow himself to be corrupted.

Serena had known that simply by looking at him, in spite of her rather sheltered seventeen years, nary a year beyond the protective cocoon so carefully assembled by her father.

No ... not her father. By Pedro Zambrano, she reminded herself, knowing he had reared her but had not fathered her.

So who is my father? she wondered. And in her zen of minds, she knew she was a child of the Universe, born of forces unbeknownst and unknowable to her.

She heaved a sigh and nibbled on a slice of roll.

The next message was a vid from the Mother Priestess Hisaka Tomi. Serena turned down the screen brightness, noting a distinct thinning in the passers-by and a dimming of ambient light. She started the vid.

"Child, Daughter, Priestess, the blessings of Buddha upon you, may the eightfold path guide you toward Nirvana. I contact you only with great reluctance and only out of great necessity. They told me to be truthful, yet they watch even as I record this message to you. Forgive me my metaphor and ambiguation, as I cannot refer directly to those who have asked me to contact you.

"First, forgive me, as I was not as convincing as needed to see that they thought what you wanted them to think. In other words, we have been found out, not officially, but by those who count the most on this brine-soaked ball of God Turd.

"Maybe I was too convincing.

"Anyway, I've been coerced into being intermediary between you and them. They'll probably skewer me for revealing that much. I'd rather commit seppuku first.

"So, my masters require that I arrange a meeting between you and them. I have been provided with encryption in all messages to accomplish this, and your replies will have equal encryption.

"The time and place of your meeting must be proposed by you, to insure that you feel safe. Yes, they know about all three attempts to speed your entrance into Nirvana. I'm being asked to apologize for the first of those, by the way. The person responsible is so remorseful that seppuku was requested but denied.

"Please choose a date, time, and place to your satisfaction, but one of utmost discretion for the good of all involved. I look forward to hearing from you soon. Namaste."

And the Mother Priestess Hisaka Tomi bowed low, touching forehead to floor.

Serena could almost hear the laugher of Buddha. What the Nirvana are you up to? she asked, glancing at the sky. She then saw that while she'd been viewing that message, another had arrived. The street was dark, the waiter had since packaged her remaining roll, and he stood beside her table clearing his throat indignantly.

She dug out her fictitious paycard, swiped it, picked up her leftovers and headed down the street.

Few other pedestrians were out. A local curfew? she wondered. Being cautious, she used the side streets, making her way slowly toward the spaceport. Her short black hair provided little insulation from the cold, and she felt her scalp crawling. The houses were traditional Japanese, shoji screens lit from the inside, some shadows visible, the streets a raked gravel, which she floated across without a sound, her kimonos rustling like the night wind.

Subdued voices ahead caused her to freeze. She stepped into shadow.

Two figures conversed in low tones just around the corner. If she'd kept going, she would have walked right into them.

"She wants it done sooner, though. How're we to do that, Omi-san, if he's halfway across the galaxy, eh?"

"Better now than trying it when he's on the Iberian side, eh? What are you afraid of?"

"Nothing! I'm afraid of nothing. Those stinking pirates are thick as thieves out there."

"Of course they are—they're pirates. But they're thicker further in. Out at the end of the Orion Arm, where the next stop is Andromeda, you won't have to worry in the slightest. But listen, she also said we should try to pick up the trail of the person he's following."

"How are we going to do that?"

"He must have some kind of tracer, or else how would he know to go way out there?"

The sound of crunching gravel.

"Sssst ..." And the voices were silent.

A passer-by walked past her, not seeing her in the shadows, and the gait continued down the street, the sound regular and fading.

"Let's go, Omi-san," the first voice said, and two sets of footsteps followed the passer-by.

Serena peered from behind the building, only a shoji-paneled corner having separated her from the two interlocutors. They appeared to be moving in the direction of the spaceport as well. She thought about what she'd overhead.

Outer Orion Arm, but no indication as to who "she" and "he" were.

She chose a path parallel to the interlocutors, hoping to pass them and get to the tarmac first.

At the gate to the small spaceport, a bored guard glanced at her tarmac pass and waved her through, the retina and fingerprint readers giving her a green light.

Behind her, two beetle-browed eidolons of classical Neanderthal extraction approached the bored guard. Serena paid her docking fees, ordered her yacht to warm up with her remote, and requested permission to liftoff.

A tarmac jockey pulled up in a gravcart. "Two galacti to save you a hike?"

"No, thank you," she said, strolling away, her yacht not far.

"Never shoulda' given up my spot at Kyoto," he muttered.

Serena stopped. "Two galacti to give those two gentlemen a lift."

"Done!" he said.

"Just get me their names."

"Uh ..." His eyes shifted left, then right. "Hai!" And he grinned and swung the gravcart around.

He'll probably charge them five galacti, she thought, walking up to the yacht, its engines at a low hum already.

Inside, the infrared vids showed the two interlocutors just climbing on the gravcart. The tarmac jockey headed out toward a scout. Serena noted the registration numbers on the side of their ship.

The tower gave her a liftoff in ten minutes. The yacht humming softly under her, Serena was eager to get off this puny village planet.

The tarmac jockey pulled away from the scout, angling out and away, circling nonchalantly toward her yacht.

She stepped out to meet him.

"Omi Kamanuki and Kasa Watana, both of Kyoto," the jockey said. "I know these slope-heads, seen 'em many times. They didn't recognize me, though."

"Who do they work for?" she asked.

"That'll cost you a hundred."

"Twenty," she said instantly.

"Seventy-five, or it's a waste of my time."

"Extortionist. Fifty."

"Done. Foreign Ministry Undersecretary Takeshi Gahara."

"Thanks." She handed him a chit and climbed back in, two minutes to liftoff. Where have I heard that name before? she wondered, frowning. The tarmac jockey had seemed quite informed, and she wondered why he'd given up a lucrative gig like Kyoto for a backwater like Miyaki.

All systems green, the yacht leaped off the tarmac and headed for the space lanes.

Half-watching her readings in her retinal, Serena pulled up her neuramail.

New message. From Papa Zambrano.

She still hadn't looked at the dozen messages from the last four years or so. After the first couple, the begging and pleading for her to return had become too much for her, and she had stopped looking at them. The apologies for what he had done—minus any clear explanation for an act so "opprobrious as to be unforgivable"—had worn thin for her after the third message.

Serena considered carefully. It appeared that he too didn't believe she was dead, despite the body at the monastery and the reports of her death. And in light of the two other messages she had just received prior to liftoff, Serena was now curious about this third one.

Just text, as his previous messages had been.

"My precious child, I write not on my own behalf but on behalf of one whom you know from an excursion six years ago. Forgive my ambiguity and imprecision, but despite the coding that keeps away eavesdroppers, no system is without flaw. Care must be exercised in all our communications.

"College was a time filled with too much book learning and not enough socializing, and my entreator is asking to meet you again at a time and place of your choosing. Because of station, this person is requesting as discrete a location as possible, and it would please this person greatly if offered the opportunity once more to see you fence. En garde!

"Please reply at your earliest opportunity, as I think this occasion will be one of great joy for you both. If I am excluded, so be it. I understand and will ask no more. Papa."

Serena blinked back a tear, unable to imagine not seeing Papa Zambrano ever again.

What am I thinking? she wondered, realizing that of the three people who had just contacted her, all three mentors to her, all three admired by her, all three an integral part of her, that Papa was the one person who loss would devastate her most.

"Oh, Papa," she said aloud, and shed a tear.

* * *

Xavier Balleros cursed and smashed his fist against the dash.

She evaded me again! he thought, finding no sign of Serena on the asteroid. The transponder signal had led him to a small, bleak, red-primary system ringed with just one gas giant and a hoop of asteroids. And in that asteroid belt, he had found the one where Serena had landed, the rock scarred with burn marks.

Nearby, he'd also found little plastic pieces, so small he'd barely noticed them. Under analysis, they'd turned out to be wire insulation.

Hovering above the asteroid in his own yacht, a four-engine model capable of carrying eight passengers, Xavier considered his next option.

Where would she go? he wondered, a question he'd asked himself a thousand times.

Balleros had planted informants in all the likely places and if Serena Zambrano showed up in any of them, he could have guns on her within minutes.

With the exception of the Mitsubi Empire, of course.

There, due to politics and language and that stubborn Japanese pride, getting an assassin dispatched took at least a day. They want to argue about everything! he thought, remembering how argumentative *she* had been at the outset of this enterprise gone awry.

Thirty years ago, at a time Xavier still fought for his majesty Maximilian Iberia as sub-commander of the Fourth Fleet guarding the Iberia-Mitsubi border, a young man had approached him on Azores II while Xavier was on shore-leave.

Xavier had had one too many and was headed back to the hotel room alone, none of the over-painted harlots at the bar having appealed to him, when a shadow stepped out of deeper shadows.

"Xavier Balleros, a moment of your time."

He could see the faint sparkle of an airshell, the atmosphere too sparse to breathe. "What do you want?" he said, irritable that he was alone on this godforsaken ball so far from the gentle hills and steep seaside cliffs of Galapagar.

"Step this way, before you're seen." The other man gestured him into the alley.

Xavier followed, his mind befogged with Sangria.

"I have a proposal for you, one that could get you the recognition you deserve."

"What's your name?"

"Cage Gaheri, but my name's immaterial. You do what I ask, and you'll be lauded by the upper echelon of the Iberian military, guaranteed."

His brain tried to make sense of the name, but could not. The face was too dark to see. The man's Spanish was clipped, not soft like the Spanish spoken on Madrid—attributed erroneously to a sixteenth century king with a reputed lisp whom everyone was supposed to have imitated for fear of angering him. Spanish from the colonies, Xavier guessed, but which one? His ear could not discern.

"What's it going to cost me?"

"Why nothing, sub-commander Balleros, nothing at all," the other man said quietly. "All that you need to do is to be in command when Princess Mariko Mitsubi attacks your outpost. On this mnemo-chip are codes—com codes for a first mate. This first mate will betray Princess Mitsubi in the midst of battle, and your task will be made much easier by that betrayal."

"What task? What am I supposed to do?"

"Kill her. Kill the Princess Mariko Mitsubi. That is all my mistress wants." The man handed him the mnemo-chip and faded into darker shadows before Xavier could object.

Three years later, just before the Mitsubi Armada under the pregnant Princess's command had attacked the Fourth Fleet's last foothold on the rim of the galactic core, Xavier had activated the codes given to him. The first mate had contacted him, puzzled. They'd conversed briefly over a channel distorted by encryption.

"What do you mean by contacting me—now of all times?" Mitsubi forces were assembling for attack.

"I mean you'll follow my next set of directions to the letter," Xavier had replied. And then he'd outlined his small variation on the original plan.

"But that's not what she told me," the first mate had said.

"Last minute change of plan," Xavier had told him, and then he smoothed over the other man's concerns.

Then the battle had gone almost as planned, except that the first mate had died.

Now, despite all his hard work, his protégé had decided to pursue some other course, and Xavier Balleros was not about to let Serena Zambrano become an agent of the Iberia Empire's destruction.

He turned his yacht toward the galactic center and was about to retract the weapons bristling from its sides when a scout dropped out a jump in front of him.

The barrage of pulsar cannon startled him but not his ship, which slammed into auto-evade, hurling him backward and to one side, the shields absorbing the initial salvo.

Warnings lit up his retinal, shields down to ten percent, drives hitting a hundred percent thrust, the bio-lobe calculating that evasion was better than absorbing the shots. The ship danced away, tucking down and under, around an asteroid. A "jump imminent" flashed, and in the asteroid's shadow, his yacht popped into jump and dropped him at the edge of the mid-Scutum Arm.

Someone's after me, Balleros thought, and he jumped again to throw off any pursuit, his mind working through possibilities. Had Serena turned the tables on him? Or someone much more powerful, such as his co-conspirator in Princess Mariko's betrayal and death. He requested analysis of the scout that had attacked him, and then set a course for Galapagar.

"Scout make and model, Mercedes SC class four four two," the ship told him. "Weapons are Nissan Pulsar Rapi-load T one two O, standard Mitsubi Naval armament. Probable Mitsubi origin."

Which narrowed the possibilities considerably.

Fuming, Xavier wondered what to do. If she's after me, I'd better stay out of Mitsubi territory, he thought, knowing even that wouldn't likely stop her.

His yacht dropped into Galapagar space. Thank the Virgin Mary I'm home, he thought, the sight of the bright blue primary comforting.

But the squadron of Imperial police orbiting his home planet was not comforting.

His com lit up, and the signal override opened the channel. "Xavier Balleros, you're under arrest." A tractor beam locked onto his yacht. "Please surrender peacefully and—"

"By whose order!" he demanded.

"His eminence the Lord Emperor Augusto Iberia."

* * *

Near a small isolated star, a tropical world simmered, its humid atmosphere and half-normal Earth gravity giving flora license to flourish in profuse and myriad ways. Located in the Lago Tio Castillo region of the Matamoros Province of the Nahuatl Empire, in the region between the outer Norman Arm and the mid-Scutum Arm, a place nearly devoid of stars, the tropical planet occupied an area adjacent to territory once claimed by the Mitsubi Empire but ceded six years before to the Nahuatl.

Serena stood on the balcony, drinking in the sights, sound, and smells of the bounteous world around her. She delighted in the rainbow of flowers, their scents heavy on the moisture-laden breeze wafting up from the foliage-obscured beach below, the surf audible but barely visible. Like the insects and the plants, the mammals here grew to prodigious proportions, their mass unburdened by gravitational restrictions. The predators were likewise astounding, but without the attendant ferocity, as though the abundance of prey and ease of killing had dulled the edge of their hunting acumen.

The room behind her was spare, the furniture purposively simple to limit the places that the local insects might hide, proliferating rampantly upon this fecund world. On the way from the spaceport, she'd ridden to the hotel resort on the back of a feline that stood taller than she at its shoulder, its handler riding just behind the great cat's head.

A streak lit the northwestern sky, and the bright point dropped toward the spaceport.

That'll be them, she thought, wondering what she was going to say to Emperor Augusto Iberia and Papa Pedro Zambrano.

Life is suffering, and detachment is peace, she thought. A brief chant and a deep breath restored her calm. So different from the guilt-laden Catholicism that she'd been reared with, Buddhism helped her find that place deep inside where the river of life flowed without obstruction.

She had seen neither of them in six years. The loneliness in between had been assuaged in part by her studies under the Mother Priestess at the Lotus Flower Monastery. The sting of betrayal had muted, mitigated in part by the knowledge that Papa Zambrano had not fully known the purpose of what he was doing.

As though I know the purpose myself, she thought.

Upon her arrival, she'd seen the news reports about the arrest of Xavier Balleros, former Foreign Minister and sub-commander of the Fourth Fleet, and widely honored among Iberians for stopping Princess Mariko and the Japanese juggernaut at the Iberian outpost Tarifa.

Somewhere deep, Serena knew his arrest was connected, and that it was reason to rejoice, but it bewildered her that she didn't know how.

In time, she told herself.

She had chosen this world in Lago Tio Castillo for its obscurity and blended origin of name. Likely deep in its history it had once been claimed by Iberia and Mitsubi alike, despite its nominal governance by Nahuatl.

A knock at her door. The hotel did not have electronics.

"Aga?" she said, stepping in from the balcony.

"The party you asked about has arrived, Señorita."

Even the native language was a mixture of Spanish and Nahuatl. "Thank you," she said, taking her hand off her lazgun. She wouldn't be needing the weapon.

Just for everyone's comfort, Serena had reserved a private dining area on the ground floor, an intimate setting that she had alerted Papa Zambrano to, so the Emperor's security personnel could examine the room and assure themselves of his safety.

She knew she'd be searched.

Serena set aside the lazgun, slipped the stiletto from her kimono belt, undid the hair-thin garrote from her hair, removed the poisoned darts from her earrings, took the tanto knife from her sleeve, unclipped the razor toenails. She wondered about the hollow, poison-gas tooth, and decided to remove it as well.

The pile of hardware on the dresser reminded her just how bizarre her flight from Teotihuacán had been. A year spent wandering the edges of the galaxy had given a sharp edge to the blunt bludgeon that she'd been reared as.

She sighed, blinked back tears, and begged Buddha for reprieve.

Even now, I'm not the person I want to be.

Chapter 16

Serena waited at the window, beyond it a wall of jungle that threatened to encroach upon the small clearing behind the hotel. In between boabs and palms, glimpses of surf peeked through the foliage.

The Emperor's guards had just left, having inspected the room and its lone occupant with the meticulousness of crime-scene investigators.

Hotel servants set out the buffet behind her, then departed.

Serena felt rather than heard Papa Zambrano behind her.

"Child …"

She turned into his arms, and he covered her with kisses, weeping without reservation and apologizing profusely. A tear slipped down her cheek, and finally he pulled back, held her face between his hands, and beamed at her.

"You have become much more than I could ever have hoped, Serena," he said breathlessly. "The person you always wanted to be."

She felt surprised both that he knew and that he could see. "It's all I've ever wanted."

He nodded. "I know, I know, and the forces in your life have always conspired to make you something else. You have not given in to them. Good! Ah, but forgive me my part in molding you to their designs. I knew not what I was doing."

"I forgive you, Papa," Serena said and wiped away the tears as he began to weep anew. "You couldn't have known, Papa. You couldn't have known."

"Aye, but I did know and I helped anyway. Oh, it hurts me so!"

Serena held him while he wept and consoled him as he had her a thousand times, when she'd fallen or stumbled or hadn't reached that impossible goal she'd set for herself.

"You couldn't have done different, Papa."

"No, I suppose not, and when I'd heard you'd died, it broke my heart, and then somehow you appeared again near Tarifa, and I was filled with hope, oh child, what you've been through!"

"It's all been worth it to see you again," she said.

"Oh, that's so good to hear, for you know, there's your destiny still, that one great goal yet to—"

"Stop it, Papa," she said sternly. "That's mine to decide."

"Among the Aztecs," said a voice.

Serena turned, and she almost didn't recognize—

The Emperor Augusto Iberia smiled. "Among the Aztecs, there's the notion of Tonali—one's destiny, a string wound round the tree of life, a string which leads a person through their journey until they die and enter Mictlan. It is your Tonali, Serena, to remake the galaxy, of that I have no doubt."

"Emperor Iberia," she said, bewildered by what he'd said. "Well met, Lord Emperor. So good to see you again."

He had broadened through the shoulders and looked more chiseled in the face, his visage that of a Greek God. " 'Augusto,' please, and so good to see you." He stepped up to her and took her hand. His eyes had not left her face as though mesmerized.

"Odd for a Spanish Emperor to describe a Nahuatl philosophy."

"Do you subscribe to the Buddhist reincarnation, that each life we live holds a lesson to learn?"

"And that not learning the lesson brings us ever more opportunities to learn it." She smiled, not minding that he hadn't let go of her hand.

"And what is your lesson in this life, Señorita Zambrano?"

"To live by my own counsel. Lord … Augusto. And what is yours?"

"To live the life that was wound around the tree of life for me, a life far more difficult than any I would have chosen."

Serena laughed and nodded. "So many people would place themselves in your shoes, not knowing the choice the most treacherous they could make. I must say, Augusto, I do admire the grace with which you live it."

His eyes held hers. "And you have a grace and stillness inside you uncommon even among priestesses."

Serena wondered why he had not long since married. "You're much too kind."

"Not at all," he said. "Señor Zambrano, you're to be congratulated. Your daughter reflects your teachings well."

"Thank you, Lord Emperor," Papa said, "but as you know, she had many teachers."

"Ah yes, and just how did you afford all those teachers?"

Such an innocent question, Serena thought, and she waited for the answer.

Pedro Zambrano stuttered and stammered and finally sighed. "Pardon, Lord Emperor, but as you know, another person paid all those expenses."

Augusto nodded. "As I suspected." He gestured at the buffet. "Shall we eat while we explore that further?"

"I'll serve," Papa Zambrano said. "Please, the both of you have a seat." He shooed them over to the table and spoke as he assembled a plate for each of them.

Serena sat, watching how he busied himself to defuse his anxiety.

"Yes, dear Serena, all of it paid by another. The private schools, the clothes, the lessons, the trips, the sports. Even the furniture in your room, all paid by him. Who, you ask? Of course, you would ask. He who was just arrested. Such a relief, I tell you, oh let me tell you, that he now resides behind bars, not that that will protect you, child, not at all, but it does limit what he can do."

"Xavier Balleros?" Serena asked.

"Sí," Pedro said, nodding. "Him."

"Why? To what purpose?"

"What we're all wondering," Augusto said.

Papa Zambrano shook his head. "His Excellency Señor Balleros came to me some thirty years ago and reminded me of my family's ancient allegiance to him. In Castile, the Balleros have ruled since our origin on Earth, and all families who live in the province owe their allegiance. My line is ancient, dear Serena, and the bonds between my family and his are deep. When he asked me to do this thing, I could in no way refuse, and of course, it became all more difficult when I saw how small and helpless you were."

"When was this, Señor?" Augusto asked.

"Ah, yes, an important point, Lord, and thank you for the reminder. Just after the battle at Tarifa, he brought you to me, told me your mother had died in battle."

"He never said who she was, did he?" Serena asked.

"No, child, he never did."

She nodded. "Why do I look like Princess Mariko?"

Papa Zambrano wouldn't look at her. "I don't know. Serena, I truly don't know."

She saw she could force it out of him. "You suspect something but don't know it."

He sighed and looked at her finally. "Yes, that's it." He brought their three plates over to the table and set hers in front of her. "That's a local pheasant, sautéed in an indigenous citrus."

Serena wondered how far to push him. "You cared for me even while I was an infant?"

"Oh, I had help—Carmen Hernan helped during that first fragile year, just like a woman to think a man can't care for a newborn, but they insisted and I was grateful. Can't have too many caregivers for a child that young."

"I met Maria Theresa on Tarifa." Serena said.

"She was well?"

"Well enough, I suppose. Distressed by what she had to do. It was she who alerted ... Balleros that I'd landed." Serena found it strange to pronounce a name heretofore unknown to her. Now she knew where to place responsibility—or at least most of it. As no one would be able to carry out such a plan alone, Serena suspected others had been involved.

"It was her alert that enabled us to track its source," Augusto said.

"She'd said she would get me his name." Serena ate slowly, her mind elsewhere.

"The fish is fabulous," Augusto told Pedro.

"Isn't it? Locally caught, I'm sure."

She realized the two men watched her closely, and she found she was comfortable with their scrutiny. "I'm grateful you've both come. I guess I needed to see you, Papa, and I didn't know how to tell you that. Thank you for everything." She let the vestiges of old betrayal send a tear down her cheek.

He thumbed the tear from her cheek, his hand under her chin. "Words that make it all worth it. You're welcome. It was and continues to be a delight."

She smiled and thumbed the tear from his cheek, "And thank you, Augusto, for bringing Papa and me back together."

The Emperor Iberia just nodded and blinked.

Serena sighed, feeling a comfort and belonging that she hadn't felt for many years.

"By the way, Augusto, you asked me to meet with you. Why is that?"

He smiled at her, looked away, and then brought his gaze back. "A great wrong was done to you in the name of the Iberian Empire. It may have been done with my father's tacit consent, and he certainly knew later what Balleros had done. Ultimately, the deed was done under Iberian rule, which means I am responsible for restoring the balance. I asked you here to beg your forgiveness, and to offer redress, if you will have it."

Serena smiled. "Your coming personally speaks to your integrity and by itself restores some balance. Redress isn't something I desire, but there is something that I would ask of you?"

He nodded and gestured.

"Princess Mariko Mitsubi had almost captured the galactic core when she was betrayed and killed. Just before Iberian fighters came after me at Tarifa, I looked upon the core and saw the face of Buddha.

"And Jesus Christ, the Virgin Mary, and God the Father.

"And Allah and his Prophet Mohammed.

"And Yahweh.

"And Olorun.

"And Shiva the destroyer, Ganesh, Krishna, Ram, Kali, and Lakshmi.

"I looked upon the face of the Universal Spirit in all its manifestations, and I wondered why mankind has colonized worship and Balkanized God, I wondered why mankind had divided up the galactic core, and then I stopped wondering. Why don't we cooperate? Why don't we share?

"What I ask is simple—get everyone's agreement to share the galactic core. Iberia is the most extensive civilization ever to exist. You are its Emperor. You of all people can bring all the Empires together. You can forge a coalition to share the galactic core."

He blinked at her, and then chuckled. "You don't dream small."

"Never have."

Still chuckling, Augusto nudged Pedro. "Has she always been like this?"

"Always," he replied, grinning at Serena.

"All right," Augusto said, sighing. "Very well, I will certainly try. Now, as much as I admire your selflessness in this, there is a small thing I would like to offer you personally, and Papa Zambrano, if you would like as well."

Serena sighed with relief, having asked the one thing that had most concerned her and knowing she had little need for much else. "What small thing?" she asked.

"Amnesty." He smiled at her "Which I would have granted anyway."

"For what?" she asked, laughing.

He looked indignant. "Don't you remember? For kidnapping me six years ago, of course!"

"Since I didn't kidnap you, I didn't think I needed amnesty. I'd forgotten."

"And restoration of your freedom inside the Iberia Empire."

"A freedom I didn't find lacking, but all right."

"And the opportunity to live in the palace for as long as you like, as close or far from the workings of government as you like."

Taken aback, Serena frowned. "Whatever for?"

"Well, for one, to help me with that little task that you've set me to. Simple but most difficult." He shook his head at her. "And secondly and most importantly, so I can watch you fence at least once a week."

"Just to watch me fence?" Serena threw her head back and laughed, remembering the handsome but lanky boy who'd come to her fencing practice every day for two months.

He blushed and smiled. "And maybe talk afterward, have lunch, or whatever."

It's the closest he'll come to asking me out on a date, Serena thought.

* * *

The fur-lined parka that cloaked her from head to foot might have been a cocoon. Serena looked up the slope in between the twin peaks, where the glacier glistened like a river of diamonds. Her breath fogged the air in front of her, condensing on the rim of her hood and giving her a frozen cowl.

Had she turned on her airshell, she might not be so cold.

Below, ice-loaded conifers crackled with the slight warmth cast by the cold yellow primary, a pinprick in the turquoise sky. On the glacier, a line of figures could be seen, their tiny forms giving the ice river a gargantuan perspective.

Serena sighed and retreated into the room. She shed the parka, already beginning to sweat. A half-hour ago, the royal shuttle from Teotihuacán had arrived, and its passengers were en route from the spaceport via subterranean tube, the planet so cold that underground tubes were the most viable transport.

Two days ago, she had met with Papa Zambrano and Emperor Iberia. Two days hence, she would meet with Mother Priestess Tomi and her "masters," whoever they were.

But Serena knew what that was about: the assassination attempt and this peculiar resemblance she had with Princess Mariko. She hadn't realized until she'd stepped aboard the lift on the outpost Tarifa that she'd taken the portrait of the Princess with her.

Of the three meetings, this one held the greatest mystery for Serena. She was baffled by the "great truth" that Emperor Fire had learned that had caused him unremitting remorse. She simply could not discern what information he might have for her that was of so great an import.

She trusted Xochitl, who had been as much a mentor to her as the Mother Priestess, Xochitl's expertise being interstellar relations and political acumen.

Serena considered what she had told Emperor Iberia, the goal that she had set for him and which he had requested her help with. In their subsequent conversation, he had suggested the formation of an independent entity overseen by the six empires or their representatives, one granted authority by them to manage the resources. "A joint-powers authority district, such as those that often manage sewage systems or water systems," he'd said. A way to depoliticize its governance. Highly familiar with the idea through her studies, Serena also knew that nothing on such a scale had been tried before. Such an entity would eventually take over all core resource extraction activities, which included energy, heavy metals, and trans-uranium elements.

She glanced over at the portrait of Princess Mariko, where it stuck out of her bag, the face half-visible. A picture of her, Serena, except with a full head of hair.

Her hair still short from her days keeping her head shaved, Serena wondered if she should don a wig.

A knock on the door.

Why didn't they use the com panel beside the door? "Hai?" she said from behind an aimed lazgun.

"Your visitors have arrived, Miss Sato."

She hurled herself over the bed but the blast still blew her against the wall. She hit the floor, firing over the top of the bed, spaying the door and opposite wall with burning light. She flung one, two shuriken, fired off another lazgun blast then readied a tanto.

No motion except settling debris, no sound except the sucking of a dying breath, the air thick with burnt cloth, burnt flesh, and chemical explosive.

Fire alarms began to go off, sprinklers in the room and hall-way, and she was soaked in a minute. No going outside now, she thought.

She kicked up the bed and sprayed more lazgun fire, leaped to kick out a stud, and shoved a table lamp shade through the hole into the hallway.

When it drew no fire, she poked her head out, then kicked away more wall to make an egress large enough for herself. In the corridor, she kicked open the door across from hers and re-treated to the bathroom, the suite thankfully empty. She hurled towels and other items into the bathtub, yanked the curtain down, then spread the curtain over them. Then she climbed to the ceiling and plastered herself above the door.

Footsteps, two pair, stopping. Quiet. A creak. A shadow.

Two men leaped into the bathroom, their guns blazing auto-matic fire into the bathtub.

Serena pop-popped them, and their bodies crumpled.

She dropped to the floor and slipped into the master bedroom closet where she set a hangar swinging, and then she climbed onto the shelf, tucking herself into the darkness.

A gasp from the other room. Footsteps, three maybe four pair. "No!" a female voice, older, somewhat hoarse, somewhat famil-iar.

"No, Lord Shield, don't!" Multiple pairs, perhaps ten.

"Lady Hernan, please, go with them!" A male voice.

"I refuse," the older female voice. "Serena! I'm here with the Emperor's guard. No one else. Your pursuers are dead. It is I, Carmen Hernan, Dolores's mother. You're safe now, Child."

So like Dolores, that voice, and yet familiar in other ways, as though from a dream, one of warmth, comfort.

Serena waited a moment.

The closet door opened. "Please, Serena, it was at my behest that the Emperor Fire is here."

Knowledge.

This woman knows me, Serena thought. "All right," she said, and she added, "Step back, please."

The figure retreated.

She dropped from her perch, weapon at ready.

The kind eyes of Dolores beheld her. Older, but still the same eyes.

Serena ventured a faint smile. "Dolores died that I might live."

Carmen nodded. "She died in the service of her Patrón." She turned her head and spat. "The pendejo, whom the Hernan shall serve no more!"

A man stepped to the door. "Necalli Chimali, Señorita Zambrano. I am to escort you to the Lord Emperor Fire, when it is safe."

"Battle Shield," Serena said. "An apt name. You have personnel who've secured the floors above and below?"

"Sí, Señorita."

"And the Lord Emperor has been removed to a safe location?"

"Sí, Señorita."

"Bring a female volunteer, about my size. Get her a parka, surround her with guards and send her to the Emperor. Get me her clothes, and I'll follow her in the second contingent."

"Sí, Señorita." He left the room.

Serena looked at Carmen.

"I'll go with the first group, child."

"You can't do that," she objected.

"I must, and you know it."

Serena blinked away a tear, awed. "Your obligations to your former master are fulfilled. El Jefe Pendejo commands you no more."

"It is you I now serve, if you will accept my fealty," Carmen said. "And in the ancient tales, Zambrano commanded in the absence of Balleros."

"So now that Balleros commands no more …"

"Sí, Lady Zambrano."

A young Nahuatl guard proportioned similarly to Serena appeared with a parka over one arm. "Here, Lady Zambrano," she said in perfect Spanish. "Here's an extra Nahuatl uniform of mine."

"Thank you," Serena said, and changed clothes quickly. "Now, go."

The Serena substitute and Carmen Hernan followed the guard Captain, leaving her with three males.

"Here, hold the gun like this," one showed her.

Two minutes later, they followed the first contingent, and a third one followed them.

The fire was out and hotel guests on the lower floors looked bewildered at the activity, stepping aside for her uniformed guards. The lobby had been cleared and secured, and Serena saw the slim volunteer in the parka step into a tube capsule with escorts. The capsule shot away, and her uniformed group stepped onto the loading platform. A dome shielded them from the worst wind, but the temperature still frosted their breath. The capsule had six seats designed for comfort and speed. The belts buckled her in, the cabin pressurized, and the capsule shot forward, her stomach and facial skin not wanting to follow. Lights raced past so fast they flickered like strobes. The capsule slowed rapidly, and Serena was grateful she hadn't eaten. The belts retracted, and she stepped onto a platform ringed with guards.

She marched in perfect synchronization with the other three guards toward the exit, the signs indicating the direction to the spaceport. At the base of the steps leading up into the terminals, a door marked "private" opened and the foursome entered.

A long corridor ribbed with piping led eventually to another "private" door.

Beyond was a small entry, six guards at attention. An attendant at a desk, his vague gesture indicating the door behind him. A parka was thrown over the chair back.

The three guards joined the six at attention, and Serena entered the room alone.

Carmen greeted her with a sigh. "Longest ride of my life."

"Thank you, Carmen. I would have felt horrible if you'd have been hurt."

"I'd have felt horrible if *you'd* have been hurt. Dolores admired you so much, you know, and gave her life willingly and gladly. I want you to know that."

Serena blinked back tears. "She was like a sister to me."

Carmen pulled her arm. "Now, let's get you out of that uniform."

"No," Serena said. "No, not … not yet. I've put the Lord Emperor Fire in danger. It's only right I should guard him."

Carmen looked at her deeply. "Very well." Then she gestured to the doorway into the next room.

The two guards stepped aside.

"Serena, child." Xochitl Olin wrapped Serena in her arms and held her close. "You've been through so much and now this. Frightened us all, by Coatlicue, bless the Earth goddess you're safe."

Serena looked at her closely, saw she had aged but behind that age was a happiness borne of fulfillment. "You look well, Lady Xochitl. Empress suits you."

"Emperor Fire suits me, a fine man with deep integrity. Admirable in a thousand ways."

"You're happy with him."

"Yes, indeed, child. Now you, you look peaceful. How, when you were nearly killed less than an hour ago?"

"I'm a priestess, remember? Those years brought me a wa that is rarely perturbed."

"But four assassins?"

Serena shrugged.

"How do you wish that portrayed?" said a deep voice across the room. Almost invisible in his Ocelotl print against the

Ocelotl-patterned couch, was Emperor Naui Quiahuitl Xiuhtectli, his age visible in his face but his eyes alight with delight.

He must be seventy years old, Serena thought. She bowed to him in the Japanese way. "Lord Emperor Xiuhtectli, an honor to see you again."

"The honor is mutual, Serena Zambrano," Emperor Xiuhtectli said. "News of an incident involving the Nahuatl Emperor and a certain famous Priestess has already spread across the galaxy."

"That was less than an hour ago," she said.

"And I'm afraid it's already being twisted to suit the designs of your enemies. They're saying you attacked me, killed four of my guards."

Serena shook her head.

"Again, how would you like this portrayed?"

"I am attacked while on a mission to unite all six Empires in a coalition to share the galactic core."

"Eh? What?"

Serena smiled. "Princess Mariko died in her attempt to bring the core under the control of a single government. How many hundreds of Empires have aspired to do the same? And for what purpose? Mastery of the core means mastery of the galaxy. All that energy. All those heavy metals. Limitless resources!

"It's all chimera," she said fiercely. "A shadow of a dream, lasting an eye blink, an illusion. There is ample for all, and no one needs either to conquer the core nor to suffer for not having access to its resources.

"If all six empires can reach some agreement to share those resources."

Emperor Fire stared at her for a moment, then laughed aloud, then stopped. "You think and dream on a galactic scale."

She gave him a slight smile. "You can help."

"Eh? What?"

"I want you to make it your goal to unite the Empires in an effort to share the galactic core."

203

"You've been taking lessons from Xochitl."

The two women exchanged a glance and a chuckle.

"An admirable dream. I will make it a priority. Señora Hernan, please join us and help our warrior priestess in her becoming."

He gestured Serena to sit beside him, the other two women across from them.

Serena did so dutifully, and she looked into his eyes, kind and wise.

Eyes that seemed to know her, eyes that she herself seemed to know. Nine years ago, in a corridor in Teotihuacán Palace, she had met this man's gaze for a moment and had known similar things. But she had lacked the experience to form a plan of action from the amorphous knowledge. She now had the experience. Now she had the knowledge.

Serena Zambrano took the hand of the Emperor Fire. "You said in your message you knew a great truth, and even two hours ago I didn't know what you meant. Now, when I look in your eyes, I know with great certainly what that truth is. I know those eyes. I knew those eyes when I first looked into them on Teotihuacán, in a back palace corridor, as I looked away from a portrait of Cuauhtémoc. I didn't know what to do with that information, nor even how to reconcile what I thought to be true and the truth that confronted me then. I bid you not to weep, Emperor Fire, for there wasn't a way for you to tell me what you knew then. There wasn't a way for me to hear it.

"No, no need to speak. Your eyes tell me all I need to know. I know those eyes because I look into them every day in the mirror. You gave me those eyes. Those eyes are my eyes. You gave me life."

And Serena pulled her father close and held him as though she'd known him all her life, and he wept out his remorse, explaining to her in broken sentences how he'd hidden even from himself the certain and undeniable knowledge that she was his daughter.

And the two of them spoke deep into the night of the things they wished they had been able to do together, and Serena told him about Papa Zambrano, and Emperor Fire wept with joy that someone had been there to give her what he wished he had been able to give.

An infinite silence of time had passed between them when Serena noticed that Xochitl and Carmen were nowhere around.

"Carmen told us how you came into Señor Zambrano's care," Naui said.

"Carmen who served former Foreign Secretary Xavier Balleros," Serena added. "The sub-commander of the Fourth Fleet who defeated Princess Mariko Mitsubi and kept the Japanese from capturing the galactic core."

"Yes," Naui said. "A pity he did it with treachery, like a coward."

"He will burn in his Catholic Hell for all eternity and be reborn as a tapeworm in some mongrel's back passage."

"He will wander Mictlan for all time."

Serena smiled. "Thank you, Father. May I call you that?"

"I'm honored that you do. There is no greater honor than hearing that from you, daughter."

"It's been ... difficult these past six years, not knowing, feeling cast adrift, finding out Papa Zambrano wasn't really my father. Thank you for welcoming me, and for honoring the bond we share."

"It is my hope, Serena, that we can come to know each other. You have a home on Teotihuacán. Will you come to stay with me for a time?"

And Serena knew for a second time in three days the certainty of her place in the galaxy.

* * *

The planet of San Sebastian floated at the eastern edge of the mid Car-Sag Arm just shy of the Iberia-Mitsubi border. A temperate world of mostly grasslands, San Sebastian was notable for its excessive gravity—a hundred-fifteen percent of Earth normal—and for its short, squat flora and fauna.

Serena looked over the setting. A gazebo stood half a click from the main resort. A low table sat amidst six cushions, the white silk tablecloth rustling in the gentle breeze.

The visiting party had balked at the location until Serena had secured the personal assurances of Emperor Augusto Iberia. Until then, Mother Priestess Tomi had fulminated her disgust in a most un-Buddhist manner about the arrangements and afterward had practically purred with satisfaction.

Serena wondered that she had learned anything at all from the Mother Priestess.

Sighing, Serena glanced one last time at the arrangements, then walked another fifty yards to the bluffs overlooking the bay below.

The surf was audible from here, and it brought her comfort. The waves were small, the heavy gravity keeping the sea tamed. An alert on her neuralink told her her guests had arrived. Serena adjusted her swords, pulled her kimono tight, and turned. Now the rituals begin.

Four people in brightly-colored kimonos descended the slight slope from the main resort, a wedge of warriors in the Mitsubi black and orange preceding them.

The guards stopped at fifty paces from the gazebo. One guard strode ahead, inspected the layout, and bowed toward the quartet.

The guards marched to formed a ring around the gazebo, all of them facing outward.

The quartet approached the gazebo but stopped at the steps.

Serena walked up the slope toward the ring of guards, stopped and bowed to the one blocking her way. In perfect Japanese with a Nagasaki accent, Serena said, "Lord Warrior, thank you for guarding my guests so diligently. I am Priestess Midori Sato."

"It is only my duty, Lady Priestess." The guard stood aside and let her enter the circle.

Serena mounted the gazebo back steps, strode to the top of the opposite steps and bowed, lowering herself to her knees and carefully putting her forehead to the floor.

The rustle of silk was the nod of acknowledgement.

Serena straightened but remained on her knees, her gaze at their feet. "Thank you and welcome, Lady Princess Mitsubi. I am deeply honored to have my modest and inadequate arrangements accepted, please forgive me their paltriness." Serena dipped her head again and raised her gaze for the first time to look at them directly.

The two women stood to the fore, the two men behind them. The older woman to the left was the Mother Priestess Hisaka Tomi, the younger woman to the right the Princess Keiko Mitsubi, reputed to be the smarter of the two surviving Princesses. The two men standing behind them were respectively General Riyo Takagi and Admiral Nobu Nagano, the latter looking hale and hearty and fully recovered from the assassination attempt.

Serena felt the scrutiny of the Princess Keiko Mitsubi and received it with aplomb. If what she suspected was true …

"Thank you for your welcome, Lady Priestess," Keiko said. "On behalf of the Empire, and on behalf of the Regent Empress, my sister Lady Yoshi, thank you. Your saving the life of Lord Admiral Nagano has preserved not only the integrity of our naval forces but an institution near and dear to the Empire itself. I am curious, Lady Priestess, about the feint in your having dressed one of the assassins in your clothes. May I ask why you did that?"

Serena was surprised at how directly the princess was asking. "Certainly, Lady Princess Mitsubi, I am honored at your asking. It pleases me that you have so much interest in my motivations.

But first, if I may, I would like to offer greetings to the Lords Admiral Nagano and General Takagi, and to the Lady Priestess Tomi. With your permission, Lady Princess Mitsubi?"

The younger sister looked amused. "Certainly, Lady Priestess Sato."

Serena exchanged pleasantries with the other three, congratulating Admiral Nagano on how well he looked, and thanking Priestess Tomi for her assistance in arranging the meeting today and for her five years hospitality and tutelage.

"Lady Sato," Princess Keiko said after the five of them had settled themselves at the table, "I must say I so admire your manners and patience. Your refinement is a glorious example of your culture and upbringing."

Serena did not smile, but she might have. "Pardon, Lady Princess Keiko? Forgive me, but I was reared on Madrid, and my native language is Spanish. I am not Japanese by upbringing. I learned the language in school, and the Nagasaki dialect at the monastery. If anyone is to be admired, it is the Lady Mother Priestess, who taught me all I know about your incredible culture. The refinement is only what she taught me, and the credit belongs to her."

Princess Keiko's eyes were wide. "I am surprised, Lady Sato. Clearly, you are ethnically Japanese. Forgive me, but are you not?"

"I was reared an orphan, Lady Princess Keiko. For many years, I knew nothing of my true origins. Even now, I do not know the identity of my mother, and the identity of my father is something that I learned but two days ago."

"Lord Admiral Nagano," Keiko said, turning to the man on her right, "Describe what you saw as you climbed the monastery stairs the night before the assassination attempt."

"Yes, Lady Princess Mitsubi," Admiral Nagano said. He looked directly at Serena. "Perhaps it was a trick of the light, Lady Priestess, but I saw your profile, and I thought I saw a full head of hair. With that hair, I thought for a moment I beheld once again the deceased Lady Princess Mariko Mitsubi."

Serena nodded, serene, feeling a tremendous peace, a tremendous wonder. "It must have been a trick of the light, as you said, Lord Admiral."

Princess Keiko shook her head. "I think not, Lady Priestess Sato. The still provided by Priestess Mother Tomi to the media looked enough like Mariko, that when I added hair and enlarged it and placed it in front of my mother the Empress Lady Fumiko Mitsubi, she—" Keiko choked on a sob and held her hand over her mouth, tears seeping from her tightly closed eyes.

"The Lady Empress spoke," General Takagi said. "For the first time in twenty-six years, she spoke. The Lady Empress said, 'Mariko-Chan, is that you? Who put Mariko's picture there?' "

Serena watched Keiko, feeling sad for the tragedy that had struck this family. "When Princess Mariko died, Lady Princess, you lost your sister and your mother. I'm very sorry for your loss."

"Princess Mariko was nine months pregnant when she died," General Takagi said.

"Did the baby survive, Lord?" Serena asked.

He shook his head. "No one knows." He dropped his gaze to the table. "For my part, Lady Priestess, I beg you to forgive me, for it was I who ordered your killing on Teotihuacán. I begged permission to fall on my knife for my transgression, but that was denied me. Truly, I did not know who you were then. I simply wanted to stir up trouble between Nahuatl and Iberia, and perhaps force the Nahuatl to return the outer Car-Sag Arm to Mitsubi control. Again, I beg your forgiveness." He lowered his head to Serena.

"Enough groveling, old friend," Admiral Nagano said. "It is my turn. Please forgive me, Lady Priestess, but it was I who ordered the kidnapping of Prince Iberia from Azteca University, although I had no part in your being blamed for it. Like my friend

Lord Takagi, I sought only to stir up an interstellar incident between Nahuatl and Iberia. Please forgive me all the trouble that I caused you, as my remorse is treble for your having saved me from those assassins."

Serena smiled and feigned bewilderment. "Both of you, Lords Nagano and Takagi, are apologizing for acts that impinged up my person or reputation, but I don't understand. These acts were taken to forward the interests of your empire. What apology is needed for that?"

The two men glanced at each other and dropped their gazes.

"Perhaps I don't yet understand. But thank you, both of you, for offering your apologies." Serena saw that Princess Keiko had recovered her composure. "Lady Princess Keiko, earlier you had asked me my motivation in dressing one of the assassins in my clothing. Simply put, Lady, it was I, not Lord Admiral Nagano, who was the target of the assassination. Someone tried to kill me for reasons I still don't understand. I was attempting to make it appear that they'd succeeded.

"Likewise, when I rescued Prince Iberia from his kidnappers—who were fellow Japanese, if I'm right, Lord Admiral?—one of them looked directly at me and said, 'Princess?' And I took advantage of his hesitation to kill him." Serena felt sad for him and prayed to Buddha to grant him a better life than this incarnation.

"Four times they have sought to kill me, the last time just two days ago. I had thought that the arrest of former Foreign Minister Xavier Balleros would stop the attempts. As he is being held incommunicado, it baffles me that the attempts continue. There must be a coconspirator, but I don't know who it is. And the why I can only suspect. You asked to meet with me, Lady Princess, and I am honored by your interest. But you did not ask to meet with me to clear up these questions." Serena held her thoughts still and composed, feeling that there was more.

"No, Lady Priestess," Keiko said, "None of those questions are central to my asking to meet with you." She gathered herself, almost visibly summoning the chi to ask. Her eyes rose from the table and met Serena's eyes.

And she knew. Again it was the eyes. "I know those eyes."

"I know those eyes," Princes Keiko replied. "You know what that means?"

"I know," Serena said matter-of-factly. Her voice was calm. Her mind reeled with the implications.

"Others will know, too," Keiko said.

"Of course they will. And they must be drawn out."

"Yes, they must. You have my support, but I cannot act against those others. You understand."

"I do. Here. We must communicate." Serena offered her neuralink address.

Princess Keiko balked. "Forgive me. I cannot. You're resourceful. The Emperor Iberia's assurances are evidence of that. There must be no indication of collusion. Forgive me, Child."

"No forgiveness needed. My apologies for asking. Of course, you cannot. But there is one thing you *can* do."

"What would that be, Mei-Chan?" Keiko asked.

The other three looked at the Princess sharply, startled by the address.

Serena smiled, feeling warmed by the welcome shown her by the Mitsubi Princess. The term she had used was one of endearment used by an aunt to a niece. "I'd like you to sit beside me, Oba-Chan." Serena used a similar term in return, that of a niece to an aunt.

Keiko rose and settled herself beside Serena.

She leaned into her relative's embrace. "Until recently, I'd never known the comfort of family," she said, feeling Keiko relax and pull her close.

"Child, no one should endure what you've endured. You will see resolution, that I know."

211

Serena nodded, suspending her doubts, not knowing but trusting that Buddha would provide her with guidance. She pulled back to looked at the older woman. "If I may, Oba-Chan, I would like to ask something important of you."

"You may ask anything, Mei-Chan. Buddha willing, it will happen."

"Princess Mariko . . . " Serena said, hesitating. "Oka-Chan tried to conquer the galactic core. She . . . Her intentions were good. Her goal was to bring the core under the control of one government, to harness the full potential of the galactic core under the auspices of a single entity. Oba-chan, I want you to make that your goal, with one small difference. I want you to help forge a coalition among the Empires to share the galactic core."

Keiko threw her head back and laughed, but her laugh faltered when Serena just stared at her, placid and unrelenting. "Mariko told me she did it to end constant bickering between Empires."

Admiral Nagano said, "To end treacherous dealings in stealth and poison, to end the tides of conquering and capitulation."

General Takagi said, "To end whole worlds being denuded to stamp out rebellious populations, thousands of years of culture ending abruptly in annihilation."

Keiko frowned. "To end two centuries of constant warring."

Serena stared, placid and unrelenting.

Keiko's brows drew together. "Mei-Chan, you're as stubborn as your mother."

Serena allowed herself a small smile. "Thank you, Oba-Chan. That's high praise indeed." She bowed to her aunt.

"I will do all I can, Child."

Serena nodded and looked at the other three. "My mother died pursuing a dream. It is my destiny and obligation to see her dream fulfilled."

The three others looked at her wide-eyed.

"But that," Admiral Nagano said, whispering, ". . . that makes you the heir, the Mitsubi heir." Nagano suddenly bowed and pulled his sword, scabbard and all, from his sash. "Lady Empress Regent, allow me to offer my ..."

"No," Serena said, more sharply than she wanted, afraid this might happen. "I am my mother's daughter, but I am neither Empress Regent nor heir until the Lady Empress Fumiko Mitsubi says that I am. Until then, I am and I remain Serena Zambrano."

Keiko shook her head. "No, Child, you are much more than that. You're Mitsubi, Mei-Chan, and never forget it."

"Yes, Oba-Chan, I will never forget it. Thank you for reminding me."

"And because your mother never had the opportunity to name you, it's my duty to do so, if you will accept it, of course."

"I'm humbled and flattered, Oba-Chan," Serena whispered, the universe opening in her heart.

"Akira—meaning clear and bright—Akira Mitsubi, welcome back to your family."

And Serena knew for a third time in five days the certainty of her place in the galaxy.

Chapter 17

From inside her bunker, Serena watched the two warriors stumble out of their scout.

The bunker was made of the surrounding sod atop planks milled from the native wood. She watched from inside as they approached the pit she'd dug below, covered with that same native sod, imperceptible to all but the trained eye.

Omi Kamanuki and Kasa Watana, the two drudges on Miyaki whose conversation that Serena had overheard.

The Emperor Augusto Iberia had announced the release of former Foreign Minister Xavier Balleros on his own recognizance, and the news media had reported his return to Galapagar, the tall, thin figure just escaping mobs of reports at the spaceports on both Madrid and his home planet, his features obscured by his hands and a wide-brim hat.

Serena had obtained the transponder codes for the Foreign Minister's yacht, had located a likely planet between San Sebastian and A Coruña, and had set her trap.

Balleros was still held captive and incommunicado, of course.

The drudges stepped gingerly forward. "I don't see anything," the taller one said, looking at a handheld. "It says his ship should be twenty feet away."

"Probably got a secret base. She warned us he'd be slippery." The shorter one looked back at their ship, an armed scout bristling with electronics. "Maybe I should guard the ship."

"Coward," The tall one said. "Go ahead. We'll both know who captured him and who hid behind the ship with shit running down his legs!"

"You're the one who pissed himself when he fired on us in that asteroid belt."

"If you hadn't missed with that first shot, he'd have never got away."

Sighing, she wondered how much of their invective she'd have to listen to. Serena silently urged them closer to the pit.

The short one pointed his finger at the tall one, and the tall one grabbed it and yanked it.

They're so close, she thought, aiming her lazgun at the ground beside them.

Suddenly, one slipped to a knee. "What?" And dragged the other on top of him and both tumbled into the pit, the edges collapsing. A strobe flashed, and smoke mushroomed from the pit.

Serena was out of her bunker and down the hill just as the gas changed color, now harmless. She jumped into the pit and bound the unconscious forms at wrists and ankles. With her neuralink, she summoned her ship.

She climbed out and set up a pulley, leaped into the pit to haul one out, using herself as a counterweight, then tied the rope to the other, and hauled him out similarly.

A few minutes later, the four-passenger scout that she'd borrowed from Augusto came over the horizon and landed smoothly a short distance away. The gravity light, Serena carried both bound men over to the ship and loaded them aboard.

Plugging in their neuralinks, she set the ship to monitoring their vitals, keeping them unconscious on a mixture of melatonin and opioids.

Then she set course for Okinawa, just across the Iberia-Mitsubi border, a flight of less than twenty minutes.

Under a young blue star, the rocky planet without atmosphere housed a simple military outpost webbed with communications equipment, the base having a small contingent of scouts and one or two fighters.

Her transponder codes already registered with the outpost, Serena landed on the small tarmac without requesting permission. Two workers with a gravcart awaited her. They took the two supine figures from her scout and loaded them into the gravcart.

"Did they see you, Lady Mitsubi?" General Riyo Takagi asked.

Serena shook her head, feeling his gaze, knowing he was trying to match her face to that of the Princess Mariko, whom he'd revered.

"Good, and those Iberian interrogators are ready."

She could see the distaste on his face. "Lord General."

"Eh, Lady Mitsubi?"

Serena decided gentle persuasion was preferred. "They're our allies. Whatever they've done in the past, it's past. I need you to work with them now, please."

"Uh, yes, Lady Mitsubi."

"For Oka-Chan, for Mother."

"For Princess Mariko," he replied, looking sad. "For her, I would do anything. My apologies for letting my doubts show."

Her hand tucked under his arm, Serena accompanied him to the interrogation theater. She saw how it invigorated him, this simple gesture, marveled at the depth of loyalty her mother the Princess had commanded. Serena wondered what leverage Xavier Balleros had used on the first mate Hideo Kobaya to cause a Japanese officer, normally the epitome of loyalty, to turn against his Captain, his Commander, and his Princess.

They seated themselves with four other Japanese officers in the darkened room, the adjoining room visible through thick glasma. Only two chairs and a bare glowglobe occupied the room.

The two warriors were brought in, still unconscious. Their bindings were cut away, and they were draped over their respective chairs. Then the neuralinks were removed, and with them the metabolic suppressors, allowing the two men to rouse on their own.

Within a few minutes, the taller one was stirring. Quickly, he sat up and looked around, then roused his companion. They talked in hushed tones, as though that might deter any eavesdropping. They inspected the nearly seamless walls, finding no flaw. They looked for vents, cameras, windows, anything. One suggested smashing a wall with one of the chairs, until they discovered that their chairs were fixed to the floor.

In Spanish, a voice boomed, "Sit down!" The instruction was then repeated in Japanese.

The two men looked around and slowly returned to their seats, looking bewildered.

Two men of clear Spanish descent in dark glasses entered. They wore the uniform of the Iberian Armada, but bereft of insignia or rank.

The questions began, one Iberian asking in Spanish, the second repeating in Japanese.

The prisoners stayed silent.

The questions became badgering. "What are your names? Who sent you? Why are you here? Why won't you talk? What are you afraid of?" The questions got louder, the interrogators screaming their questions, their faces sweating, veins and tendons bulging.

Suddenly the questions stopped and they left the room.

The two prisoners looked at each other and sighed. "I thought the fat one was going to blow a blood vessel," the thin one said, and they both burst into laughter.

Soon their giggles faded, and one got up to inspect the wall where the door had appeared, trying to find the seam.

In Japanese, a voice boomed, "Sit down!"

The two men returned quickly to their chairs, again bewildered.

Two men of clear Japanese descent entered the room, both wearing kimonos of the Mitsubi armed forces but without insignia or rank.

The questions began, one asking all the questions.

The prisoners stayed silent, but their frequent glances at each other spoke volumes.

The questions became badgering. "What are your names? Who sent you? Why are you here? Why won't you talk? What are you afraid of?" The questions got louder, the interrogator screaming the questions, his face sweating, veins and tendons bulging.

Suddenly the questions stopped and they left the room.

Serena prepared herself. Her kimono was nearly identical to the last one worn by Princess Mariko. Her wig resembled Mariko's most frequent coif. Her swords were positioned in the same way that Mariko had worn them.

The effect was startling as she strode down the corridor toward the interrogation room. The base crew crossed themselves, bowing abjectly as she passed.

On her retinal, she saw Admiral Nagano enter the room.

The two prisoners instantly leaped to their feet and bowed.

"Lords, a misunderstanding, I'm sure." His manner though brusque was friendly. "How did you get to Okinawa?"

"Eh? Okinawa?" one said.

"You didn't know you were on Okinawa, Lord Kamanuki? Where did you think you were?"

The two men looked at each other. "Iberian territory, Lord Admiral."

"Oh, I see." Nobu's brow wrinkled. "Then you'll have orders and passports, I presume. Still begs the question, how did you get here?"

The pair exchanged a bewildered glance.

"And what were you doing there? I can't remember authorizing any reconnaissance mission, or at least none recently."

"Reconnaissance, yes, Lord, uh, for the Lady Foreign Undersecretary, Lord," the short one said.

The tall one gave him a look.

"I'm sure it'll be in your orders, of course. Very well, although it disturbs me I wasn't made aware of the mission. It would rattle the ghost of the Princess Mariko to know I wasn't informed. Very well, Lord Kamanuki, Lord Watana." He nodded to them.

They both bowed deeply. "Lord Admiral."

He left, and the two prisoners sighed. "Why'd you tell him that?" the tall one asked in a hushed whisper. "She'll cut off our balls with her pinky nail!"

The short one looked ashamed. "How *did* we get here?"

"They're watching!" the tall one warned.

"Of course they're watching. I just can't figure out *who's* watching."

"Bizarre, wasn't it? Like some Kami decided to bedevil us."

Serena stepped into the room.

Screaming, the pair backed into the farthest corner, clutching each other in fright. "Please, please don't hurt us, Kami Princess," the short one whispered.

She whipped out her Katana and held the point an inch from his nose. Instantly he shat himself, "Tell me who sent you!"

The tall one pissed on himself. "The Lady Foreign Undersecretary Takeshi Gahara," he said, his bladder squirting all down his front.

"Who told her to send you?"

"I don't know, I don't know, I don't know . . ." the high pitched chant sounded like the protestations of a child about to be punished.

"Who, by Buddha's bulging belly!" she yelled.

The pair slid down the wall and cowered helplessly in their mixed feces.

Serena felt sorry for them. And the smell was horrible. "Find out, and I won't chase you through all eternity! Find out or you'll be licking Buddha's balls forever!" And she stormed out, trying not to laugh.

In the corridor, Admiral Nagano was clutching his sides and covering his mouth, his face split by a rictus, his eyes leaking tears. The two of them stepped further down the corridor and into an office three doors down. Then Serena burst into laughter.

General Takagi came into the room, red-faced and chortling. "That'll be one Kami they'll never forget!"

"That was just like the Princess Mariko, Lady Mitsubi, just like the Princess." Admiral Nagano smiled at her. "Feels like old times, eh, Riyo-san?"

The General nodded. "Indeed. What now, Lady Mitsubi, now that it's apparent these drudges know nothing?"

"Now, we spook the foreign Undersecretary," Serena said.

* * *

The cell deep beneath the Iberian Palace on Madrid looked nothing like the kind of place she'd thought she'd meet her benefactor, El Patrón. The dungeon was spare, the walls carved from naked bedrock, a chill upon the air that reached deep into bone. Despite the chill, everything sweated, and her airshell sparkled in its efforts to repel the nearly double air pressure.

His laughter echoed among the empty cells and corridors before she even saw him. Chains hung from shackles at wrists, ankles, and neck, the metal padded but beginning to chafe anyway. The chains led to a roboservelet, its five arms each controlling a chain. They loosened and tightened as Balleros paced the cell, his head turning to remain facing her as his body bounced from side to side like a metronome, like an animal long since resigned to the cage.

Serena knew the roboservelet would prevent any effort by the prisoner to take his own life or to assault his captors. But that was only in extremis, since the attached neuralink could administer a neurablock and render him immobile even faster.

"You've come to find out who colluded with me," Balleros said.

"Such an effort would indicate I am still bound to your designs."

A smile might have shadowed his face briefly. "Of course, you are. You are your mother's daughter. My designs were built upon who you are. I thought that would be obvious."

"Who helped you?"

His laughter echoed once again, and then faded into silence. The rustle of cloth and tinkling of chain were the only sounds.

"Whose plan did you subvert to achieve your ends?"

He stopped mid-stride. "Now you begin to see."

Serena didn't expect an answer—not uncoerced. "What do I need to do to get that information?"

"Become everything that I intended you to become."

Again, the expected response. "Did you also intend that I would become Empress over half the galaxy?"

His face twitched. "I intended that you would destroy the Mitsubi Empire entirely. Failing that, I intended to kill you."

A piece fell into place for her. "Your coconspirator didn't expect me to survive your assassinating my mother."

"You're so naïve. How have you managed to live this long? Have you no idea what your plans for the galactic core will bring? Much wider the destruction than what *I'd* intended."

How had he heard about that? she wondered. Serena kept her face still as the realization sank in. She extended her awareness.

An air flow where none should be, the hum of machinery underneath the rustle and clink, a scent of ... paella ... rice and seafood.

A visitor—despite the isolation.

He expects me to walk out alive, Serena thought; otherwise he'd have told me the name of his coconspirator. A secret told will only stay secret if that person dies.

"Your only hope," Serena said, "is that I become what you intended all along. You've never really sought to kill me, have you?"

"Your vision clears as you emerge from your fog."

"Only to spur me into action." She knew she would get nothing further from him. Unless ... "What would you bargain for clemency?"

"Clemency?" Balleros laughed aloud and stopped abruptly. "You've no power there. Or didn't you know? Emperor Augusto is more the tyrant than his father Maximilian. He'll have me put to death quietly, without trial or charge. Clemency is possible only when established judicial procedures are followed. Clearly, your political science education has lain dormant too long."

Will he simply not divulge who his coconspirators are, or is he just so pessimistic he holds no hope of his ever being free again? Serena wondered. Either one confirmed how utterly irredeemable he'd become. Further, his attempts to kill her would either result in her death or in sharpening her killing acumen. Again, beyond redemption.

Knowing she would get no further, she walked off.

"You can't avoid your fate, Serena Zambrano!"

* * *

Foreign Undersecretary Takeshi Gahara yawned and crawled into bed, her day too long, all her time consumed by this fruitless pursuit. Her two henchmen had disappeared and all her efforts to find them had gone awry. She had to be discreet, not wanting to reveal her role in their chase of the former Foreign Minister, Xavier Balleros.

She'd always thought it ironic that she'd been tasked to pursue someone who'd once occupied a corresponding position in a neighboring Empire.

Ironic and appropriate.

She'd never learned the reason for the pursuit. Her mistress, the person to whom she owed her loyalty, had not told her the motivation. She had simply told her, "Kill him."

Subsequent instruction had also indicated a need to find out the person whom he himself pursued, but the primary objective was simply to have Xavier Balleros killed.

Then, a week ago, the Iberia Empire had announced the arrest of her target.

Takeshi didn't blink. She'd then set her sights to finding where he was being held.

Oddly, two days ago, the Iberia Empire had reversed itself, announcing the release of Xavier Balleros.

Maneuvering close to the Iberian Capitol Madrid was a tricky business, made all the more difficult by the former Foreign Minister's surely being surveilled, but she'd managed to get her two drudges to the planet Galapagar anyway.

Then they'd commed her to say they'd detected his transponders taking him to a small grasslands planet between San Sebastian and A Coruña.

Then, to Takeshi Gahara's infinite frustration, the two drudges had disappeared, the transponder on their scout indicating it remained on the grasslands planet. Her agents had located the scout, empty, and no sign indicated what might have become of them.

She pulled the silk quilt up to her chin, her windows open, the chill night air of Kyoto relaxing to her, and closed her eyes.

She couldn't sleep, her thought preoccupied with finding her curmudgeons. She'd selected the two dullards for precisely that quality, not wanting anyone to ask too closely into the reasons for her activities.

Where did they go? Have they betrayed me? Have they been suborned by someone? Is someone seeking revenge for my idiot brother's sticking his head up six years ago? Captain Tani Gahara had disrupted the negotiations between Nahuatl and Mitsubi, where the outer Car-Sag Arm had been ceded to the Nahuatl without a fight.

Like him, she had felt demoralized and ashamed that their great Empire would have to kowtow to these "beak-nosed foreigners with the birds nesting on their heads." Unlike him, she wasn't such a fool as to say so publicly. Unlike him, she wouldn't disrupt interstellar negotiations.

The infernal idiot! she thought for the thousandth time. Lucky I didn't lose my position because of his imbecility! What mental infirmity or character weakness caused him to waste his life like that was beyond her. She'd immediately repudiated him and had gotten herself adopted into the Matriarchy of the Empress Regent but of course wouldn't presume to adopt the Imperial name. But at least it had staved off her being extirpated like every other descendant of the Gahara lineage for the stupidity displayed by this one fool member, for of course all his descendants and ancestors had been systematically executed.

Unable to shut off her mind, Takeshi decided to watch a vid, rather than introduce a melatonin through her neuralink.

She ordered up a romantic comedy, one of those American imports with the impossible plot about a young man stumbling over his own cupidity in pursuing a young lady too far above his own station to merit her possibly even noticing him, and yet somehow, she does. Completely incongruous, and delightfully stupid as a result.

The opposite wall was a life-size screen, real enough for her. Why would I want to immerse myself with a neuralink?

Her eyelids heavy, the screen dimming in response to her dimming attention, she heard a voice that wasn't quite right, the dialogue a bit too incongruous.

"You didn't know you were on Okinawa, Lord Kamanuki?"

Takeshi snapped awake.

There, on screen, was her pair of pathetic scoundrels, both of them looking at their interrogator, both of them sweating droplets the size of pistachios.

She froze the vid. Okinawa? And what's this doing in my vid? She rewound the vid until it showed the usual characters, and then set it to play again.

The vid continued, the besotted male lead hurling himself helplessly at the feet of the indignant if attentive female lead. It continued to play long past the point she'd rewound from, but no scoundrels.

Did I just imagine that? she wondered. I must really be tired.

The plot wound itself toward its inevitable and predictable end, boring but for its impossibility.

The two miscreants leaped to their feet and bowed at the entrance of a third person.

"Lords," that off-camera person said. "A misunderstanding, I'm sure. How did you get to Okinawa?"

Takeshi sat bolt upright and froze the vid. I'm not dreaming! What evil Kami is persecuting me like this? Donning her neuralink from the bedside table, she injected herself into the vid.

With the neuralink, she rotated the camera, able to move it any direction, zoom close enough to inspect a pimple, or choose to see the scene from any character's perspective.

The screen before her was clearly from the interrogator's perspective. Takeshi switched it to the tall one.

The image of the interrogator was greyed out.

Careful not to interrupt the playback, Takeshi tried to record the vid, but the neuralink reported she didn't own the copyright. Frustrated, she played the vid through, hoping for some clue about the interrogation. The two curmudgeons seemed to hang on the third person's every word, and the accent was Kyotoan, but the voice seemed unusually high-pitched, as though modified.

"Reconnaissance, yes, Lord," the short one said, "for the Lady Foreign Undersecretary."

Takeshi screamed, tore off the neuralink and hurled it at the short one on the wall.

The vid continued, uninterrupted by her rending.

"Very well, Lord Kamanuki, Lord Watana." And the interrogator left the room.

The scene cut away to the young man bringing the young woman a bouquet of red roses, which in Japanese culture would have been an unpardonable insult, but the slavish young woman accepted them with overplayed delight, and managed to throw her arms around him without scratching him with the thorn-studded flowers.

Takeshi would have found it ludicrous if she'd been watching.

But she was comming her Matriarch, the Empress Regent Yoshi Mitsubi.

Chapter 18

The spaceport at Kyoto was among the largest in the galaxy. When the six-person yacht belonging to the Admiral Nobu Nagano landed, it attracted its share of attention, but its passenger roster received no attention whatsoever.

The quartet who disembarked received little scrutiny at customs but garnered odd looks from everyone else.

The woman strode through customs dressed in elaborate kimonos whose formal, tiara-topped coif might have graced a fashion publication. She held her katana in both hands, her right on the intricately wound and bejeweled hilt, her left on the matching scabbard. In between gleamed a good foot of steel, the blade etched with the figure of a squirming dragon. Her face was stark, her eyes distant as in meditation, as though she were preparing to kill.

Or to die.

She followed three men whose garb was as penurious as hers was extravagant.

One man kept his shackled hands as close to his face as possible, his head tucked so far down as to nearly obscure his six-four height, his dress the barred tunic and breeches known to be worn in some Spanish prisons. The other two men wore coarse gray linens of the kind used in Mitsubi Prisons, "Kyoto Penitentiary" emblazoned on their backs in black. One tall and one short, they were notable for their sloped foreheads, crooked teeth, and general slovenly appearance. They too wore shackles at wrists, ankles, and neck. A roboservelet floated just behind the trio and right in front of the woman, its fifteen arms each firmly controlling a shackle.

Hushed whispers and silent, startled stares followed them through the spaceport. A few older passers-by bowed deeply until the quartet had passed, some of them going to their knees. Some crossed themselves, other blinked away tears.

The whispers were all the same: "Princess Mariko."

By the time they reached the spaceport entrance, a large crowd followed, and spaceport operations had ground to a halt. No one stopped them or questioned them. Everyone stepped reverently to the side and watched enthralled as the quartet passed.

"A gravcar, please," Serena said to no one in particular.

Several valets scrambled to find an appropriate vehicle, disappearing into the subdued throng.

During the wait, a uniformed man bedecked with insignia approached, an assistant in tow. "Forgive me, Lady-Sama," the man said, bowing. "I am Josan Hiroto, Director General of Kyoto Spaceport Authority. Is there any assistance I might offer?"

"An open-topped gravcar with your most trusted driver and room for my three prisoners, Lord Director Hiroto."

"Certainly, Lady-Sama, immediately." He nodded to the adjutant who stepped back and spoke into his neuralink. Director Hiroto turned back to her. "May I ask ...?"

"You will know my name in time, Lord Director. My apologies for my unannounced arrival, and thank you for your hospitality."

A gravcar pulled up, sans top. The four rear seats had been arranged in a diamond shape. Serena directed the roboservelet to seat the prisoners, the tallest Latin prisoner in front, the two Japanese prisoners next. Serena nodded to the director. "Again, my gratitude for your assistance." She climbed aboard and stood behind the three prisoners. "Kyoto Palace, please."

The driver looked sharply over his shoulder, as though to object. She paid him no attention. Director Hiroto gestured sharply at the driver to do as directed. The gravcar accelerated.

"More slowly, please."

The driver nodded and slowed down.

"Still too fast."

He slowed again.

"Half this speed, please."

Again the driver slowed. "Lady-Sama, at this speed we will block traffic, forgive me for speaking up."

"No apology necessary, Lord. Thank you for maintaining this speed." The pace was one of a brisk march. Her sword still held between her hands, she stared straight forward, oblivious to the stares she drew.

The wide boulevard cleared ahead as word spread, many of the people whom she had passed having contacted relatives and friends on their neuralinks, sending either live or recorded vid of the strange quartet, the brief conversation at the spaceport entrance transmitted by a hundred different observers to their several hundred friends, and thence to several thousand associates.

Behind them followed a throng, most of them on foot.

People lined the street on either side. Building tops bristled with bodies. Faces crowded windows. Hovercraft buzzed overhead, among them numerous press vehicles.

A police patrol cruiser floated over the crowd from one side, two smaller hoverscooters escorting it.

A voice blared from a hood-mounted speaker. "Kyoto city police. Please halt."

She didn't even glance at it. "My apologies, I cannot. Driver, please continue." She could see he was beginning to sweat, glancing fearfully between her and the patrol vehicle.

The cruiser settled in front of the gravcar. "You are ordered to halt."

"Give me the controls, Lord Driver."

He stopped the vehicle and brought her the handheld.

From where she stood, she looked directly at the cruiser, seeing the officer through the window. "I formally request that you either get out of my way or escort me to the palace, Lord officer. Decide!"

A crowd began to form around his vehicle and a low chant was heard. "Escort! Escort!" and someone pushed on the patrol vehicle. More people joined in.

"Take your hands off the vehicle!"

Serena edged the gravcar forward, and the crowd began to push the patrol cruiser aside.

Soon, the way was clear and the crowd cheered as Serena pressed forward, returning the gravcar sans driver to its leisurely pace toward the palace.

Multiple police cruisers came alongside, hovering above and to each side. As they did not attempt to block her progress, Serena ignored them.

"Mariko! Mariko!" floated through the crowd, and thrown chrysanthemums began to appear on the wide boulevard in front of them, the crowd thick on all sides, the people in front parting respectfully. The fragrance of the inches-deep flowers soon overpowered all the other smells.

Imperial patrols soon replaced the city police, but like their city counterparts, they hovered at the respectful distance but did not intervene or interfere.

The wide boulevard widened farther and turned toward the palace complex. Near the gates, the boulevard spread out into a plaza.

It was already full, the noise deafening, the people chanting the name of their deceased Princess.

The crowd parted peacefully for the gravcar, now so coated with chrysanthemum petals that it might have been a parade float.

Behind locked gates, Kyoto Palace stood resplendent, the ancient architecture majestic, the interlocking tiled roofs now covered with people, every ledge, balcony, balustrade, and window bursting with bodies. Visible between wrought iron bars, guards blocked the entry for as far as Serena could see. Guard towers bristled with weapons, all of them aimed at her. Two destroyers dropped from orbit, porcupined with guns of every shape and size.

Serena stopped the gravcar at the gates.

She held her sword over her heard, the blade scintillating in the sunlight.

The crowd grew silent.

"I am Princess Akira Mitsubi, daughter of Princess Mariko Mitsubi, and I bring proof of great treachery to submit for the personal inspection of her majesty, the Lady Empress Fumiko Mitsubi, my grandmother." She lowered the sword.

Noise spread like gunpowder set alight

Serena stood immobile while the information sank in.

Patience, she told herself. I will wait for the count of two hundred, she told herself.

Beyond the gate, nothing stirred, the thick assembly of guards showing no motion.

The crowd grew agitated, subsided, agitated again.

She raised her sword and waited until the crowd grew silent. "I am Princess Akira Mitsubi, daughter of Princess Mariko Mitsubi, and I bring proof of great treachery to submit for the personal inspection of her majesty, the Lady Empress Fumiko Mitsubi, my grandmother." She lowered the sword. I will wait for the count of two hundred, she told herself.

The crowd around the gravcar began to get restless. "Forgive me, Lady," an eight-year-old child said, "Lady Princess Mariko died before she gave birth. How can you be her daughter?"

Seeing that the girl had on a neuralink, her hair not having yet fully grown back from its installation, Serena smiled. "Stand beside me, Child-Chan, and I will tell you the tale."

The girl climbed into the gravcar and smiled up at her. "My name's Akira, too. Akira Uraga."

Serena sent an instruction to the roboservelet. The robot arms lifted Xavier Balleros out of his seat and turned him to face Serena.

"This man, Xavier Balleros, attacked the flagship Yamato, which my mother commanded," Serena said. "He bribed the first mate to betray my mother by disabling communications between my mother's ships, and when this man's ship was close enough, the first mate killed my mother—but kept her body alive through her neuralink. When this man boarded my mother's ship, he cut me out of her womb and took me back to Madrid, the Iberian Capitol, and had me reared among the Spanish. But he wasn't supposed to keep me alive. His orders were to kill both my mother and me."

"Who ordered him to do that?" The girl asked.

"Who indeed?" she said, frowning. Serena directed the roboservelet to return Balleros to his seat.

"One moment, Akira-Chan." She stood to her full height, looked again beyond the gate, and raised her sword over her head.

Serena repeated her litany into the silence, and then lowered the sword.

She had the hapless pair stand and face her. "These two pathetic creatures were caught following Señor Balleros and revealed that they were sent by the Mitsubi Foreign Undersecretary, Takeshi Gahara. Lady Gahara was tricked into contacting the person who ordered her to have those two gentlemen follow Señor Balleros. And do you know who that person was?"

Akira Uraga shook her head, peering up at Serena.

"The same person who conspired with Señor Balleros to kill my mother and me." She had the machine reseat the pair.

"Bad person," the girl said.

A disturbance among the guards on the other side of the gate indicated someone approaching.

"I agree. Oh, look, someone's coming." Serena couldn't tell who it was.

The person shoved through the last layer of guards and looked at her from between the bars.

Keiko.

"Forgive me for disobeying you, Akira-Chan. Lord Captain, open this gate!"

A large man stepped toward her, his subordinates clearing the way. "Lady Princess Mitsubi, forgive me, but I cannot." He bowed to her.

"Then give me the key, Lord Captain, and I will."

"Forgive me, Lady Princess Mitsubi, but I cannot give you the key."

Keiko pulled out a blaster and blew the gate latch into a million pieces, then struck the barrel under his throat. "You'll assist my niece the Lady Princess Akira Mitsubi through the battlements and into the palace, Lord Captain."

He swallowed, sweating, his dilemma clear, his life forfeit no matter what his choice. "Please forgive me, Lady Princess Mitsubi, I humbly request permission to commit Seppuku, as I cannot bear having to choose between obeying my orders and obeying you."

"Lord Captain," Serena said. "I am the Princess Akira Mitsubi. I would beg you to comply with my Aunt the Lady Princess Keiko Mitsubi. After following her orders, you may then release your soul into the great beyond, if you think that is still required." Serena bowed to him and held it, honoring him.

"Hai, Lady Princess Mitsubi," he said, nodding, his shoulders straightening. He turned to bark orders at his guards.

Serena bade the child Akira Uraga to step off the gravcar. She turned and raised her sword over her heard with both hands.

Silence fell.

"Your faith and devotion to Princess Mariko will always be remembered."

She lowered the sword and turned, the gates now open, the Captain leading a contingent ahead of her gravcar.

Chants of "Akira! Akira!" followed her into Kyoto Palace.

* * *

Serena looked on in wonder as the last set of doors opened upon the Imperial audience hall.

Seven chandeliers hung from the ceiling, three on either side of a center chandelier whose girth exceeded that of a space-fighter. She estimated ten thousand crystals comprised the center chandelier, which she suspected was suspended by gravu-nits. The undulating walls were papered with multicolored silk cloth, many of the patterns in the Imperial colors. The chairs on either side of the central walkway were each rich enough for a king, the black-lacquer, cherry-wood frames upholstered with bulging cushions covered with brocaded silk, their head-rests carved into the shapes of animals and trees sacred to the Japanese people. Every chair was occupied, and all eyes were on the strange quartet, the captive Spaniard at their lead.

At the other end of the central walkway stood a platform raised three steps, and on that platform sat three chairs, the largest in the center. More elaborate in design that those on the floor, the two side chairs faced inward at a slight angle. The third chair, the most elaborate yet, with silken wings and a canopy, and a blood-red rising sun on a bright white background, framed the Empress Fumiko Mitsubi.

Serena nudged her prisoners forward, feeling underdressed for the occasion despite her elaborate headdress and formal kimonos.

She felt the eyes of the observers on her, in a way she hadn't before arriving at this room, despite being watched by thousands of people, and through their neuralinks, by billions more throughout the galaxy.

Ten paces from the platform she stopped.

The roboservelet made the prisoners prostrate themselves. Then Serena herself did so, lightly bringing her forehead to the floor.

The silence stretched.

Serena wondered, her head to the carpet, why the delay.

I'm being reminded of my inferior status.

"What interloper rudely intrudes with ludicrous fictions of preposterous proportion?" The voice had come from the right.

As much acknowledgement as I'll get, Serena thought, rising from her bow. She looked only at the Empress. "My name, Lady-Sama Empress Mitsubi, is Akira Mitsubi, daughter of—"

"Liar!" Yoshi yelled from the right-hand chair, tendons standing out on her neck, a vein pulsing at her temple.

The woman in the center, the Empress, held up a hand.

To the left, watching closely, sitting forward in her chair, was Princess Keiko Mitsubi.

Serena kept her gaze on the Empress, feeling the fire in the stare of the elder princess from the right. "I am Akira Mitsubi, the daughter of Princess Mariko Mitsubi."

"Pretender! Fraudster! Guards, take her to the dungeons! Torture the truth out of her!"

The Empress turned her head to her left, her gaze burning.

Yoshi's eyes went wide.

"I bring proof of great treachery—"

"You spout foolery and confabulation! You're—"

"Silence!" the Empress hissed.

Yoshi recoiled as though struck.

It was the second time in twenty-six years that the Empress Mitsubi had spoken, Serena realized.

"I bring proof of great treachery for your personal inspection, Lady Empress."

A disturbance behind Serena caught her off guard, and she spun, startled.

"Get out of our way!" a gruff voice growled from behind a partially-open door. General Riyo Takagi and Admiral Nobu Nagano strode into the room, herding a Japanese female prisoner in front of them, a woman behind them. "Forgive our untimely arrival, Lady Empress Mitsubi," General Takagi said. "We bring proof of great treachery for your personal inspection."

Serena sighed, grateful. She moved her prisoners and herself to one side as the Admiral and General approached the throne.

Another disturbance at the door interrupted their obeisance to the Empress.

"Lady Empress," the doorman said, "The Lord Emperor Naui Quiahuitl Xiuhtectli and Empress Xochitl Olin request immediate—"

The door opened behind him as though possessed.

"Forgive my intrusion, Lady Empress Mitsubi," the Fire Emperor said, "the Empress Olin and I bring proof of great treachery for your personal inspection." A Hispanic woman followed them.

Before the doors had even closed, another person pushed his way inside. "Forgive my untimely interruption, Lady Empress Mitsubi," Emperor Augusto Iberia said. "I bring proof of great treachery for your personal inspection." Beside the bronzed, handsome Emperor stood a plainly-dressed Hispanic man, as short and pudgy as the Emperor was tall and slim.

The observers were in an uproar by this time, and the veritable pantheon of supplicants crowded the forward portion of the audience hall.

Keiko strode to the head of the steps and raised her white Imperial Sword above her head. Slowly, reluctantly the noise level decreased. "On behalf of the Empress Fumiko Mitsubi, I hereby declare this an Imperial Inquest into the betrayal and death of Princess Mariko Mitsubi.

"Lady Akira, who is your first person to testify?"

"Lady Princess Keiko, I call upon the man—"

"This is a farce!!" Yoshi screamed.

"YOU WILL REMAIN SILENT UPON PAIN OF BANISHMENT!"

Head instantly to the floor, Serena felt ashamed at her grandmother's outburst. Dead silence had spread through the hall, everyone looking at their feet. Serena spoke, her voice quavering, "Forgive me, Lady Empress Mitsubi, for causing such discord. My humble apologies."

"It is not your fault, Child. Sit up and look at me."

Serena did so.

The eyes of the Empress probed her features, then she glanced at Keiko. "That portrait of Mariko, where did you get it?"

"The face, Lady Empress," Keiko said, "was from the still of the Priestess Midori Sato provided by the Mother Priestess Hisaka Tomi. The face of this woman before you."

The Empress nodded, glancing among the petitioners. "Proceed, please."

"Thank you, Lady Empress. I wish to call upon the man whom I knew throughout my upbringing as my father, Señor Pedro Zambrano."

Papa Zambrano stepped to the place directly in front of the throne and bowed. "Lady Empress Mitsubi. I am Pedro Zambrano, and I was approached twenty-nine years ago by Señor Xavier Balleros, at that time sub-commander of the Fourth Fleet of the Iberian Navy, stationed at the outpost Tarifa. He asked me to rear a child for him, and a year later, Señora Carmen Hernan brought me an infant girl and stayed to help rear her for that first year. That girl, whom I named Serena, was and is the woman before you, the one who calls herself the Princess Akira Mitsubi."

Serena smiled at him. "Lady Empress, I next wish to call upon Señora Carmen Hernan."

The Hispanic woman who had come with the General and the Admiral stepped forward and took Papa Zambrano's place. "Lady Empress Mitsubi, I am Carmen Hernan Leon de Dulce, and I received from my sister Maria Theresa Hernan an infant whom I transported to Madrid aboard the personal yacht of sub-commander Xavier Balleros, an infant whom I helped care for in the year that followed."

Serena nodded, a grateful tear trickling from one eye. "Lady Empress, I next wish to call upon Señora Maria Theresa Hernan."

The Hispanic woman who had come with the Nahuatl Emperor and Empress stepped forward and bowed where her sister had been. "Lady Empress Mitsubi, my name is Maria Theresa Hernan Leon de Dulce, and at the behest of sub-commander Xavier Balleros, I obtained personal service to the Princess Mariko Mitsubi under false pretense, and I was present when Princess Mariko was killed by her first mate Hideo Kobaya aboard the Armada Flagship Yamato, and I attached the neuralink that kept her body alive after she had been killed—"

An astonished gasp was followed by a roar of indignation. "Silence!" Keiko shouted, unsheathing her katana and running out among the spectators. They quieted.

"Please continue, Señora Hernan," the Empress said.

"And I brought her body to Commander Balleros, who cut the baby out of her womb in front of me—"

Another gasp was quickly stilled in an angry glance from Princess Keiko.

"And he handed me the infant to take to my sister. We cleaned up the child, and she left with her." Mario Theresa began to weep disconsolately, and her sister helped her away, both of them weeping.

"Lady Empress, I next wish to call," Serena said, her voice strained, "Former sub-commander and Foreign Minister for the Iberia Empire, Señor Xavier Balleros."

The tall, gray-haired Spaniard looked at her from his shackle-imposed position on the floor. "You can burn in both your Christian and Buddhist Hells!"

Serena spoke for him. "Señor Balleros conspired with First Mate Hideo Kobaya to defeat the Princess when she attacked the Iberian outpost at Tarifa, and after the Mitsubi Armada had been defeated in battle, the First Mate then slew Princess Mariko. Lady Empress, I next wish to call Lords Omi Kamanuki and Kasa Watana." Serena maneuvered the two slope-headed grunts to the place in front of the Empress.

"We didn't do anything!" one protested.

Admiral Nagano projected a vid of the pair on the back wall of the audience hall. "Reconnaissance, Yes, Lord, uh, for the Lady Foreign Undersecretary, Lord."

"Who were you following?" Serena asked.

Kamanuki looked at the floor. "Him," he said, nodding toward the Spanish prisoner.

"Lady Empress, I next wish to call the Lady Foreign Undersecretary Takeshi Gahara." General Riyo Takagi maneuvered his Japanese prisoner to the place before the Empress.

Foreign Undersecretary Gahara wouldn't look up from her bow. "Please forgive me, Lady Empress. I beg permission to commit seppuku and end all shame." Her voice was barely a whisper.

Admiral Nagano projected a vid of the Foreign Undersecretary upon the wall.

In the vid, Takeshi Gahara hurled a neuralink at the figures of her two henchmen. Then she retrieved the neuralink and commed the Regent Empress Yoshi Mitsubi.

"What are you doing, fool?" Yoshi's voice said, on her face a scowl.

"But, but, Lady, they've been found out by someone!"

"Who?" Yoshi snarled in the vid.

"I don't know, Lady—"

"Stop it!" the real Yoshi screamed, leaping from her chair. "Stop this charade! This is pointless! You're all possessed! Kamis have infected every last one of you! You people—"

Keiko's sword was at her throat. "Tell us, sister, what you did twenty-seven years ago."

Yoshi stared at her, her eyes wide, her brow glistening.

"Tell us how you contacted sub-commander Balleros through an intermediary and offered him an unlikely victory against the Mitsubi juggernaut. Tell us how you suborned First Mate Hideo Kobaya into betraying his own commander on the cusp of her conquering the galactic core! Tell us how you betrayed your own sister, that you might inherit the throne instead. Tell us!"

Yoshi stared at her sister, her breathing rapid and shallow, big drops of sweat dripping off her chin.

"Deny that you did any of this, Sister," Keiko said.

Yoshi was silent, her gaze dropping to the floor.

Keiko lowered her sword and turned to the Empress. "Lady Mother, Oka-Chan, I beg permission to remove the head of my sister for her foul treachery against my sister, your daughter, the Princess Mariko Mitsubi, and thereby set right the abominable act that this despicable creature has committed."

The Empress stood, her balance unsteady. Two servants rushed to her side to prevent a fall. She accepted their assistance until she was steady, and then waved the servants off. Gingerly, she stepped toward her eldest living daughter.

Her face inches away, the Empress looked into Yoshi's eyes.

Yoshi wouldn't meet her gaze.

"Look at me," the Empress said, her voice hoarse.

Yoshi's gaze snapped upward.

"Tell me that you didn't betray your own sister."

The silence stretched, the sweat pouring of Yoshi nearly audible. Finally, she looked away.

The Empress stepped back to her chair, her gaze vacant.

The silence stretched.

Serena bit her lip, sad for the horror and betrayal etched clearly upon the face of the Empress.

"Akira," she whispered.

"Yes, Lady Empress?"

"Please, Child, call me grandmother." The voice was stronger. "Step over here, please. Yes, right here beside me."

Serena was surprised at the strength of her grandmother's grip.

"I formally declare that my second daughter, Princess Yoshi Mitsubi, has demonstrated with remarkable alacrity that she is unfit for the position of Regent Empress and is hereby divested of the position and all its attendant privileges and responsibilities. Further, her behavior constitutes such a monumental betrayal of her family and the Mitsubi Empire that she is also divested now and forever of her position in the line of inheritance, even unto the last Mitsubi descendant, even unto the last Mitsubi subject. She will remand herself to the custody of the warden of Kyoto Penitentiary, pending trial."

The old woman closed her eyes briefly, looking suddenly twice her age. "Immediately, please."

Four guards converged on Yoshi and hauled her away, the former Princess sobbing audibly.

"Akira-Chan," the Empress said. "Kneel before me, child."

Serena did so.

"Dearest granddaughter, do you, Akira Mitsubi, daughter of Princess Mariko Mitsubi, granddaughter of Empress Fumiko

Mitsubi, agree to carry out the duties of Regent Empress to the best of your ability and in accordance with the laws of this Empire, so help you Buddha?"

"Sobo-Chan, dearest grandmother, Lady Empress Fumiko Mitsubi, I do so swear to carry out the duties of Regent Empress to the best of my ability, and in accordance with the laws of this Empire, so help me Buddha."

Grandmother Fumiko raised Serena to her feet, a hand on each of her shoulders. "I pray you can forgive all of the wrongs that have been done to you. You have been tasked with a more difficult goal than just being Regent Empress. Born in war, you must find peace. So I ask, War Child, how will you bring yourself peace?"

Serena shook her head. "I don't know, Sobo-Chan, but I will find it. Somehow."

The Empress nodded. "I believe that you will, child. For your first task as Regent, you must decide the fate of your Aunt Yoshi, she who betrayed your mother, and her coconspirators. You must also decide, with the permission of Lord Emperor Augusto Iberia, the fate of her Spanish collaborators, including this Xavier Balleros."

Serena smiled. "You give me absolute say over the fates of the two people whom I should most hate, an issue almost as difficult as attaining the peace that I seek. You are wise, Sobo-Chan, wise beyond compare. If I may, Lady Empress Mitsubi, I would like to make a request."

Grandmother Fumiko raised an eyebrow at her. "Oh?"

"Yes, Sobo-Chan, forgive me my impertinence. I would like to see fulfilled my mother's dream of bringing the galactic core under one rule."

"Child, you know not what you ask. Her dream destroyed her!"

Serena smiled. "Ah, but my approach to that dream is what differs. What I want to do is to unite the Empires in an effort to share the galactic core."

The Empress Fumiko Mitsubi smiled and nodded. "You may yet transform the universe and achieve the peace you seek. As Empress of the Mitsubi Empire, and as a servant of this War Child now before me, I will do all I can to help unite the Empires."

Epilogue

From an observation booth, Serena-Akira looked out over the assembled diplomats and smiled. *Seven long years, and I've finally done it.*

Below, the emissaries from six Empires had come together to sign the charter for the Galactic Mining and Energy Commission, a joint-powers agency that would possess exclusive rights to mine the galactic core for minerals and energy.

In the year after she had assumed her place as Mitsubi Princess and Regent, her grandmother Empress Fumiko Mitsubi and then her father Emperor Naui Quiahuitl Xiuhtectli had died, making her the Empress of both the Mitsubi and Nahuatl Empires. Thankfully, Keiko had been willing to step in as Serena's Regent in the Mitsubi Empire, and Xochitl Olin as Serena's Regent in the Nahuatl Empire. Then Serena and Augusto had married, making her the Empress of the Iberia Empire as well.

"Oka-Chan, can I see?"

Serena-Akira bent down to lift her daughter. "Certainly, Mariko-Chan, look at them all." She balanced her three-year-old on her hip.

Mariko giggled. "That woman has a bird nesting in her hair!"

"It looks like a bird, doesn't it? What would any bird do if it found itself on someone's head?"

"Poopy doop!" the girl sang.

Serena laughed and shook her head. "No, silly, it would fly away. So it can't be a real bird."

"Fly away, birdie!"

Serena smiled and sighed, handing the child off to her husband.

Augusto took her and nuzzled her.

Turning back to the window, Serena thought of all the hard work it had taken to bring the remaining three Empires into the fold. Being Empress in three Empires had freed her to focus on the other three. As Empress Mitsubi, Empress Xiuhtectli, and Empress Iberia, she hadn't had any difficulty getting the joint-powers agreement ratified in those three Empires. The other three, however—the Americans, the Chinese, and the Russo-Slavians—had been notoriously obstinate.

Now, seven years after being restored to her family in the Mitsubi Empire, Serena-Akira had accomplished her goal: Uniting all six Empires in an effort to manage the resources of the galactic core equitably.

The galactic core, the ultimate prize.

Dear reader,

We hope you enjoyed reading *War Child*. Please take a moment to leave a review, even if it's a short one. Your opinion is important to us.

Discover more books by Scott Michael Decker at https://www.nextchapter.pub/authors/scott-michael-decker-novelist-sacramento-us.

Want to know when one of our books is free or discounted for Kindle? Join the newsletter at http://eepurl.com/bqqB3H.

Best regards,
Scott Michael Decker and the Next Chapter Team

You might also like:
Bottle Born Blues by Conor H. Carton

To read the first chapter for free, head to:
https://www.nextchapter.pub/books/bottle-born-blues

About the Author

Scott Michael Decker, MSW, is an author by avocation and a social worker by trade. He is the author of twenty-plus novels, mostly in the Science Fiction genre and some in the Fantasy genre. His biggest fantasy is wishing he were published. His fifteen years of experience working with high-risk populations is relieved only by his incisive humor. Formerly interested in engineering, he's now tilting at the windmills he once aspired to build. Asked about the MSW after his name, the author is adamant it stands for Masters in Social Work, and not "Municipal Solid Waste," which he spreads pretty thick as well. His favorite quote goes, "Scott is a social work novelist, who never had time for a life" (apologies to Billy Joel). He lives and dreams happily with his wife near Sacramento, California.

How to Contact/Where to Find the Author

Websites:
http://scotts-writings.site40.net/
https://www.smashwords.com/profile/view/smdmsw
http://www.linkedin.com/pub/scott-michael-decker/5b/b68/437